THE THREAT

ALEX ROSE

BLOODHOUND
— BOOKS —

www.bloodhoundbooks.com

Print ISBN: 978-1917705516

PART 1

ONE

Wannabe parents sometimes turn a bedroom into a nursery when their baby is in the womb. Libby Mytton had gone a step further and transformed the attic room when her child was just a desire. A year ago, at the age of thirty-three, she and her husband, two years her elder, had done the work, which included widening the trap and installing a set of switchback stairs.

Six months later, while trying to get pregnant, she'd learned she was infertile. Joel hadn't wanted to foster or try medical magic, so the dream had slipped away.

Libby would have been happy to keep the bedroom intact, but Joel hadn't been on board. He had felt that Libby would pine every time she set foot in the attic, so he reversed the transformation while she was out one day. She returned from lunch with her sister to find the space wallpaper, the cartoon posters, and everything else gone. Now the attic was a bare area, used for time alone to relax. Joel liked to sit up here and read or stargaze through the skylight. Libby thought of her missing child only when enveloped by these four walls, so she avoided it when she could.

This dark November evening she couldn't. She was looking for a store receipt that she was certain Joel had used as a bookmark. Given that the floor was bare except for a black leather recliner chair and a coffee table bearing a single book, the hunt took her only a few seconds. Receipt in hand, she switched off the light and headed for the trapdoor.

Her attention was caught by a faint crunch of gravel from outside. She saw a soft brightness through the ajar skylight. Vehicle headlights. Pure suspicion drove her to the window.

Between the backyards of the houses on her street and those on the next was a twin-row of lock-up garages separated by a gravel lane. Above the top of the nearest row of garages, she saw the upper quarter of a plain white van parked on the gravel. The headlights she'd seen were now off and the lane was dark, but she recognised the vehicle as her husband's work van. Not thieves again then.

He wasn't there to park because they left their vehicles out front, to avoid vandalism. That left just one alternative. Although they maintained a garage for the sole purpose of storing junk, Joel sometimes discarded work debris there. Usually this was wood, since he was a joiner, but just last month she'd taken out a box of unused clothing and discovered three rotten internal doors. Joel had said he was holding them until a skip could be ordered to the house he was renovating, but it had taken two weeks. She was sick of complaining about it.

He got out of the van. Their garage was number five, on the opposite side, so she got a clear view of his upper body as he opened the up-and-over door with one hand. He did it slowly because the mechanism was old and noisy. The garage had no interior light, but he didn't use the one on his phone. Instead, he walked into the gloom and vanished. No doubt clearing a space for whatever he was unloading there this time.

He was back thirty-seconds later. She didn't know why, but

she ducked as he emerged, so he wouldn't see her face at the partially opened skylight.

She waited to hear his back doors open, but that sound never arrived. Instead, she heard crunching gravel. She peeked again and saw his van, still with its headlights off, back out of the lane. Had he not dumped trash after all? If he had, it was a small amount he'd carried in the hand she'd been unable to see. At least it wasn't a bulky item from the back of the van. She'd still ask him about it.

She left the attic and headed downstairs, into the living room. She put the store receipt on the coffee table, next to a kettle she would be returning for refund tomorrow. Just seconds later, Joel's front door key scraped in the lock.

'Libby, where are you?' he called out from the hallway.

'Living room. How come you're late?'

'Just a second. Need the world's biggest piss.'

'What were you doing at–'

'Hang on! Three pints of piss.'

Such a sweet image. She heard him run up the stairs. She went after him. Upon entering the bedroom, she heard the shower running in the en suite bathroom. The door was shut, which was new. Neither of them ever closed it because water damage had warped a couple of wooden boards and the bottom rail shrieked across them.

'You in the shower?'

'Yes,' he called back. 'Covered in paint, so gimme a min. Remember I said I'd be back late?'

Joel ran a six-man team of builders who were renovating a privately operated pub called Bowlers, just over a mile east on Abbey Lane. The pub's landlord continued to open for business nightly at six, so Joel's men were always gone by five. However, Joel had texted earlier to say he and the lads were going for a few drinks afterwards and he'd be back before 9pm. It was 8.18.

'You went drinking covered in paint?'

'Yeah. We stayed at Bowlers. Free pints, but I had non-alcoholic. Then I had to pop to Screwfix for a new dust sheet. That okay?'

She tried the door, but it was locked. That was strange. 'You locked it? I want to get your clothing for the washer.'

'Actually, do me a favour, babe. I left my phone in the van. Can you get it?'

She said sure and headed out. She threw on slippers stored by the front door and grabbed his keys off the hook. She checked the van's cabin first, to no joy. No phone on the dashboard, centre console, or in the driver's door pocket.

She opened the rear doors. The cargo bay was squeezed thin by shelving for his myriad tools. The floor was a mess of dropped nails and bits of wood. It was a nasty, stinking mess and she searched only with her eyes. No phone. When she returned to the house, Joel was in the kitchen, wearing only a towel around his waist.

He was two years older but looked a decade younger. His work had given him a toned body and he still had dark hair as glossy as a teenager's. Even after so many years together, she found him very attractive and looked him up and down.

'Sorry, my phone was in my pocket,' he said. 'Thanks anyway.'

Her eyes relocated to the washing machine as she heard it start to fill. 'You put your clothing in?'

'I thought I'd save you a job. I put some other stuff in, too. I'll get changed and we can do that movie.'

He headed past her, planting a kiss on her cheek on the way, and out of the kitchen. For a few seconds she stared at the washing machine. Joel had washed his own gear? Like the locked bathroom door, that was another anomaly. He hadn't done that since they were a new couple and he was still eager to play the modern man.

Maybe it was nothing. She put it from her mind and walked towards the living room, to load up Netflix for their evening with a movie. She got two steps then a foot skidded out from under her, dumping her hard on her ass with a yelp of pain.

'You okay?' Joel called from halfway up the stairs.

'Yes. It was nothing.'

The pain quickly subsided, allowing a new sensation to have the spotlight. Wetness on the rear of her jeans. She noticed that the linoleum was dappled with water. She saw a line of tiny puddles leading from the kitchen doorway to the washing machine. It was too much fluid to have dripped off Joel.

His work gear: it must have been soaking wet when he carried it to the machine. But why? Had he showered in his clothing, or washed it afterwards?

Libby got to her feet and walked carefully into the living room. By the time she sat on the sofa, there was a heavy ball of suspicion weighing in her gut. Joel was acting strange and she felt he was hiding something. He had run straight for the bathroom after coming home – door locked – and she hadn't caught a glimpse of him until he was freshly cleaned. Then he'd sent her out to his van, which she now believed had been a ploy to free his path to the washing machine with his clothing. If there had been something on him or his gear that she wasn't meant to discover, well, now she never would.

She moved to the bottom of the stairs and yelled up. 'Joel? You said it was another two weeks until the Bowlers job was done. That still the case?'

'Yeah,' he called down. 'We're on track for a bonus still. I'll buy you something special.'

That sounded like guilt talking. 'You've been there two weeks. So that means you're only halfway through.'

'Yeah. Quite a bit left to do. Why?'

'You said you were covered in paint. So how come you're painting already?'

Silence. She knew he was thinking. But inventing, not remembering. What he came up with was, 'We painted the games room. We're not working on that. It was a side job. Extra cash. That's why I needed a new dust sheet, because it got ruined by a spilled tin of paint. Libby, what's up?'

Bullshit. Just like his story of staying back for a drink after work. It all made sense now. It was probably another woman's scent he'd erased from skin and fabric. She had no doubt. Her husband was having an affair.

TWO

Joel chose a comedy for their evening movie. Libby didn't fancy any film after what she'd learned, but a comedy was the worst choice of all. She worried it would give away her mood, and she was right. Half an hour in, she hadn't laughed once. Joel flagged it.

'I'm just not in the mood,' she said. 'I have a belly ache.'

They usually sat at opposite ends of the sofa, legs up and intertwined. Tonight she had her feet planted firmly on the carpet. The empty space between them allowed him to slide close and put an arm around her. 'How's my baby? Bad day?'

His touch felt wrong. Had he put his arm around another woman earlier? While naked with her? But she didn't want to upset him so didn't object. 'I'm fine. I might head to bed in a minute, though.'

He remained in place, hip touching hers, arm around her neck, and got back to the movie. She bit the bullet for another ten minutes, until it all became too much to bear. He was laughing too much, and the smell of his body wash was a constant reminder that he'd used it to scrub away another woman's odour. She moved his arm away.

'I need a bath before bed. That okay?'

He nodded. 'If you're sure you're okay?'

'I am. I might just call Linda about the party first.'

'I thought you'd already done that.'

'Mostly, yes. I need to know about the napkins.'

Joel laughed and kissed her cheek. His lips felt cold. Or was that in her mind? She left the room. Upstairs, she got her phone and called Linda, wife to one of Joel's employees. Linda wanted Libby to do the catering for an upcoming birthday party. The details had already been finessed, as Joel had said. There was an entirely different reason why Libby needed to make this call.

It was half ten and Linda was still awake. Libby asked a few catering questions that she already had the answers to, then steered the conversation down a far more important route. 'Your Bert wasn't too drunk tonight, was he?'

'Drunk? No? Why? He's been working. What makes you ask that?'

'Oh, nothing really. Joel said he wanted the boys to stay behind for a drink after work. Didn't Bert bother?'

'Not as far as I know. He drove a couple of the lads home. Did he miss something good?'

'Not really. I just wanted to make sure Joel didn't drink too much.'

'I don't know. Sorry.'

Libby continued the small talk long enough to make sure her questions didn't raise an alarm, then thanked Linda and hung up.

So, Joel had lied. He'd said his whole team had stayed back for a drink at Bowlers, yet Bert and at least two others had gone straight home. There was no drink planned. She bet everyone had headed off home. Everyone, that is, except Joel.

She brushed her teeth, used the toilet, and opted for bed. Normally she slept naked, but couldn't face that tonight. She couldn't bear the thought of being next to Joel with nothing between them, just in case he tried to engage her in sex. She had no pyjamas, so lay atop the covers fully clothed and with a book by her side. Hopefully it would appear as if she had fallen asleep while reading.

THREE

Three years ago, Libby's sister, Emery, who was older by nineteen months, had her bathroom remodelled. The builders were a pair of handsome, single men called Joel and Andy, who made it clear they liked the two women. A double date was arranged.

A year later, the sisters married their beaus in the same month. Soon after, the builder duo started seeing another pair of sisters behind their wives' backs. It sounded like a setup from a daytime chat show.

When Libby found out that Joel had cheated, she tore him a new one and ejected him from the house. He spent a week staying with a mate, while she wallowed in hate and sorrow. Ultimately, though, she got over it.

He came back from work one day and found her parked outside. 'I'm on the fence about what to do,' she said. 'Bring me down on one side.'

They drove the streets, talking. His input was begs and promises. Hers was warnings and an ultimatum. He moved back home the same night.

The 'fence' line had been Emery's idea and, on the very

same night, she, too, gave her husband the order. But she came down on the other side of that fence. Divorce proceedings were instigated. She also convinced Joel to fire Andy from his firm. Now single, Emery downgraded her home and decided to use funds from the sale to buy a business of some sort. She was thinking long and hard about which way to swing her life when a burger van drove by. It was a eureka moment.

It struck Libby as whimsical, but Emery had a sudden bee in her bonnet and wouldn't be swayed. Six months later Emery owned a converted Mercedes Sprinter, had registered as a food business, passed the Health and Safety Executive's hygiene test, gotten the relevant licence, certificates and insurance, and even found a trading spot on Peakhigh Industrial Estate. She was all set to go except for one detail: a partner. Another female, to warrant the name of her new business: BurgerGurlz.

'You want me to be a burger girl?' Libby said.

'You're going to be. We'll be famous burger girls. Quit your job right now.'

Libby was on that job – phone work at a recruitment centre called Atlas Staffing – when she took Emery's call. She was doing the 'fence' thing when a customer insulted her, and it made picking a side easier. She walked out a minute later.

The sisters worked nine to five, Monday to Friday, and business was booming because Peakhigh Industrial Estate hosted fifty-five companies and a few thousand carnivores. The morning rush was their most profitable period and couldn't be missed, so Libby's alarm was always set for six. Today she woke ten minutes before it went off.

She was still fully clothed but now under the covers. Had Joel covered her? He was asleep beside her. He wasn't at work until midday because he had a dentist's appointment at ten. Emery wasn't picking her up until eight, so it gave Libby some free time to snoop around.

She headed downstairs and checked the coveralls he'd washed and dried last night. Clean, fresh, no smells. She checked the pockets but found nothing. No phone number. No sexy note. She checked his coat and found a Screwfix receipt for a polythene dust sheet. Just as Joel had said. The new day and fresh energy gave her pause for thought. Now she was no longer absolutely certain that Joel had another woman.

She got his phone from the bedside table and scuttled into the bathroom to check it. It was password locked and she didn't know the code. Suspicious? Well, her device was also password protected in case of theft or loss, and Joel didn't know the code. Maybe it meant nothing.

Emery's Sprinter pulled up outside at eight, as always. The two women hugged on the doorstep. Libby's detective work had put her ten minutes behind and she had yet to get her uniform on. She invited Emery inside and said she'd be a couple of minutes.

'Has Joel got a Stanley knife?' Emery asked. 'The lino is getting worse.'

She referred to a tear in the floor of the van. A portion of the lino had ripped and both women often tripped over it.

'I'll check in a moment.'

When she was dressed, the sisters headed out. Libby unlocked Joel's van and climbed in the back. She found a silver Stanley knife in two seconds, but it had a hooked blade. She knew a spare would be inside. It was an old knife, so she needed to remove a screw to separate the two halves. There were three screwdrivers on the floor.

When she lifted out the hooked blade, she noticed that its housing was stained with a tacky red substance. Blood. Someone had been silly with this thing. She swapped the blade for a standard utility one and put the knife back together. Emery took it to go cut out the loose flap of lino, then Libby replated the knife, locked up the van, and returned the keys to the hook in the hallway.

Job done, Libby got in the burger van's passenger seat. Behind the wheel, Emery raised her eyebrows. Her expression said, *Want to tell me what's wrong?*

The girls knew each other inside out. Emery had sensed something was amiss with her younger sister. 'It was nothing,' Libby said.

'I know that body language. Start talking.'

Libby shrugged. 'I'll tell you after work. We have to smile for the customers.'

Emery nodded and started the van. 'Okay, we'll put it aside for now. But that's a promise, right? End of shift, you tell me what's wrong.'

'Okay. Promise.'

FOUR

The sisters alternated the cooking and serving shifts. A Tuesday afternoon meant Libby worked the griddle. Once they'd parked in their spot and readied the van for trading, Libby asked if they could swap roles.

'Are you sure? If something's on your mind, might be best to avoid moaning customers.'

'Might be best to know other people's lives are also shit.'

Emery laughed, knowing exactly what her sister meant. Nobody queued like the British and they were world champion moaners. The sisters had heard all manner of gossip from those awaiting their turn at the serving hatch. It was fun to get a snapshot of other people's lives.

The morning rush of blue- and white-collar workers didn't fail to deliver. An elderly manager-type loudly told his suited comrade about his wife's new dog. 'Chewing everything, my friend. Including phone chargers. I want the arsehole to electrocute itself.'

A couple of women were chatting about one's recent baby. 'It was hard to bond at first. I mean, when your baby almost kills you coming out, there's going to be some resentment. Right?'

A man and woman who looked as much like sexual partners as co-workers were discussing something intriguing. 'I don't get it,' the female said, 'because she's only been missing one night. All this furore, and she's probably stayed at a friend's. I mean, I saw how many cops were at the cemetery when I was coming to work. Maybe she was depressed after going to see his grave.'

The next conversation Libby overheard was between a pair of manual labour sorts who clearly weren't on the best of terms. 'So how long should I wait for you to get over her? Ten years? No ex-girl of yours is allowed to date anyone, that it? She's gotta be celibate till you stop pining?'

The sisters took their own lunchbreak around two, when the masses were fed and gone and the road was lifeless. Emery liked to 'get high off her own supply' and had put on two stone in a year. Libby had a packed lunch of Caesar salad with bacon. They ate at a bench twenty metres from the van. It faced TGB Aluminium Services, which had a big front window with a fish tank they could stare at.

'How's Joel doing?' Emery asked.

The girls knew each other inside out for sure. Libby had no doubt she'd read Emery's tone correctly. Big sis wanted to know what had been bugging her kin and figured Joel was the root. So Libby dove straight in. 'I think he's cheating again.'

Emery almost choked on her burger. 'No shitting way. How do you know?'

Emery told the tale. His tardiness and a lie about staying back for a drink at Bowlers. His little distraction so he could get his clothing into the washing machine.

'Wow,' Emery said. 'Sounds bad. Not exactly concrete proof, though. What are you going to do? Grab his phone? I'd go for his phone.'

'I don't know. Keep an eye on him, I suppose.'

'You could get a listening device. Hide it in his van. Cheap these days.'

Libby didn't fancy her food all of a sudden. 'That seems tacky. Maybe I should just confront him. But I can't think how. If I'm wrong, I'll look like a paranoid wife.'

Emery nodded. 'You need some kind of plan. Let me have a think and knock something up.'

That moment happened as they were driving home after their shift. Emery, behind the wheel, pointed out the window when they halted at a red light on Abbey Lane. 'Her. Use her.'

Libby looked past Emery. In the next lane was an A-frame digital billboard truck, which displayed a missing person poster. She was one Joanne Yeowell – however, instead of 'missing', the poster said, 'Please Find'. It had a QR code and a map of her last-known location, which was Abbey Lane Cemetery around 5pm yesterday. The head-and-shoulders photo of the pretty young woman showed her blinking and moving slightly. If that effect was designed to make her appear more real, it worked a treat.

Libby remembered the conversation she'd overheard in the lunchtime queue. She was stunned that someone had gone missing so close to her own home. She lived just five minutes from Abbey Lane Cemetery. In fact, they would pass it in a minute or so.

'Libby. You hear what I said?'

She looked away from the poster. 'Yes. Use her, you said. The missing woman? What do you mean?'

'She's local. Look at the poster. She was meant to be at the cemetery at six last night. So the cops are going to want to talk to everyone who lives round here. Like within two miles or so. That pub Joel was working at was just a couple of minutes back there. The cops will want to know what people there might have seen. So tell Joel to call the cops.'

She was puzzled. 'To tell them what? I don't understand.'

The light turned green and Emery left the A-frame van behind. 'Witnesses. The cops will want to talk to everyone who was around and about last night. But they'll also check everyone's story, so they can... what's the word? Eliminate people from their enquiries.'

'I still don't get it. The police will want Joel's story?'

Emery nodded. 'And he'll know they'll check it out. So he's not going to lie.'

Libby still wasn't following, so Emery broke it down. Libby would call the police and say, 'Hey, my husband was at Bowlers last night. Him and his work pals might have seen something. Come on round and take a statement.'

'Sitting there, in front of coppers, there's no way your man's going to spill some yarn about drinking at the pub all evening. It would take the cops about eight seconds to find out that's bullshit. So I reckon he'll just straight out admit another woman. Right in front of you.'

Libby's eyes widened. 'I can't do that.'

'What, you think Joel won't just unbosom himself?'

She almost laughed at her sister's strange choice of word: *unbosom*. 'I mean I can't waste police time like that. I can't just use a missing woman to get my own way. That's immoral.'

A kid with a death wish blew across the road on a BMX. Emery cursed the day he was spat from a womb and raised a middle finger. 'Okay, just confront him, then. Just come out and say you know he's fucking someone else.'

Libby had no response. They drove in silence. Now that a missing woman called Joanne Yeowell was in her mind, Libby was more attuned to the references to her. They seemed to be everywhere. Standard paper missing person posters were in three shop windows. A speed limit sign had been plastered with stickers showing her face. A woman who might be a relative was standing on a corner, handing out flyers. A little way further on, in a bus lay-by across the road from Abbey Lane Cemetery, police had set up a mobile police office.

It was a giant van with a welcome sign and a ramp to an open side door. Nearby was a sandwich board boasting a different image of Joanne. A digital sign on the side of the van asked for help in finding her and promised confidentiality. But what captivated Libby most of all was a store mannequin standing beside the ramp. It was dressed in a pair of green jeans, a blue T-shirt with a dragonfly image, and a white leather jacket. That must have been clothing similar to what Joanne was wearing when she went missing. The mannequin even had a long, curly brown wig.

'I'm not sure that doll would work if someone went missing naked,' Emery said.

'This all happened fast,' Libby said, turning her head to stare as the burger van drove by.

Emery grunted. 'Missing white woman syndrome.'

FIVE

When Libby got home, around 5pm, she found mail on the radiator near the front door, where Joel habitually dumped it. She riffled through it as she walked into the living room. A water bill. A pamphlet from a windows company. A letter from English Heritage seeking their membership renewal. A takeaway menu.

Joel wasn't having a TV session in the living room. She walked into the kitchen, drawn by noises, and stared out the back window. There he was, playing makeshift tennis over the low fence with their neighbour, a fiftysomething called Darren. They used ping-pong bats and a tennis ball. She opened the back door and both men waved, then immediately resumed their chat about an upcoming snooker tournament. Libby shut the door and went to the bin to dump the junk mail.

When she stepped on the pedal to flip the lid, she saw some paper scrunched up inside. A portion of a face was printed on the balled sheet, showing half a smiling mouth and a single eye that stared at her. An hour ago that face wouldn't have concerned her. Now she snatched the paper ball from the bin and unfolded it.

Sure enough, the half-smile and the eye belonged to Joanne Yeowell. In Libby's hands was a missing person flyer. Someone must have delivered them to all the homes on the estate. Soon the police would come, but not with flyers. They'd knock doors to interview residents. The story was getting bigger.

Libby realised she knew next to nothing about the woman herself, so she grabbed her phone and scanned the flyer's QR code. It took her to a page on Missingpeople.org. Here were four pictures of Joanne, a short biography, and a message from her mother: *Hope you're well, baby. Please contact us. We live in hope.*

Eager for more, Libby grabbed a tea, sat in the living room, and googled the missing girl. She was twenty-one years old and last evening after a reception shift at a pallet firm, she'd gone to visit her grandfather's grave at Abbey Lane Cemetery. And she hadn't been seen since.

The fact that Joanne had a standard job was a puzzle, for she was the daughter of Devin Yeowell, a mega-rich CEO of Arcadia Streams, a mining royalty company with offices on five continents. He was worth £90 million and had homes in Monaco, Hong Kong, New York, and his main hangout of London. But not Sheffield?

The puzzle was answered when she read that Joanne had moved to the South Yorkshire city to live with her dying grandfather, who'd met his wife here. Joanne had opted to forgo a jet-set lifestyle in order to help the old man through his final days. Very honourable. After his death, she remained in Sheffield because she'd met and fallen in love with a man. She'd even taken on a regular job and bought a small house.

Every Monday after work, she would visit her grandfather's grave. Yesterday, November 10th, had been no different, yet there this routine had changed. She had not returned home to her boyfriend. No one had heard from her. Her vehicle was found in Abbey Lane Cemetery car park, but of Joanne there was no sign. CCTV at the entrance did not show her leaving, yet a search of the grounds yielded naught. She had simply vanished. Her mobile phone was traced to the graveyard, but the battery had run out by the next morning. It still hadn't been located. It was all a big mystery.

Due to her father's influence and big-time contacts, Joanne's disappearance became a priority one event immediately. He played golf with the Metropolitan Police's senior national co-ordinator, so he was able to put pressure on someone who could give their South Yorkshire counterparts a kick up the ass. By 10pm last night, just five hours after she went radio silent, fifteen detectives were on the case. By morning it was fifty. A news article dated just an hour ago put the new number at 120.

Teams of police searchers had been at the cemetery and nearby beauty spots. The case was trending on social media and there was already a £50,000 reward for information. Only the vanishing of the Princess of Wales would have garnered a heftier response.

Libby was reminded of Emery's plan. Now, she would have to do nothing to set it in motion. No tricking the police or taking advantage of a lost girl's plight. The police would come and they'd ask questions. As long as she was by Joel's side when he spoke to them, she'd get the truth.

A few minutes later, Joel shut the back door and entered the living room with a glass of milk. 'How's things, babe?'

The flyer was on the arm of the sofa. She held it up. 'Did you throw this in the bin?'

He barely gave it a glance. 'Yeah. Just some junk through the door.'

'It was a woman who went missing from round here. Last night.'

'Okay. Didn't even look. Anyway, what we got for dinner? Have we got any of that quiche left.'

He walked into the kitchen, perhaps to go check for quiche. Libby followed him. 'The police are asking for help. From people who were around Abbey Lane last night. Have you called them?'

Squatting before the fridge, hands fiddling inside, he said, 'No. Why would I?'

'You were at Bowlers that evening. Maybe you heard something. She might have walked past the pub.'

'Didn't hear anything. Apart from a bunch of foul builders swearing. We were all inside. Doubt I could help. I wouldn't have seen someone walk past.'

'The police, they always said people should call them. Even if people think what they know isn't important.'

Still he seemed more interested in his belly than their conversation. 'My information isn't important. I was stuck in a pub. Saw nothing, heard nothing. I can't help. Did you eat the last of that quiche?'

Maybe it wasn't a lack of care, but nervousness. Because she was attacking his carefully laid lie. She pushed it. 'I think you have to tell the police that you and your mates were at the pub. It's only half a mile from the cemetery. They'll be knocking on all the doors around here soon, so you'd have to tell them eventually. Then they can check your stories out.'

He stood up and slammed the fridge door. 'I need to take a piss.'

He headed upstairs, fast. Clearly she had him rattled. He was between a rock and a hard place and knew it, and she wasn't about to ease the pressure. She went up the stairs hot on his tail.

He had gone into the en suite bathroom. She knocked. 'Joel? We need to talk about this.'

'Some privacy would be great here.'

No way. 'I could give the police your statement if you don't want to. You were at Bowlers, right? After work? Then you went to Screwfix for a dust sheet. I saw a receipt for that, but it was at almost seven o'clock. So what about before? Did you go anywhere else? Any other shops?'

'Trying to take a private moment here, Libby.'

'What about at Bowlers? Did you play pool or anything at the pub? Use the jukebox? Buy crisps?'

'Jesus Christ, let me take a damn piss in peace, woman.'

'The police will want all the details, Joel. Everything you did, everywhere you went, everyone you saw. They'll want to talk to all your mates as well to see if the stories match. Are you listening?'

No response. She was annoyed now. His demeanour reeked of guilt. 'If any part of your story was different to what your mates and the pub landlord said, the police will know and it will look bad.' She rapped on the door again, louder. 'Joel, are you listening? Talk to me. Tell me exactly what you did last night.'

She jumped as Joel gave the door a strike of his own, but a much, much more powerful one, perhaps with a foot. It thudded in its frame hard enough to make the whole wall vibrate.

'*Fuck off,*' he screamed.

SIX

Libby sat in the living room, unsure what to think. When she was upset, noise bothered her, so she put the TV on with the sound muted. Joel often got over an anger burst quickly and followed it with an apology. She waited. He came down a few minutes later, bearing the standard sheepish expression.

He sat at the other end of the sofa. As always when they fell out, she waited for him to go first.

He started with, 'We weren't the only ones in the pub that evening. Regular goers didn't come in until about half seven. So it was just me and the lads. And some actual lads.'

She waited for more.

'As in, thirteen-year-old lads. Four of them. They came in to ask if they could clean the windows for money. They ended up buying beers and playing on the pool table. The landlord said the pumps were busted and they had to buy bottles. At extra price.'

She wanted to hang fire some more, but puzzlement pushed her. 'I don't get what that has to do with anything.'

'That's why I can't tell the police. If they talk to us, or they look at the CCTV, they'll find out the landlord served alcohol to under-age kids. He'll get shut down.'

Libby nodded, but only to give the message that she had understood his story. Belief was another matter. 'So you won't be telling the police you were at the pub? Not even if they knock on our door?'

'They won't.' He got up. 'Look, I was going to pop out. I said I'd meet Johnny for a pint. You mind?'

'Are you sure it was Johnny?'

'What do you mean?'

She'd taken a risky move with that semi-accusation. But sailing that close to the wind felt good. She wanted more and decided, sod it, she would have this out with him right now. 'I mean, are you fucking another woman?'

She watched his face for the primary reaction. What she got was awe and the line, 'What on earth gave you that idea?' But was the emotion real? She couldn't tell. It wasn't like last time she'd accused him of cheating. That had involved dejection and an immediate confession.

'Your pub story, Joel. I called Linda. She said Bert came straight home after work yesterday. But you said all the lads stayed back.'

'Is that what that crap with the police was about? Telling me I'd get in trouble if I lied? You don't believe I was there?'

She lifted her phone. 'If I call Bowlers, will the landlord say you all stayed back?'

'Call him. Or will you just assume he's in on it if he said I was there?'

She loaded Google, to find the number. Joel stepped forward and took her phone. 'Okay, look, I was there, a few of us were... but I popped out for a bit towards the end. I went to get a dust sheet, like I said. But I went somewhere else, too.'

'Are you going to make me ask? Or will you just say it?'

Joel got to his feet. Got his shoes. And car keys. She expected to hear the front door open and close, but her husband returned to the living room. 'There's another woman.'

She turned her head towards the silent TV, so he wouldn't see her face. The pain on it. It was hard to hold back the tears. 'Who was she?'

'No one you know. A girl who comes into the pub. It was a one-off thing.'

'One-off sex behind my back?'

He sat on the edge of the sofa. Even though Libby was at the far end, she pressed herself against the arm for more distance. It probably looked a little immature, but of course he couldn't show it. He went right along with the pantomime by standing up again and taking two steps backwards.

'It was just a date, Libby. She was at the pub. After about an hour, I got talking to her. I left the lads behind and took her out for a drive. We drove around, just talking. I took her to Screwfix, but don't ask where we went after that.'

'Oh, I'm sorry,' she spat. 'Is that too awkward for you?'

'Don't ask what she looked like or how old she was or anything else. It'll only hurt you more.'

'So that's where you're going now? Back to her?'

He shook his head fast. It was the only one of his actions that she could definitely label as sincere. 'No, no. The Johnny part is true. I'm going to see Johnny, honest. The girl was a one-off. And I didn't sleep with her. There was just one kiss at the end.'

'No arrangement for more?'

'No arrangement for more. I promise.'

'Your promises mean nothing.'

That one got through his armour and stung, she saw. 'I

know. I hope to change that at some point. Shall I leave for a bit?'

Libby nodded.

'Shall I come back tonight?'

She slapped the sofa. He got the meaning: *you'll be sleeping down here.* She then pointed at the door, and he understood that message, too.

SEVEN

Ninety minutes after Joel had left, Libby sat to watch the 7pm local news. Of course, Joanne Yeowell was the feature. She'd been missing for over twenty-four hours now, and things had progressed at rocket-pace.

A second search of Abbey Lane Cemetery, this time conducted by Joanne's friends and volunteers, had uncovered her handbag in a bush forty metres from her grandfather's grave. On the bank of a stream another hundred metres away, they'd found her dead phone. South Yorkshire Police was getting slaughtered on social media for missing these items during its own search.

There was no CCTV of the graveyard, but plenty of other cameras had captured important events. Police had released footage showing Joanne's car leave work, drive south a mile, and enter the grounds of Abbey Lane Cemetery just after 5pm. The car would not move again until it was hauled onto the back of a truck.

There was more. North of the cemetery was Packway Road, which had a lay-by that was connected to the burial ground by a footpath running through the woods. Just off the footpath police had found a man living in a tent. He was a wheelchair user, so quickly eliminated as a suspect. However, he became a prime witness.

He told police that at around the time Joanne had visited the cemetery, he'd seen a vehicle pull up in the lay-by and had glimpsed the driver on the footpath. He'd viewed this activity through a heavy mesh insect screen across his doorway, so visibility was impaired. After that, he had thought no more of it and headed out to beg for money. All he could attest to for certain were two details. The first was that the driver was male.

With a shaking hand, Libby called Bowlers. A barmaid answered with, 'We're not doing the karaoke tonight, love. If that's what–'

'I want to speak to the manager,' Libby cut in. 'It is very important.'

He was on the line forty seconds later. Libby told him who she was, then said, 'What time did my husband and his men leave your pub on Monday?'

'Oh, about half five, same as always. That's the cut-off because we're still open in the evenings.'

'They didn't stay behind for a drink?'

'Those guys? No. Not sure I'd let them anyway. I mean, we don't really have a dress code, but guys in dirty overalls? That's not good. Why, was there a problem?'

Oh, there was a problem all right. She hung up. She looked at the TV, which showed a detective standing outside Abbey Lane Cemetery, talking to a bank of journalists. He was asking for witnesses who had also seen what the homeless man had spotted.

Detail number two: the vehicle parked in the lay-by had been a white van.

Like Joel's.

Libby suddenly had a throat like a desert. She rushed to the kitchen and gulped water. Her legs were wobbly, so she sat right there on the floor.

Joel's van? Could it really have been his, though? Why would he have parked in the lay-by near the cemetery? Libby got up and hunted for her phone. Standing in the living room again, she loaded Google Maps, then searched for Abbey Lane Cemetery.

She saw the graveyard and Packway Road about fifty metres north of it. Between them, Marriott Wood and the footpath running through it. There was a housing estate close to the lay-by on the other side of the road, which was good news.

Libby felt her thumping heart calming. Just for a moment she'd been unable to shake the idea that her own husband had murdered Joanne Yeowell. But it was paranoid and obtuse. She knew her own man and he was no killer. She was such a fool. It was obvious now why Joel had parked in the lay-by. It was the perfect spot to stash the vehicle and walk to the housing estate. And why would he do that? Because his new woman lived there, and she had a husband and gossiping neighbours. So Joel...

But according to the statement of the homeless man, the van driver had ventured down the footpath. On the map, that footpath led nowhere but into the back end of the cemetery.

The same hollowness in her chest returned. The world seemed to flicker and buzz like a mistuned TV image. 'No,' she said to the room. 'It wasn't Joel. He wouldn't. Couldn't. He...'

But he'd left Bowlers at the standard time of five, roughly the same time Joanne Yeowell reached the nearby cemetery. White van. White male. He didn't go to the DIY shop until seven, which leaves over three hours unaccounted for. He was acting suspicious when he came home.

'Because of the woman he's seeing,' she said, countering that inner voice. 'That's why he showered when he got in. And washed his clothing. To get rid of her perfume. That's why he's so secretive. He's never heard of Joanne Yeowell...'

But he had. Her face was everywhere, including on a missing person flyer posted through their door. Joel had stacked the mail on the radiator, as always. He hadn't disposed of a takeaway menu or a pamphlet from a windows company, neither of which they had use for. Yet he'd screwed up and binned Joanne's missing person flyer.

'He's not violent,' she said. He could raise his voice, but never a hand in violence – in her experience, at least. Joanne's killer was a psychopath and a wife would know if her husband was sick in the head...

But she'd found blood on a Stanley knife.

EIGHT

After collecting the keys she required, Libby went to the back door, where she paused with her fingers gripping the handle.

She tried to tell herself she was being stupid. Her own husband, a murderer? It couldn't be. That kind of thing only happened on TV. It only happened to someone else.

But that was what other people would say about her.

She hauled open the door and walked down the yard, then unlocked the gate in the back fence. Across five feet of grass was the back wall of the first row of lock-up garages. The patch of green land was lit by a streetlamp curiously placed dead centre. Again she halted.

This time, however, her mind offered no argument against what she was doing. She had come too far. She had breached a bubble by leaving the house, and now onward was the only path available. She had to see this through.

She skirted around the row of garages, crossed the gravel strip, and approached block number two. She stood before their garage, key in hand. A third lingering moment. She wanted a rational part of her brain to object, to send her back indoors. No voice of reason existed. Or it had already said its piece when it told her to investigate what Joel had been up to in the garage yesterday evening.

It took some effort to haul up the door, which squealed as if annoyed at being disturbed. When it was high enough for her to duck under, she entered the cold, dark storage area. The light from the streetlamp beyond the other row of garages cast her shadow across the concrete floor, but the door blocked illumination beyond a few feet. She should have brought her phone to use as a flashlight. She wanted to run back to get it, and hopefully abandon this mission once in the bright warmth. Something inside refused to turn her around and instead made her step deeper inside.

Despite the gloom, she could see the familiar shapes and bumps of everything they'd stored here over the years. In the last twelve months she might have ventured into this chilly space three times, yet her eyes immediately latched onto an anomaly. Something different about the interior. A new addition since last time.

It was a plastic supermarket bag sitting under their old dining room table in a corner. It brimmed with something. She approached, bent down, and recognised what lay at the top of the bag. Green denim. Jeans. Joel had stored a bag of clothing?

Of course. For his new woman: he had bought her gifts. Or they were for him, purchased by her. Either way, they had to be hidden from Libby. She pulled the bag from under the table and grabbed the bottom, to upend it and dump the contents onto the concrete floor.

The clothing fell in a neat pile, with a T-shirt on top. That garment was crusted and tough, like something that had got soaked and been left to dry in the bag. But an image on the front was neat and flattened, as if from a movie scene that wanted the audience to recognise it. And recognise it Libby did.

The world wobbled again as her head seemed to fill with air.

Her eyes were locked on that image, willing it to change, to become the word *love* or a whale or a flower. But it didn't transform.

It was still a dragonfly. The very same one displayed on the T-shirt worn by Joanne Yeowell when she vanished.

What little light there was suddenly rippled, and she knew something had moved between the garage and the streetlamp.

Someone.

She turned, already aware of who that someone would be. Locked solid, she watched as Joel ducked under the half-open door and entered the garage.

NINE

Joel stood just inside the doorway, seemingly taller than normal. That would be her mind playing tricks. His face was in shadow, so she couldn't see his eyes. But for sure those eyes were on the clothing piled to one side of her. She felt a wave of fear and guilt, as if she was the one who had done something wrong.

'You've got an idea in your head,' he said. 'But it's bizarre.'

He'd entered the dark space silently, ghoul-like, but the imagery was fractured when she heard his voice. Monster or not, he was just a man. Her man. It allowed her fear to seep away. 'In that case, enlighten me. Tell me how that missing girl's clothing got here.'

'I found it.'

The only thing bizarre here was her laugh. It did not belong at this terrible scene. Maybe it was due to fear after all.

Joel read it for what it was: mockery. 'I promise it's true,' he said. 'I was seeing another woman. I admitted that. I met her that night at the cemetery.'

He paused here to await her response. Perhaps he had given this snippet of explanation in order to gauge the potency of his full story. She was willing to hear it. 'Go on.'

'I drove her around, like I told you. But what I left out was that we went to the cemetery. We knew it would be quiet there and we could have... sex.'

Libby waited. He read it as consent to continue.

'We had sex on a grave. It was quick, not very good. I regret it. It was wrong. When it was over, we went separate ways. I didn't see it at first. It was on the ground. The clothes, I mean.'

He pointed, as if she might be confused as to what clothing he referred to. She waited.

I tripped over it. I landed on it. My hand touched the clothing. Then I saw her body. Joanne's. Close by. I panicked after that.'

Another pause to determine the success of his tale. Libby waited.

'I knew she was dead. I knew it was murder. I mean, no way had she stripped off to kill herself. And I knew my fingerprints would be on the clothing. Fibres from her own clothing, too. My DNA. I knew I would be blamed. So I did something silly...'

He fell silent again, watching her. Maybe he had the boiling frog syndrome in mind: if he offered up his bullshit piecemeal, she might acclimatise by the time the fanciful end arrived. This time she prompted him: go on.

'I ran, Libby. I panicked and I scooped up that clothing and I ran. I didn't call the police. I knew they'd blame me. I just wanted to hide away and forget it all.'

'What about her body? It's still missing. It isn't in the cemetery.'

'I honestly don't know, babe. I promise. She was there when I ran away. I don't know what happened. Someone else must have moved it afterwards. Maybe the killer came back to take her away.'

Boiling frog syndrome, while a silly fable, was a metaphor for acceptance. If someone's life deteriorated, they would accept that downward spiral if it was gradual. But in reality frogs jump out of slowly heated water. And Libby was not going to fall for outlandish lies. She would not adapt to life with a vicious murderer of young women.

'I don't believe you. You killed that girl. You're evil. And I'm a fool.'

She saw his head shake in the dark. 'No, I promise. It wasn't me. You're no fool. *I'm* the fool for panicking and–'

'Stop,' she cut in. 'Look, if your story is true, we tell the police and get through it.'

'No. They can't find the killer. They don't have a suspect and so they'll blame me. The country is in uproar and they're under pressure. They'll serve me up like a fine meal.'

'What did you do with her body?'

He took a step forward, arms out, as if he actually thought there was a snowball's chance she'd hug poor old him for his bad luck. When she stepped back, bumping into the dining table, he stopped. 'It wasn't me, Libby. I couldn't do such a thing. Not ever. I'm Joel, the man you married. The man you love and know. And you know deep down that I'm telling the truth.'

'I don't know you. I'd say *anymore*, but that's not right. I never knew you. I just knew the mask you wore to hide the monster below.'

He folded his arms. 'So you want to send me to prison? To rot? That missing woman–'

'Joanne,' Libby yelled. 'Joanne Yeowell. That's her name. The name of a young woman with a life ahead of her.'

'She attacked me, Libby. Okay, you want the real truth? She came at me with a knife. That bitch tried to kill me and I had to defend myself and...'

It was all more lies and his words seemed to dissolve in her head, as if her brain had closed its doors against the assault. He saw it happen and abruptly shut up.

'You're an animal,' Libby said into the subsequent silence. 'A monster. I can't imagine how anyone could do what you did. I can't imagine what that poor girl went through before she died. You deserve to rot in a cell till you die. And you will if I have anything to do with it...'

She tailed off, realising that her lack of fear had made her too bold, too forward, too mentally clumsy. With that final threat, she had pushed too far, exposed too much, and backed Joel into a corner. She saw it in the way his shoulders slumped. There was just one way out of here, and he stood between her and it.

He reached back, grabbed the inner handle, and shut the garage door with a shrieking rasp, plunging them into abyssal darkness.

'Let me show you exactly what she went through,' Joel said, and she heard his feet step towards her.

TEN

Vicious murderer of a female or not, Joel had never before raised a hand to his wife. That meant he expected no offence as he crossed the dark garage and grabbed her.

The punch knocked him backwards. Libby heard his feet scrape on the concrete, then a grunt and a thud as he fell to the ground. He must have tripped somehow because the strike hadn't been very powerful. No matter the reason, the result gave her the opportunity she needed. She ran for the door. Right into it.

'Where are you going?' Joel yelled, as if she was acting irrationally. She ignored him and threw her hands across the metal, seeking the small length of rope attached to the top for opening the door. When her fingers closed on it, she gave a hard yank. The metal panel shifted slightly and an oblong of space appeared at the bottom. Enough to roll through, and that was about all she had time for. She dropped flat to the ground.

She was through and up in two seconds. But not free yet. Like a scene from a cheesy horror movie, Joel's arm snaked out of the ten inch gap and fingers clapped around her ankle, tripping her. She stumbled forward, out of his grasp, and fell flat on her face two metres away. Pain enveloped her left knee and right elbow.

'The hell is this shit?'

The words of a man approaching down the gravel lane with his dog. He was young, hooded, and carried a can of lager in the hand that didn't hold a dog lead.

Libby got up, turned, and saw Joel's fingers wrap around the bottom edge of the garage door, ready to haul it up. She would never outrun him, never keep her blood if his hands touched her flesh, and she saw only one, desperate option. She threw herself at the angled garage door, bending low in order to strike the bottom with her hip and shoulder. Her weight and momentum dragged it from Joel's fingers as it slammed shut with a mighty clang.

The dog walker just stood there, fascinated and scared. Even his Labrador was absorbed.

The garage door shook as it tried to open. Joel must be tugging on the rope. Libby sat against it, feet glued to the gravel. 'Open this damn thing, Libby,' Joel yelled.

'I need a phone,' she shouted at the dog walker. But he didn't move. He seemed possessed by the kind of numbed awe that could only be exhibited by those snatched from routine and dropped into hell at a moment's notice.

'Help me block the door. Now,' she screamed at him.

Joel pounded against the door, sending thunder through the night air. This, rather than her shout, seemed to trigger action. Still utterly confused, the dog walker released his pet's lead and rushed to her. The dog bolted. He jammed a foot where the door met the ground. He now seemed to have his wits back. And he'd kept hold of his lager can. 'Jesus fuck, what the hell's going on, missus?'

Before she could ask again for her saviour's phone, she saw part of it sticking out of his pocket. She snatched it. From inside the garage came new noises. Not the striking of metal, but violence unleashed on other materials. Tornado-like, Joel was blindly taking his rage out on everything around him. Was this the beast Joanne Yeowell had faced in her final moments alive?

'What the fuck you got in here, a tiger?' the dog walker yelled. He might not have been joking.

Worse than a tiger, she thought as she dialled 999. *A lot worse.*

PART 2

ELEVEN

In December 2012, three men kicked in the door of a house to rob a drug dealer – a practice known as taxing. The trio of intruders ransacked the house for cash and dope, assaulted the dealer, and fled with a fiery parting gift. As his house burned, the dealer had a choice to make: get out now, or rescue a secret drug stash in the attic. He was not a wise man.

The subsequent murder investigation unearthed only one suspect: Mike Voyzey, local dropout, hoodlum, loser, and general shitbag. Nominally a dead drug dealer wouldn't trouble the front pages, but Voyzey's brother was a multi-millionaire businessman. The media jumped all over the fact that such a wealthy family had a member involved in low-level crime.

The truth was that Voyzey had no access to those riches, for he'd long before been ousted by his family due to his criminal lifestyle. For over a decade before the killing, the black sheep had lived on the streets and funded himself with burglaries and muggings, drug dealing, and other illicit endeavours. By the time his brother started to earn big money, Voyzey hadn't seen him or the rest of the family for years.

When his brother's wealth quickly got real serious, Voyzey

tried to re-enter his life, but that bridge had been burned. When, years later, Voyzey sought financial help in his manslaughter trial, his brother supplied not one penny. As he told an inquisitive reporter, 'Blood might be thicker than water, but it means nothing to me.' Voyzey got basic free legal assistance and was sent down.

Voyzey had no clout in the outside world, but behind bars it was a whole different planet with different rules and different ways to make your name. He'd built a reputation and garnered powerful friends across the country. He had the means to make an impact outside the prison.

Prison life was one of inertia, especially for a man with others at his beck and call. Added to the fact that Voyzey loved sugary treats, he now weighed 300lbs and had diabetes and sleep apnoea. Of all the ugly folds and bumps of his flesh, his neck embarrassed him the most, so he'd grown his hair long and wild to hide it as best he could. Unfortunately, it was prematurely grey and added ten years to his unkind forty-eight.

The prison had an ongoing anti-obesity programme, because eighteen per cent of inmates were overweight due to inactivity and unhealthy food, but Voyzey had declined to enter it. The therapeutic and well-being meetings were too much hassle and, besides, it wouldn't do well for his pride to admit that something was out of his control.

Amongst those who would do his bidding were some prison guards. At just after 9pm that Monday, one of the staff approached his cell and unlocked the door. 'You hear the news? Your niece went missing.'

Voyzey struggled to sit up on his reinforced bunkbed. Joanne? What? 'What do you mean, missing? Start talking.'

The guard knew little more than what was in the news and gave over his phone so Voyzey could see for himself. He spent ten minutes reading various stories, to get a fuller picture.

Joanne had been reported missing only a couple of hours ago, but already it was a major story. Because of her suave, handsome, rich dad, of course.

But Voyzey didn't learn enough to satisfy him. Joanne lived in Sheffield and he knew some unpleasant people there. He dispatched the guard and got his burner mobile from its hiding spot. He always got wind of prison-wide cell tosses a week in advance.

He called his fixer on the outside, a man who knew how to get things done. That guy contacted various Sheffield-based hoodlums. None of them knew any more than had been reported already.

'You're going to have to try your brother,' his cellmate said from the top bunk. He was an Italian guy in his early thirties nicknamed Nando.

Seven years ago he'd been given thirty-three years for a double murder. Two men tried to steal his car, so he chased them, naked, down the street, cornered them a few hundred metres away, and kicked both to death with his bare feet. As an enforcer for a local gang, he entered prison on the back of a serious reputation for violence. To provide for his wife and children, he let it be known he would play slave to the 'highest bidder'. And that was Voyzey, who paid £2,000 a year for Nando's services. Nando called himself a broker.

Voyzey punched his bed five times, and stopped only because the exertion made him a little dizzy. Nando was right: wherever the hell he was, Devin would have a high-ranking cop by his side to impart developments as they occurred.

'Nando, let me use your phone.'

'Why?'

'I called my damn brother off mine before. He's blocked it.'

'Best not have him block mine in case you need it in an emergency. I'll go get you one.'

HM Inspectorate of Prisons expects to see prisoners spending ten hours a day out of a cell for mental well-being, but since the great Covid lockdowns things had changed. Here inmates rarely got four hours unlocked. But Voyzey had clout and could organise things. The governor allowed him some leeway because he could stamp out insurrection far better than the staff could. His cellmate called the guard back and it was arranged for him to visit the showers. Instead, he went in search of a mobile phone.

When Voyzey had a new device – handed over by someone who knew better than to object – he called a number from memory. Hong Kong was eight hours ahead of the UK, which would make it very early in the morning over there. He got the housemaid, who had broken English made worse by the fact that she'd been woken by the ringing phone. But she was able to take his message and make a call of her own.

Voyzey got the call he'd been awaiting forty minutes later. The moment he answered, his brother said, 'I know you care. I know you want to help. But it's all in hand.'

Devin sounded annoyed. Was that because Joanne was missing? Or because his jailbird brother was sticking his nose in? 'I just want to know what's going on. Tell me everything you know.'

Devin claimed to know very little so far, and nothing beyond what the newspapers had broadcast.

'Bullshit. You'll have a hotline right to the chief constable. I'm her uncle, Devin. This ain't fair.'

'Not fair? Where were you when she got pneumonia and spent two days in hospital? You didn't call, didn't send a card. She receives no card at Christmas. What day is her birthday, Mike?'

'Fuck you, Devin. That mean I don't care? Since when was a lung illness the same as going missing and maybe being dead?'

'You only care about your pride and your ego and your reputation. If Joanne's been hurt, it shows that the almighty Mike Voyzey isn't untouchable. You're probably more concerned about having your shady empire damaged or challenged.'

Voyzey wanted to rage, but Devin could cut it down by simply hanging up. So he bit his tongue and cycled down the gears. 'I do care and that's why I called you. Besides, you poisoned the whole family against me. I'm the scumbag criminal black sheep, remember? Did you ever consider that I stay out of touch because I know nobody wants anything to do with me?'

Devin paused. His next words suggested he felt a little guilt... but not enough to apologise. 'You'll get updates as I get them, Mike. But I'll call you, not the other way round. I have to go now. Don't talk to any reporters if they try to contact you.'

Voyzey hadn't considered such a thing. 'I want to help. If Joanne got lost somewhere or she's hurt in a car crash, you have the means to find her. But if some sick fucker took her, then we're in my world, aren't we? And you can't get answers the way I can. Have you considered that this might be for ransom? Have you had a note? Is that what you're hiding? People would love to strip some of that mega money from you.'

'You think this is my fault?' Devin snapped. 'Joanne might be missing because of *you*, Mike. You make vicious, erratic enemies. Don't call me again.'

He hung up. Voyzey called back, but the number was blocked. Again. What was that, five phones now barred by his brother?

Devin's words, while harsh, had come from a place of intellect. Voyzey was a bad man, existing in a world full of them. Ransom was definitely plausible, but maybe Joanne was the innocent victim in a simple case of payback instead.

Was this his fault?

TWELVE

'Joel has admitted it.'

Libby barely heard the woman's words. Her eyes were still fixed to a framed overhead photo of a hedge maze. She had needed something to take her mind off the sweetness of the family room at Woodseats police station. It had been furnished like a living room, probably to give a sense of comfort to victims of crimes and the families of such. But Libby hated it. It felt like camouflage. Like pretending nothing was wrong.

'Libby?'

Libby dragged her eyes from the maze on the wall and looked at the family liaison officer who'd been assigned to her. The middle-aged lady was sitting on the other end of the sofa, watching her. Libby hadn't noticed her return.

'He admitted killing Joanne Yeowell?' Libby said.

Detective Constable Sally Monroe nodded. 'Just now, from his cell. Before interview even. I think he knows the evidence against him is substantial.'

A clock on the wall said it was 9.49, which meant it had been almost two hours since Joel's arrest. They'd been whisked away in separate police cars. Nobody had asked her a thing until she reached the station and was formally interviewed. After that, she had been paired with this FLO, who'd described herself as a conduit between victim and investigators. Monroe had then left Libby here alone and gone off to do... whatever.

Libby had had no idea what was going on beyond these walls, but she'd fretted that somehow the police wouldn't be able to charge Joel, and he'd be released. She had even wondered if he was already back home and she was still here for safekeeping.

Now, hearing that he'd confessed to murder – or *unbosomed* himself, as her sister might have said – she should have been happy, or at least relieved. But she didn't know how to feel. Had part of her hoped that she'd gotten this all wrong and Joel was innocent? That they could continue their normal married lives?

Just to be certain she wasn't delusional, she asked Monroe two questions. 'Joel's here, right? At the station?'

Monroe failed to hide her puzzlement. 'Yes.'

'And Joel's been arrested for murder and has admitted it?'

'Yes. He'll still be interviewed soon, and we won't charge him until after that.'

There. It was all real. No hallucination. Life had forked. Everything she'd been before this moment was now different. Delayed shock would probably hit her soon. 'What did he do to her?' she asked.

'He said he can't remember,' the DC said. 'He said he blacked out during the crime. No memory of what happened or what he did with her body. He's told us that much outside of interview.'

'Does that mean he's insane?'

Monroe looked uncomfortable at the question. Libby realised how silly it was and waved it off. 'Ignore me. So what happens now?'

'We'll still do his interview shortly. After that, he will

probably be charged. If so he'll go to the magistrates' court tomorrow.'

Libby knew next to nothing about the court process, but somehow she'd learned that magistrates' courts dealt with less serious offences. Weren't magistrates just volunteers who weren't even legal professionals? 'Magistrates? I don't understand. He killed a woman.'

Monroe explained that all criminal cases first went before magistrates, to decide if the circumstances warranted a referral to crown court, which dealt with serious crimes. Murders always went to crown court, of course, but that initial hearing at the lower tier still had to go ahead.

Joel would attend to confirm his details. He could not enter his guilty plea at that stage, but he could indicate his intention to do so. Brownie points were up for grabs for those admitting their crime at the earliest opportunity.

His case would then be sent to the crown court, and there, at his next hearing, he could enter that guilty plea. If he did so, he would either be sentenced immediately or recalled on another day to learn his fate.

So, court tomorrow morning. Libby rubbed her face. Everything seemed to be moving so fast. 'I don't get why he won't tell you where her body is. I mean, he's not denying he killed her.'

Monroe didn't get chance to speak. The look that came across her face told it all.

'Because of what he did to Joanne, right?' Libby said. 'I get it. If police see the body, they'll know what happened. Perhaps rape. Mutilation. Joel wants to hide the evil he did to her.'

The DC paused, but she might as well have nodded furiously. Libby sighed. 'But we don't know anything for sure yet,' Monroe said. 'Hopefully Mr Mytton will give us more in his interview.'

Libby took a deep breath. 'I think I want to go home.'

'I think you should stay a while.'

'I think I just want to sleep.'

'You can sleep here. I could get you a blanket for the sofa. We can keep you updated better.'

Just hearing the word 'sofa' made her feel sleepy. This station felt like the core of everything, the mechanism that had turned her life to dust, and she wanted out. But she also couldn't face an empty house. Besides, she couldn't return home yet. The police had cordoned it off and were searching it.

'I have to get out of here,' she said.

'Then we can arrange a hotel. No problem.'

Libby shook her head. 'I'll go see my sister. I have to call her. We need to talk. She doesn't know anything yet.'

That same concerned look passed across Monroe's face. This time she didn't hide what was on her mind. 'Libby, I have to tell you, but I don't want to worry you. What happened at the garages tonight... Local residents saw Joel's arrest. They've put two and two together and–'

'And they know,' Libby said. It wasn't a question. 'The story is out, isn't it?'

Monroe nodded. So, word had travelled, and fast. Her neighbours knew, and her few friends knew. And soon the whole country would know that her husband had been arrested for the high-profile murder of Joanne Yeowell.

'This is why you don't want me to go home, isn't it?' she asked. When Monroe nodded, Libby said, 'Are journalists there? Are they camped outside my house? Are they outside this police station right now?'

Another nod. 'But we'll keep them away from you.'

'Will Joel be front-page news? Will I?'

Another nod.

There had been a massive seismic shift in her world over the last hour or so, while she stared at a maze picture in the comfort of this faux living room. Monroe expected her to wilt like a thirsty flower, but Libby planned to be stronger than that. For no reason she could fathom, she thought of the dog walker. Her saviour. 'Where's the man who helped me? Is he here? Do reporters want to talk to him as well?'

Monroe had a surprising update. The dog walker had fled the scene upon the arrival of police. They didn't have a name for him yet. 'I suspect he's got no interest in being labelled a hero. Or he's wanted by police for a crime. Either way, it appears he wants nothing to do with this.'

'That makes two of us.'

THIRTEEN

The role of a family liaison officer was werewolf-like. Libby needed Monroe in order to be kept abreast of the murder investigation. To that end, the detective constable would answer questions and pass along to her superiors any concerns Libby had.

But the police also needed someone to relay information provided by the wife of their murder suspect. At first Monroe had acted like her best friend, but suddenly the full moon came out and the DC transformed. She wanted Libby to talk about her feelings ever since she'd first suspected Joel was having an affair. It was fishing for something juicy via an innocent remark or a seemingly insignificant detail that hadn't emerged during earlier questioning. The family room and Monroe's smile did little to sugar-coat what was basically an interrogation.

Libby cut it short once she'd realised she was being pumped for evidence. She told the DC she would talk more after she'd called her sister. Monroe let her use her mobile phone.

Emery, like the rest of the country, was connected to the internet and, more important, social media. No longer did people wake up to news of events that had happened the night before. Now they had live access at their fingertips. Emery had not only heard about Joel's arrest, but she had seen mobile phone footage of it taken by Libby's neighbours. She had read comments from people playing judge, jury and executioner. And she knew Monroe was right about the new interest in Libby as the wife of a killer.

Emery had also learned of a rumour going viral on social media. Someone unknown had promised to put £100,000 into the pocket of whoever killed Joel.

'What?' Libby barked. 'Who would do that?' She immediately cursed her own silliness. Who would want to kill a man who'd murdered an innocent young woman? Probably one in four or better.

As for an actual name: many had fingered Devin Yeowell, Joanne's father and a man who could dump a hundred grand and barely notice the dent. Clearly he'd heard the rumours or had been accused by someone because he'd already replied.

'You should know this isn't my doing,' he had said through his solicitor. 'If I was so inclined, which I'm not, I would have put up twenty million.'

There were other theories. Inmates across the UK had been making plans to get at Joel once he was in prison. A local criminal gang had said they would not perform the assassination, but would happily hide the recipient of the prize for a fee. There was even a claim that a professional hitman from Brazil had already entered the country. So much gossip, so insanely fast. Libby wanted a sinkhole to open beneath her feet and swallow her forever.

Emery asked, 'I mean, how on earth would someone pay the bounty? The killer will be a wanted man.'

Libby wanted to change the subject, so they talked about anything but Joel and Joanne for a few minutes. But when it became obvious that both sisters were forcing small talk, Libby told Emery she'd call her later, and then hung up the phone.

Monroe had left the room to give her peace. She used the opportunity to search Google. It was a bad idea. She checked over a dozen online newspaper stories and social media threads, and every one that featured Joel mentioned her name, too. Even some legit, big newspapers were involved. She closed down the search.

When Monroe returned, Libby immediately said, 'Are the media allowed to slag me off like this?'

Monroe took her phone from Libby. 'Did you check online? That's not a good idea, Libby.'

'People are saying I'm involved. They seem to be hating on me more than they do Joel. I did nothing wrong.'

Monroe sat by her. 'Joel is in the court system now. Reporters could be charged with contempt of court if they say anything that could influence his case. But you haven't been arrested. So, much as I hate to say it–'

Libby said it for her: 'I'm fair game for abuse.'

Monroe nodded. 'It's not nice, I know. But it's a big, developing story. It's too early for anyone to really know anything, including us. At this stage people only have their own guesswork.'

Great. She knew the police always kept things under wraps until after a trial, which meant Libby could look forward to months of hassle and accusations. Hopefully there would come a day, after he was locked away and interest in his crime had waned, when she could get her wheels back on track. Become anonymous again. Walk the streets without pointing fingers and snide whispers in her wake.

Or perhaps not. Maybe, like her husband, she would be hated and abused for the rest of her life.

She remembered Monroe's promise of a hotel and now asked about it. 'I just want to hide away until tomorrow.'

'That's a good idea. I've already made enquiries and I've found a place.'

The hotel was called The Summer Palace. It was on Abbey Lane of all places and just a half mile from Libby's home. The route there from the station would take them past Sanders Road, which her street ran off. It gave her an idea.

When the unmarked car bearing her, Monroe and a driver was close to passing Sanders Road, Libby reached forward and tapped the DC on the shoulder. 'Turn right here. Go past my house. I want to see. Please.'

Monroe turned to look at her. 'Why?'

'Pure nosiness. Please.'

Monroe didn't object. Maybe the DC wanted to see how Libby reacted to seeing the crime scene. Maybe her bosses had told her to keep an eye out for clues that Libby had aided Joel somehow, perhaps by hiding evidence. Everybody else seemed to bloody well suspect her of keeping a secret. The driver made the turn onto Sanders.

An unmarked car would alert nobody if it cruised by a crime scene. Libby sat in the centre of the back seat, to be less visible through the windows. When the car drew alongside the entrance to her street, Libby asked for a dead stop. The vehicle paused in the junction, allowing Libby to peer down the road she might never call home again.

There was activity. The road seemed to be blocked by onlookers standing around. After seeing a flash of yellow, Libby realised the group milled at a cordon marked by tape. Beyond it were law enforcement vehicles and the moving shapes of people in plastic coveralls, suits, and police uniform.

A van in a neighbour's yard blocked her view of the lower half of her house, but there was no doubt that the important people inside the cordon were dealing with the place where she and Joel had built a life. Where they held everything important to them. Crime-scene technicians and detectives would be crawling all over that home, searching drawers, lifting carpets, poking here and there to find a weapon, bloodstained clothing, a diary with frightening admissions.

It was a horrible sight. How many times had she watched such scenes on true crime and fictional TV shows? How many times had she wondered what it was like to be the neighbour of an infamous killer, watching all this unfold right across the road? How many times had she wondered what a killer's wife must be going through?

How often had she pitied such a woman?

'Drive on,' she told Monroe, who was watching her intently. The car started moving away. Libby didn't look back.

Home. That word no longer applied. She wasn't sure she would ever be able to go back to that building. The place felt cold and remote and alien, as if a killer had not just slept there but buried multiple victims under the floorboards. It would have to be sold, if a buyer could ever be found. If the council didn't demolish it in order to wipe away an imagined evil aura.

Her husband had ruined that house, her life, everything. It angered her. It put an impulse in her. 'Has Joel been asking about me?'

Monroe looked round at her. 'Yes. He told us he'd like to apologise to you. But he's in custody so there's no visitors, I'm afraid. Maybe—'

'Let me talk to him,' Libby cut in. 'I'll get him to talk. Don't tell me the idea hasn't already occurred to someone above you. Turn the car around.'

FOURTEEN

Hours before the story broke, detectives on the case finally came to speak to Voyzey. He was having a particular bad day with aches and pains and couldn't walk, so the meeting took place in his cell, and he didn't give a shit who saw. The detectives weren't there to offer updates, of course. They wanted to know about people in his orbit who might wish harm to him or his loved ones.

'That's a long fucking list, pal,' Voyzey said. 'And you ain't getting it from me.'

'What's this, the Omerta?' one of the tecs said. 'This code of silence shit still applies, does it? Even when someone might have slaughtered your niece? You'll protect the guy who did that because you don't want to be a snitch? How honourable.'

'How professional, talking to a grieving family member like that. Fuck you. You fools haven't got a clue what happened to Joanne yet. I'm not going to rat out a bunch of guys when they might all be innocent. If you get a suspect and he's a definite, come see me again and I'll dish the dirt. Now piss off and do your job.'

The other detective said, 'Sure thing. But how about you keep your people from getting in the way?'

Last night Voyzey had sent men to Sheffield, to ask questions. The cops were knocking on the doors of regular people, because those types would always talk. Criminals never spoke to the police, and that was a fucking shame. Because the slimy, callous, thieving, deceptive people of the world were the ones with information. Bad knew bad.

Voyzey's heavies had gone into the dark recesses of the city, to crack the heads of crackheads and show local bad boys they were small fry. Sometimes this type of endeavour yielded little nuggets of information and sometimes it dropped a jackpot like a benevolent fruit machine. But this time Voyzey didn't even get a pair of lemons. Nothing. Nobody had a clue who had snatched Joanne.

One of his guys had been arrested for assault, though, after kicking in the door of a drug den only a half mile from Joanne's house. Voyzey had gotten word that the cops had tied the arrested man to him.

'How about you leave my people alone to ask questions?' Voyzey said. 'Why stop them? Does the glory of solving the case mean more than finding my niece? My people can get the sort of answers you can't. You should fucking welcome it.'

'Well, we don't.'

That whole day was the worst in all his time as a prisoner, more so even than his first night as an inmate. He hated the walls because they prevented him from getting out there to find her. He spent hour upon hour angry, and some of it was directed at himself, because he had failed to protect Joanne. He should have realised that danger always lurked around the families of people like him. He had been complacent. Where the fuck was she? Jesus! And Devin hadn't called him back.

Voyzey had tried his brother's number again and found it disconnected.

But he remained optimistic, and it paid off in the evening.

Sometimes Joe Public with a social media account could break big news before the authorities and major media outlets. Voyzey heard about the arrest of a man for Joanne's murder on X, from a profile with nine followers. There was video of him being released from a garage and then snapped up by cops.

A name was mentioned, so Voyzey ran it through Facebook. Joel Mytton had an account but it was private and Voyzey could only see a profile picture. It was enough. He stared at the man's face for a long time. Here was the fucker who'd killed Joanne. He almost punched his phone.

Staring down from the top bunk, Voyzey's cellmate said, 'Yep. He's got that look about him.'

The look of one who'd rape and murder young women? If only it was that easy. Voyzey made calls to a handful of people on the outside and barked orders. One of the recipients was told to find him a reporter who'd be willing to interview Joanne Yeowell's jailbird uncle, right there in his prison cell. Could a newshound pass that up?

Apparently not because Voyzey's phone rang half an hour later. On the line was a reporter called Dan, who worked for a national tabloid. First question out of the man's mouth: *'How do I know you're who you say you are?'*

'Publish the story and see if the real Mike Voyzey objects. Besides, you're a tabloid, so you like the sensational. Would you like to end this call and do some research? You could call me back tomorrow like the others.'

Others? Other journalists who might run this exclusive instead? Too risky, and Voyzey knew it.

So he smirked when this journalist said, 'Did you know a man's been arrested for Joanne's disappearance?'

'I did. Joel Mytton.' Saying the name disgusted him. The creature didn't deserve a name.

Did Voyzey believe Mytton was guilty and would be convicted of kidnapping? Or murder, even though there was no body? There was no proof she was dead, right?

'She is, and they'll find her. As for a conviction. If he survives long enough, he'll go down.'

'If he survives? Are you saying you plan to kill him? You have a reputation as a man with connections. I heard you were once labelled as an orchestrator of carnage.'

Voyzey had never heard that description. 'I've heard the same rumours about me. All bullshit, my man. I'm a God-fearing man and I don't believe in revenge. But prisons are full of bank robbers and gangsters. Guys like that like to protect sweet young women. And they don't like blokes who hurt them. Mytton has a ticking time bomb stuck on his back. There's a lot of hard cases banged up who can't wait until this shitbag gets delivered right to their door. He might be a dead man before his trial.'

'Wouldn't it be better if he was convicted and sentenced to a lifetime in a cell?'

Voyzey laughed. 'Prison scares the hell out of everyone at first. Don't matter if you're a hard case or not. But you know what, you get used to it. Then it becomes routine. Do the routine for enough years and these places become who you are. When this shitbag gets locked up, it'll be hell on earth at first. But he'll get used to the food. He'll get used to the daily grind. And when this bullshit all dies down, people will get used to him. He'll make friends. He'll get comfortable.'

'What's your point? Do you mean he'll become institutionalised?'

'It's a thing. And guys who become that thing aren't serving time any more. They're at home. This shitbag could get thirty years, but he won't serve that. He'll be in a cell, but he won't be suffering. Those of you who think he'll be in pain and horror 24/7, think again. He'll be right at home. And that ain't justice.'

'What would justice be? Death? Would you want capital punishment brought back?'

'I hear there's a bounty on his head. Which means someone has already decided Mytton's fate. As for me, I wouldn't touch him. God will have plans for Joanne's killer.'

Voyzey had said what he needed, so he wrapped up the conversation after giving bland answers to a few more questions. The first guy he'd called, his fixer beyond the prison walls, had been told, 'The cops got some fuckwit for my niece. Start spreading the word that there's a price tag on his head. Hundred thousand.'

'You're gonna pay a hundred big ones to whack this guy?' the fixer said. 'You could have someone inside do that for a Twix.'

'There's no money. Just make sure that rumour goes around. It's nothing to do with me.'

Voyzey knew that, as a bad guy connected to Joanne, of course he'd be a suspect when Joel Mytton got whacked. At least now, with a bounty story as camouflage, there would be a smidgen of confusion and doubt, and it might just keep the cops from his cell door.

Now, his call with the reporter done, Voyzey got hold of his fixer again and asked for a certain man's number. When he contacted the latter, he said, 'Job for you. You won't like it. I won't give a shit.'

After learning what was being asked of him, the man on the other end of the phone panicked. 'I can't do that. That'll be the end of me. I'll go to prison and–'

'I release what I've got on you, you go to the nick anyhows.

But this way means your family doesn't disown you. They don't have the shame of knowing what you are. You can tell them you killed Mytton for the hundred K bounty, so your kids will be well off. Better to go to prison as a killer of a killer, eh? Or would you prefer the truth to be in the hands of all those lunatic lifers you'll be inside with?'

The man cursed, and he begged, but he might as well have tried to wring blood from a stone. Ultimately, he had to agree.

'And you'll do it tonight,' Voyzey ordered him, then hung up.

A couple of years back, Voyzey had set up a team called Stingray, which used adults to pose as children online, in order to trap paedophiles. It was a burgeoning subculture. When a grown man turned up to meet a child, he'd instead find himself surrounded by adults with cameras and pelted by accusations. The recordings, sometimes including foot chases as suspects fled, went online and to the police, who hated such vigilante action but happily sent the offenders to court.

Six men had been prosecuted so far, with two being given custodial sentences. Others had avoided conviction due to a lack of evidence, but had been shamed and ousted by their friends and families. One guy had topped himself after being mistaken for a child molester, so sure, yes, the cops were right about the odd innocent man having his life ruined. But Voyzey wasn't in this game because he worried about his moral fibre.

One member of Stingray had joined a chatroom as a boy of eleven called Morris, and he had successfully arranged to meet a man for sex. Getting paedos off the streets was just a bonus because what Voyzey truly sought were powerful people to blackmail. And this latest was a gem. He was a police officer, and now he was in Voyzey's pocket.

The cop would kill Joel Mytton. In prison he'd wallow in

suffering because of his job, so why heap suffering atop anguish by also being known as a kiddie fiddler? Both were bottom of the scum ladder in the slammer.

All calls done, Voyzey hid his phone and settled back to watch TV. He felt good, eternal body pains notwithstanding. The ball was rolling. Joanne would have her vengeance soon.

FIFTEEN

Woodseats police station had an exercise yard locked in by blank walls. No windows to climb through, no handholds to scale the walls with, and a single iron entrance door impossible to breach without permission. In the yard itself there were no chairs, no trees or bushes, or anything else that a prisoner could use to harm themselves or others.

Actually, one wall did have a feature: a small iron ring for restraining the most unpredictable and violent criminals. Libby had been married to the prisoner they brought out at close to midnight, but they weren't going to take any chances. She was the one who'd delivered him into their hands, and it wasn't unlikely he might have a sweet-tooth for revenge.

So not only was Joel handcuffed to the solid ring, Libby was also ordered to remain outside a three metre distant semi-circle chalked around it. It reminded her of an old cartoon about a dog tied to a stake. These procedures she accepted, but not an escort. An officer was stationed by the door, but she asked for privacy.

'Leave? Me? Can't do it,' the officer said.

Libby didn't like being rude to people just doing their jobs, but she felt deserved of some leeway. She wasn't here purely to help the police. 'Then I won't talk. Take me back inside.'

The officer had to get on his radio for the opinion of someone with a higher pay grade. The answer was no surprise. Libby and Joel were alone sixty seconds later. Clouds suddenly obscured the moon, making the yard blacker, the world more surreal, and her optimism a piece of history.

Joel hadn't said a word yet. His first ones were, 'Any chance you've got a station key in your pocket?'

'Where would you run?'

'Somewhere far. You coming?'

'The running life isn't for me. Besides, why would I go anywhere with you? I don't even know you.'

Joel looked hurt by that. Good. She wouldn't abide any attempt by him to pretend this was nothing more than a hitch in their marriage. He sat on the ground, which forced him to keep his cuffed arm raised. 'Look at me. What do you see?'

What she saw was a cute kitten standing next to a ripped-apart bird. Here was Joel, the loving husband and good friend, but also a man who'd murdered a young woman. It played tricks with her mind, much like if you heard a dog meow. She had to replay his attack on her in the garage just to remind herself she didn't have this wrong.

And then she gave her answer. What did she see? 'A wild animal shaped like a man.'

He shook his head. 'No. You *do* know me. I'm no monster. I just did one bad thing.'

'So you weren't always like this, that's what you're saying? You turned into a monster one day?'

He seemed to miss the sarcasm as he paused to consider his response. 'Maybe that's something that actually happens. Something in the genes at a certain age. Maybe it really is as simple as an overnight change. Remember how I always wanted to be an astronaut? Then one day I swapped it for tennis superstar.'

'I remember you saying you were born to play tennis. You just didn't know it until you picked up a racket.'

He read between the lines, and hung his head. 'That's harsh. I'm not a killer, Libby. I killed, but I'm not a killer.'

'So you became a monster just for one hour or so? And now you're back to being the old Joel again.'

'I promise, Libby, that's not me. I will never harm anyone ever again. I couldn't.'

'I think a courtroom is going to make sure of that.'

Joel said nothing. The moon returned, and he raised his eyes to it. He was probably eager to gaze anywhere but at her, that was all. But she couldn't help wondering if there was something... *lycanthropic* at play. Lunar cycles affecting human behaviour – that was a thing, right? Hadn't she once read that Brighton Police had put extra officers on shift during full moons?

She looked around the yard. The dark, the cold, the high walls: it felt like a giant, roofless cell, and she hated being here. Time to cut the chitchat, even though Monroe had told her to tread slowly so as to not unsettle Joel.

'Why won't you tell the police where Joanne's body is?'

He leaned forward, as if to make sure she could see his eyes. 'I can't remember. That's the truth, babe. I blacked out. I think my drink was spiked with some weird drug. I don't remember anything. I just know I did this because I came to with blood on me. And I had that bag of clothing in my van.' He paused. 'Do you believe me?'

'No. No one will. The police think you did some nasty stuff to the body and that's why you won't give it up. Because they'll know how evil you are when they see what damage you did.'

'I didn't have sex with her,' Joel said. His words came out in

71

a whine and contained more emotion than his earlier murder admission. It was as if he thought rape was despicable but cold-blooded slaughter was fine and dandy. Or he believed a faithful wife might forgive the latter but never the former.

It made her fume. 'I came here to get you to tell me where Joanne's body is. That's it. The police wanted me to sweet-talk and trick you into it, but I can't stand here any longer and–'

'I don't know, Libby. Honestly, I don't know where the body is. But I knew you wouldn't believe me. And that hurts, since you're the only friendly face in my life now.'

His final sentence was one that sweetly segued into her next utterance. 'Take a good look at this friendly face, because right now might be the last time you see it live and in the flesh. But if you give up what you did with Joanne, I'll make you a promise...'

SIXTEEN

Joel asked for a pen and notepad, which an officer brought to the yard. He sat against a wall and wrote for roughly fifteen minutes, not a word spoken. Libby stood before him and watched, remembering a time when Joel had called her a bitch because he was angry.

On that occasion, he had not verbally apologised but had written down his feelings. Back then he'd said he could explain his emotions better on paper. But was this like that? Or did he feel he could lie better if he didn't have to look at her?

When he was done, he gave her the pad and remained seated, eyes now on the ground. She also sat, but beyond the safe white line and with her back to him so she could read in peace.

You never knew this, but sometimes I like to sit in the graveyard. It's peaceful. I like to help out by scraping moss from the gravestones. So the people there don't seem forgotten. Some of the older graves have no loved ones still around. So I parked in the lay-by on Packway and I walked in. I didn't follow Joanne. I didn't know she was there. I just bumped into her when she was there.

I don't know why, but I chose to speak to her. She was the only one there. She was at her grandfather's grave. That's what she told me. She said, 'This is granddaddy. He died of cancer. I always come here. Who are you visiting?'

I said I wasn't here to visit. Just for some peace, and to help out.

We started chatting about this and that for a few minutes. I got my Stanley knife out and scraped away some moss from her granddad's grave. She said thanks and that's when she told me she had fallen out with her boyfriend and wanted to leave him. She said she wanted to put some distance between them.

I said, 'Are you moving away?'

She said no. 'By distance I meant having sex with other men.'

I was surprised because it seemed like a come-on. She then said, 'I just had a guy on the way here. There was a man thumbing a lift. I picked him up and we fucked in my back seat. He was quite rough, and he didn't use a condom.'

I didn't know how to react, what to say. All I could think of was, 'Did it work? Are you over your boyfriend?'

She told me, 'No. Just one shag won't do it. I need to have more. You're handsome. Fancy helping a girl get love out of her system?'

I told her no, I couldn't, because I was married and loved my wife. I could tell she didn't like that and asked me again. I said no and that seemed to upset her.

Before I knew what was happening, she started to strip. I just stood there in shock. She took all her clothing off and stood there, naked.

She then said, 'How about now, handsome?'

I think she believed that seeing her naked would change my mind, but I said, 'I'm still married. You should get dressed and go home.'

That seemed to set her off. She picked up a big rock, and she started yelling at me. She said she was going to smash my head in. And that was when she tried to attack me. She tried to hit me in the head with the rock.

Because I'd helped with the moss, I still had my Stanley knife with its hooked blade in my hand, but I didn't realise this. Instinctively, I put out my hands to block her strike, and the blade of my knife must have been pointing forward. I wasn't moving the knife, but I was holding it tight.

That was when she tried to sidestep my arms, to get at my head with the rock. But she misjudged it and ran straight into the knife. I couldn't believe it. Before I could stop it, she moved into the blade and it got her in the throat, and it cut her wide open because she was moving sideways.

She fell backwards, onto the ground. I could see the wound was big, and I knew an ambulance wouldn't get there in time, not with the rush-hour traffic. All I could do was close that wound and stop the blood, so I knelt over her and grabbed her neck. I squeezed the sides of the wound together, but it didn't work. She still bled badly. I was terrified. I was talking to her, trying to soothe her, and promising that she would be okay, that I would get her to a hospital.

And then, suddenly, she stopped thrashing. I knew she was dead. I got her phone so I could call for help, but I realised it would be quicker to take her to hospital. I thought there might be a chance of saving her because I'd read that people could be brought back to life up to forty minutes or so after dying, and I think there was a woman in

America about ten years ago who was revived after half a day or so.

So I picked her up. I had brought my knife wrapped in a carrier bag, so I put her clothing in it. I knew that Joanne would need it if she was revived at the hospital. I carried her out of the graveyard, and down the path that led to the lay-by. I wanted to flag down a car, but Packway Road sits higher than the lay-by, and there were bushes between the two roads and it was dark by then. Nobody could see me.

The best bet was to put her in her van and drive her to hospital myself. I knew I'd be driving fast and I didn't want her body to bang about inside the van, because I've got sharp corners and tools and wood in there. So I wrapped her in a dust sheet before putting her in the van. Then I started driving.

But when I got her phone out to call ahead to the hospital, I saw how much blood was on me. Suddenly I panicked. I knew how it would look. Her blood was all over me and it was my knife that she accidentally killed herself with. I knew it would look like I killed her. I would go to prison and my poor wife would be all on her own. Joanne's family would think she'd been murdered and that would hurt them. I couldn't have that.

I know it was stupid, but I decided to hide the body. That way my wife wouldn't be on her own, and Joanne's family could always think Joanne was still out there somewhere, alive. I drove fast and, unfortunately, her body bounced around in the back on corners and speed bumps. But I had to rush.

I found myself driving past Pacific Isle Golf Course, and I saw the woods and realised it was a good place. There's a dirt track used for maintenance vehicles or something, so I drove down that. When I was hidden in the trees, I got her body out of the van and carried her about five metres off the track, where the undergrowth was thick and it was obvious nobody walked.

I had a brick bolster in the van. It's a four-inch-wide chisel for cutting bricks. I used that to dig a hole. It took me about two hours to get a hole deep enough. I buried her in the foetal position and she was still in the dust sheet. I covered her in soil and then put leaves and bits of wood and branches over her. I am so ashamed of this, but it was the only way to make sure that she was never found, so her family could live in hope. I thought that was best.

It wasn't until I got home that I realised I still had the bag of Joanne's clothing. I knew I needed to keep it. If her body was ever found, the family would want the clothing back. So I stored it in my garage. I was wracked with guilt and sorrow. Over the next few days I was just numb, crying and unable to think. I am so sorry.

Libby wished she'd never read it. If his confession had contained atrocities beyond just snuffing out a life, it would have destroyed her psyche. But she would have accepted it as the truth. If he had tried to write something that painted him in the best light, he couldn't have done a better job than this. This tale of a woeful accident was worse than a confession loaded with gore and evil because she didn't buy a syllable of it, and now she had only her imagination to fill in the blanks.

Without speaking another word to him, Libby knocked on the heavy iron door. It was opened by three officers. One remained with her while two uncuffed Joel and led him away. His final communication to her was a smile. She didn't mirror it.

Monroe entered the yard a few moments after he'd gone, a little out of breath as if she'd run here eager for news. 'Did he give you anything?'

'Nodded, smooth, moon,' Libby said. 'A What3Words address. That's where Joanne is buried.' Her own words chilled her. Only now did she fully feel the impact of what had just happened. Her own husband had told his grisly secret. For a minute or two, only two people in the world had known where an innocent young woman's butchered body lay. She wanted to be sick.

'Thank you,' Monroe said. 'You did an important thing and I hope it wasn't too uncomfortable.'

She held out the pad. 'His confession. I don't know if it can work as a statement. Maybe you need him to say it under caution in an interview room. But here it is.'

Monroe was so eager for it she snatched the pad. While reading it, she said, 'How did you manage to get him to confess and give up the body?'

Libby rubbed her throbbing forehead. 'He needs a comforting face at court. So I have to be there every day.'

SEVENTEEN

The dodgy cop who worked at Woodseats police station had been seeking the right time to make his move and get next to Joel. His gangster boss had gotten lucky because the cop was not only clocked in until midnight, but he was on what was unofficially called Stasis. Most officers on response duty were known as Roamers and had to patrol the streets, but those on Stasis got to hang around the station and catch up with paperwork while they awaited a call to arms.

Unfortunately, the dodgy cop couldn't just lurk around the custody suite, so he tried to think of a way to get down there. Earlier that evening he'd had a run-in with a man accused of slashing a neighbour's tyres. No arrest had been made because there was no evidence beyond the injured party's claim.

The dodgy cop got hold of his boss – the official one, an inspector – and said he wanted another chat with the accused, so he was let out of the station. It was just after eleven. Round at the possible offender's home, the cop banged on the door.

The offender answered it topless and hissed at the cop. 'You again. What do you want now?'

The cop whipped out his cuffs and grabbed the man. 'I'm nicking you for criminal damage, twat.'

Bang. Job done. Now the cop had to process the prisoner. And he'd take his damn time with it so he could hang around the custody suite and fathom a way to get into Joel Mytton's cell.

In the rear yard of the station, he parked and left his prisoner in the back of the vehicle while he had a chat with a couple of officers who were taking a smoke break. They were talking about the big new guest, of course, so the dodgy cop hoped to learn something new. What he discovered made him desperate and he stepped aside to make a phone call.

'I just heard Joel's wife just had a meeting with him,' he said to his gangster boss.

A pause. 'What do you mean?'

'Out in the yard. Just the two of them. And now I'm hearing a buzz that he's given something up. And people here are in a twist. I reckon it's the body. I think he's just given up the body. Or maybe the murder weapon. Something big, definitely. The wife swayed him somehow.'

A pause. 'Get in there and sort him out when you get a chance.'

'I'm trying. It's not easy. I can't just walk into his cell and... look, there's more bad news. Apparently a detective superintendent is coming from London to talk to Joel.'

A pause. '*What?*'

'Yeah. I have no idea why. But it must be some unsolved crime he's got down in his patch. Maybe Joel's been whacking women all over the shop. This isn't good. He might get shifted down to London.'

A pause. 'Get in his cell. If he gets carted off down south, I'll blame you. And then I'll ruin you.'

'I'm trying. I just arrest–'
The line went dead.

EIGHTEEN

As Monroe was driving Libby to The Summer Palace hotel, she got a radio call that the secret was out. Monroe explained that she'd had to book the room officially, through the Crown Prosecution Service, so someone at the hotel had obviously realised a vulnerable person and a possible witness needed housing for the night. Given that Joel's arrest was the big news story of the hour, it was a no-brainer to determine that VP to be Libby.

A new hidey-hole was required. Monroe picked a Premier Inn barely a mile away from the police station. Monroe used her own money this time, to avoid the same mistake, and headed in alone to book the room. When she returned, she told Libby that a detective would be along to watch her overnight. Monroe had tasks back at the station.

When the female detective arrived, she had a baseball cap and sunglasses for Libby. 'A disguise?' Libby said. 'Is that necessary?'

'Better safe than sorry,' Monroe said. 'We don't want reporters waking you at 3am.'

Libby took the items with reluctance. Monroe bid them

goodnight and departed. Libby and the detective entered the hotel with their key. Libby kept her disguised face hidden from the receptionist, who barely glanced their way.

Their room was on the top floor but they encountered no other guests or staff on the journey. As soon as they were inside the room, Libby looked for a minibar. She didn't often drink, and had never before turned to it for help after bad news. But this was uncharted territory. A drink was all she wanted now, if only to help her sleep.

But there was no alcohol in the room. 'Can you go out and get me gin?'

'I can't do that. I think we might need you sober, too. Please don't insist.'

Libby sighed. This detective had introduced herself with a joke: *I'm your bodyguard tonight.* But she felt more like a jailer. Libby could have pushed for the booze, but she didn't have the energy.

The TV seemed to be calling her name, but she refused to turn it on. A nice comedy programme might have eased things a little, but she didn't trust herself with the remote control . She'd be a button away from a news report. Unless a terrorist group had exploded a whole country, she'd see things far too close to home and too much to bear.

Luckily, silence was a good mood enhancer. It would have been nice to call Emery again, but she didn't have a phone. The police had taken hers for analysis, which was a scary thought. It kind of said the police didn't fully trust her.

The detective wanted to talk – not about the case – but Libby was in no mood. She sat in the armchair and read a book, leaving the detective to watch a documentary about life on a cruise ship. Libby tried to tune out the annoying voices of people able to have fun because they hadn't married vicious murderers.

By 3am, the detective chaperone was asleep and Libby was no longer able to fight an urge. It wasn't for news of Joanne's body, but it did concern the dead woman's corpse. She headed downstairs to see the receptionist. A shift change had occurred at some point and a new woman was on duty. 'Can I use your mobile for a moment?' Libby said. 'To check the internet? Mine's naffed.'

The receptionist agreed, so long as Libby remained in the lobby. She sat on a sofa and loaded the What3Words website.

It was a global address system that sectioned the earth into a grid, with each 3-metre square identified by a 3-word code. There were apparently 57 million of them. The police used the very same app, since it designated an address to locations that before had had none. You could find a single rock jutting from a vast ocean. A tree in the desert.

Or a dead body.

Libby's stomach lurched as she saw where *nodded, smooth, moon* took her. The location Joel had given her was a portion of the woods between Abbey Lane and Pacific Isle Golf Course. It couldn't be. If Joel had buried Joanne's body at that location, then she'd been lying just 500 metres from his home. Where Libby had soundly slept in her own bed that same night. While Libby hummed a tune and spread tuna on toast in their kitchen, her husband, just a five-minute walk away, had been spilling a young woman's blood.

These thoughts were quickly overshadowed by the realisation that the police had mentioned nothing to her about the body itself. Maybe they were still setting up whatever equipment they needed for a search. Or they'd found nothing because Joel had lied. Maybe, though, what they'd discovered had been deemed too abhorrent for her fractured mind to deal with.

The truth, surely, would come with the dawn of a new day.

NINETEEN

The detective superintendent was a fifty-one year-old called Jones, and his arrival at the station caused a stir. Despite the late hour, one of the station's own superintendents ordered officers to run about and have a clean-up, as if royalty was visiting. They didn't want Detective Superintendent Jones returning to his Met boys and slagging off South Yorkshire Police.

Police stations were full of people who investigated wrongdoing, so of course someone did some snooping to try to figure out which crime the detective superintendent wanted to talk to Joel Mytton about. Best bet: the murder of a woman three years ago.

In Deptford, London, the fire brigade had been called to a wasteland where a sofa was aflame. By the time they'd put out the fire, the chair was just springs and metal and a charred frame, which allowed the firefighters to see what lay beneath. A blackened body. A post-mortem would divulge that thirty-seven-year-old Sarah Gretton, a prostitute who lived less than 300 metres away, had been strangled and stabbed forty-two times. No solid clues, no real suspects, and a coating of ice on the case file. Until now.

This crime was the first Jones had investigated as a detective superintendent. Fresh into the role, with something to prove, he would surely be sore about failing to solve this homicide thus far.

Jones arrived in plain clothes so he wouldn't look like a copper. He met with a fellow detective superintendent but refused to give many details about why he wished to speak to Joel Mytton, until he could confirm if the man was a viable suspect. He said only that it involved a murder three years ago, which kind of confirmed the rumours.

He also insisted on speaking to Joel alone, and in his cell. He didn't yet want to do this as a formal interview, for that would spike rumours of serial killing if news got out. The station's detective superintendent agreed with this prognosis. People were eager for juicy details and, even just a few hours in, had already tried to make Freedom of Information requests for everything from bodycam footage of Mytton's arrest to personnel files of the detectives running the investigation.

Nor did Detective Superintendent Jones want an escort, because that would set tongues wagging. He had no idea they already had been. Nonetheless, he was allowed to make his own way to the custody suite. The custody sergeant had been made aware that the detective superintendent wanted nobody within earshot when he spoke to Joel. It wasn't good practice to allow a high-ranking officer to be alone with a killer, but orders were orders. The sergeant handed the detective superintendent a portable panic button that would bring help running, pointed him in the direction of Joel's cell, and prayed that things weren't about to get breaking-news-worthy.

Joel knew nothing about the visit and sat up when the door unlocked and a burly man dressed like a civilian walked in. Jones flashed a warrant card and introduced himself.

'Metropolitan Police?' Joel said. 'That's London. What do

you want with me? Is this where coppers from all over the country try to dump old murders on me?'

Jones said, 'We'll get to that. Up you get and turn around. Arms out. I need to search you.'

He'd been searched already, of course. Once when he was arrested, again upon entry into the station, and for a third time after his meeting with his wife. He saw no problem in a fourth and stood and turned around and put out his arms.

Jones grabbed Joel's hair and punched him in the back of the neck – or so the prisoner thought. Jones had just slotted the blade of a knife hard into the flesh, where it skidded off the spine with an audible squeal and sank hilt-deep.

Joel immediately collapsed, but he didn't hit the floor because the detective superintendent's powerful arm kept a tight hold of the hair and allowed his victim only to sink to his knees. It put Joel's neck in an easier position for the following five stabs. Blood went everywhere in spurts from severed veins and arteries and spatters from the moving knife. Joel didn't make more than simple grunts upon each blow, none of them loud enough to carry beyond the room. Nobody came running.

Jones had been with the Metropolitan Police for twenty years. He'd been a strategic firearms commander, kidnap and extortion senior investigating officer, and a specialist in cybercrime. However, he'd cut his teeth chasing down violent gang members, and he'd seen his share of blood. It bothered him not one jot as he watched Joel die on the cold cell floor. He had a family to worry about instead.

His hand was coated in blood, so he wiped it on his own jacket before pulling out his phone. The device was a Zanco Babyfone, the world's smallest at just over seven centimetres in height. He made a call to the man who'd orchestrated this carnage.

'Is it done?' Voyzey answered.

'It is. Now you cut me free, okay? Because this is day one of twenty years behind bars for me. For doing this for you.'

'At least your kids will still love you. You only killed a killer. If the country learns about your liking of young boys, it won't be from me. Just make sure my name is never connected to this.'

Voyzey hung up. Jones got a small tin of petroleum jelly from his pocket and coated the phone in it. Murder wasn't even the part of this job he'd most dreaded. It was swallowing this damn phone so investigators wouldn't get it. It almost made him throw up, but it was preferable to trying to eat twenty sharp fragments. He'd get the device back probably tomorrow, but he'd worry about what to do with it then.

He also wanted to wash the blood from his hands, but was unable. As a murder suspect who'd be required to give samples, Joel wasn't allocated a cell with a toilet or sink in case he destroyed biological evidence. Jones sat on the bed to give himself five minutes of calm before the storm broke. But the dead time was too awkward, so he hit the panic button. Four officers came thundering. They froze in the doorway at probably the very last sight they'd ever expected.

Jones held his bloodied hands up. 'I just saved the taxpayers fifty thousand pounds a year. I also thought it can't hurt to help myself to that hundred K bounty on his head.'

TWENTY

At midnight, Franz turned off his computer, his work done for the day. He would have rather continued, but his wife had set limits. Midnight, maximum. One day's work should never bleed into the next. Rules. He'd built his world on them.

He left the office and opened the door of his son's room. The ten-year-old was fast asleep, but his phone was in his hand and playing a YouTube video. Franz turned it off. He had to repeat this action in his eight-year-old daughter's room.

That done, he checked on his wife, who was also asleep. Next, he checked the security system to make sure all the cameras and motion sensors were operational. That done, he went downstairs for his half hour of TV before bed. It was 12.30.

The routine had stuck even though he hadn't been able to watch what he'd wanted for the last four months. The reason why was seated on the sofa, wrapped in blankets.

'I need water,' his wife's elderly mother said.

Franz fetched it for her. He wanted to spit in it. He had a large house and there were two spare bedrooms, but Lacy's mother was infirm and didn't like going upstairs. So her bedroom was the living room, and come darkness she never left it. Her portable toilet was right next to the sofa. He had to empty it for her.

He sat in an armchair to watch on-demand *Judge Judy* episodes. He hated the show, but it was all she seemed to partake of.

At 1am, his TV time done, he got up and headed to the sunroom at the back of the house. He was waiting for a phone call and wouldn't be able to sleep until it came. He sat and read a book. He decided they needed a TV in this room, then remembered that his wife had vetoed the idea already. One of the kids would always be down here, blasting out *Teen Titans*, and Lacy would get no peace and quiet to read her books.

His phone rang forty minutes later, just as he was about to drift off in the reclining armchair. He answered it to hear:

'That fucking superintendent who came? Goddamned killed the fucker.'

Franz paused. He always took his time to create a response, even if one was obvious. 'What? Joel killed the super?'

'No, other way round. The super stabbed Joel to death in his fucking cell. You believe that?'

He wasn't sure he did. 'This is a silly dream. Why would such a thing occur?'

'I don't know. But your man's dead. I guess you're safe.'

Franz hung up and headed upstairs. He shook his wife awake. Groggy, she said, 'Always the yellow ones,' and stumbled into the bathroom. Yellow ones? Some kind of dream.

She was awake and alert when she exited the bathroom, though. She looked like someone expecting bad news. 'What's gone wrong?'

'Joel's dead,' Franz said.

'What? But you said your peeler was just going to... what did he do?'

Just going to... give Joel a warning. Yes, that had been the plan. Franz's dodgy 'peeler' on the inside was supposed to warn Joel not to talk to the police. But before he could, another police officer got to the prisoner and murdered him.

Lacy received this update with wide eyes. She rubbed them as if thinking she might still be dreaming. Her response was not to seek more details, but simply to state: 'This thing keeps getting weirder.'

She wasn't wrong.

Franz ran a business called *Go Go Karts*, which operated out of Barnsley and catered to those with a love of karts. There were two speed tracks and an obstacle course. He'd built the place two years ago and loved running it so much that he'd sold off all his other registered companies to concentrate on it. Good profits made it perfect as a front for laundering money from Franz's illegitimate endeavours, of which there were many.

To the neighbours and his staff and customers, Franz was a successful local businessman. The government didn't share that opinion, labelling him as the head of an organised crime group with its fingers in all the usual malarky: prostitution, drugs, extortion, theft, and more.

Organised crime group members needed to be of a different ilk: tough, cruel, unforgiving. Joel had been one such man. He didn't look the part, but he had a vicious streak, fearlessness, and fighting spirit that made him a perfect enforcer. If Franz needed someone threatened, or a guy to storm a drug house full of enemies, Joel had always been the man. They weren't friends, but Franz liked him.

So, he'd picked Joel for the kidnap job. Over a five-week period, Joel had gotten to know Joanne Yeowell and her routines and habits well, all without her knowing she was under surveillance. Joel had decided that the prime time and location for the snatch would be when she visited her grandfather's grave. Franz had already prepared a cell for her, where she'd wait until her rich dad handed over £5,000,000 for her safe return.

Law enforcement would go wild chasing down hunches and leads, but Franz knew they'd find it hard to look past Mike Voyzey, Joanne's gangster uncle. He and his rich brother were at loggerheads because Voyzey had been fiscally ignored, which sounded like a great motive. Even if the police didn't suspect him of involvement, they couldn't ignore the fact that Voyzey was a man with an abundance of capable, violent enemies. This muddying of the waters should have provided a forcefield that kept Franz's name off blue line lips.

Then it all went wrong. Joel had called Franz and claimed that Joanne hadn't visited the graveyard. Joel had never let Franz down yet, so he'd believed it. Even when Joanne was reported missing later that night, Franz hadn't suspected Joel was involved.

By the next morning, it seemed half of South Yorkshire Police was on the hunt. Franz was surprised the lack of blue line people elsewhere hadn't set people off looting. Still Franz hadn't even considered the possibility that Joel might have found Joanne after all and done something bad. A bad call for certain.

Someone else, though? Sure. He had been pretty much convinced that Joanne had been targeted by someone else who wanted to milk money from Devin Yeowell. Maybe fifty other guys were, like Franz, right now cursing whoever had beaten them all to the punch.

Then Joel got arrested that evening and the truth came out.

To maintain his good image, Franz didn't recruit lowlifes with known bad reputations and criminal records. His men and women were all cleanskins, meaning unknown to the police. They were also single and without children. Rules.

Joel had started as one such, but at some point he'd found a woman, married her, and even moved in with her. All without his criminal colleagues, especially Franz, having a clue! To keep a second life so secret for years showed an exemplary level of trickery and smarts.

But it also meant Joel had deceived Franz, and if he could do that, he could also sell him out to save his own hide. When his people got cuffed-up, it was always a problem. Heart and loyalty weren't bulletproof when someone faced a long stretch, and none was lengthier than what Joel had on the horizon. A rape murder was about as bad as it got.

As counter to this very scenario, Franz had dodgy officers in various police stations across South Yorkshire. So, he had tasked his Woodseats sleeper with getting close to Joel to deliver a warning to keep his mouth shut. But now someone had beat him to it and silenced Joel in a very bulletproof way. Franz should have been happy: Joel Mytton wouldn't be telling the authorities the real reason he and Joanne Yeowell had crossed paths.

But there was a new worry. Who had sent the killer? Voyzey? The gangster helmed a criminal empire of his own from a cell in a London prison. He was also known for running the kind of outrageous psychos Franz avoided. But did all of this add up to having the clout to force a detective superintendent to commit murder and end his own career?

Franz's wife believed so. After listening to her husband's theories and worries, she said, 'Voyzey must have had help from his brother. Maybe he paid. I did tell you this kidnap thing was a silly idea.'

Had she said that? He didn't think so. But he couldn't deny it was a valid point. 'It's all over now. Joel's gone and so is the plan and my involvement in it. We put it behind us.'

She raised her eyebrows and stared at him, which was her way of saying he was being naïve. 'The police will dig into Joel's history. They'll find out that he's involved with you, no matter how secret you both think you've kept it. Then that's big trouble. How do we know they don't already know everything?'

He didn't. But he had hope. 'There no way he would have unloaded already. Not this quick. He hadn't even been to court and–'

'His wife, though? You said he had a meeting with her at the station. Maybe he told her everything. Husbands do that.'

Franz had been wondering about that very thing.

TWENTY-ONE

When the detective chaperone stopped speaking, Libby waited for something to happen. For the news to change something physical within her. But it didn't happen. She felt nothing.

No grief at Joel's murder.

But was it simply delayed until the shock had dissipated?

'Are you okay?' the detective asked.

'I'm fine. Please go back to sleep now. I'll be okay.'

Monroe had called the detective with the news of Joel's death, so that Libby could hear it from a warm body standing before her rather than down the phone. It was their way, of course. But Libby would have preferred a faceless messenger.

She knew it was rude, but she turned away from the detective and stared out the window, across the city. It was a poor second best since she couldn't actually be alone in the room. She tried to picture Joel as she'd last seen him, but the image wouldn't come. All she could see was Joanne Yeowell. And there was blood.

It was Joanne she felt for. There was nothing for Joel. Their history counted for naught. His murder of a young woman and her rape – she didn't believe his version of events – had changed everything between them. Sometimes former couples turned their love into hate, and often it took months or even years.

Her change had been instantaneous. The man she had fallen in love with was a phantom, imaginary. The real Joel had been exposed, and he wasn't an entity she could – or should ever have – cared for. So she didn't mourn him. Never would. Learning he was dead by murder had hit her with all the might of being told he'd lost a fingernail in an accident.

Or, again, were her true emotions just on delay?

It was 4.30 in the morning and she hadn't slept yet, and following Monroe's call couldn't possibly hope to get any shut-eye today. But she operated like someone in a fugue state and suddenly it was after 7am and she remembered nothing of the last few hours. Had she stood here at the window, like the Terminator, for all that time? A knocking on the door had jolted her out of a reverie.

It was Monroe, and this time she had news that had a far bigger impact on Libby. A corpse had been found right where Joel had pinpointed. Joanne's boyfriend had already identified it as hers.

Libby sat on the bed, her legs vibrating with stress. How had this information hit her harder than her own husband's death? Was that normal, or did it make her a freak?

Monroe wasn't yet done unloading bad news. The discovery of the body wasn't a secret. Police digging in woods just 500 metres from a house turned into a major crime scene? Only a fool wouldn't have connected the two. So the story was out there.

Joel's death wasn't, though. It had survived being leaked to the public. Both developments would be communicated to the world at a press conference later that morning. Libby wanted the universe to freeze over and pause and never reach that moment in time.

After breakfast, which she could barely stomach, Libby borrowed the chaperone detective's mobile to surf the internet. The story had blown up even more. Various news websites told of human remains being removed from a scene close to the suspected killer's home. A cheeky journalist had managed to sneak into the woods and take photos of police and crime-scene technicians grouped around a hole in the ground. Libby found it very upsetting. Could this nightmare get any worse?

It sure could. She found a Facebook page called *Justice for Joanne*, which was a hotbed of anger. There was a drone photo of her home, surrounded by police. One of her neighbours had attached a photo of himself with her and Joel in his garden, taken a few months ago. Myriad people had posted comments calling for Joel to be punished badly. They wanted the death penalty back. They wanted time alone in a room with him. Some were claiming Joel had ties to organised crime. Jesus.

Before leaving that morning, Monroe had warned her that opinion of her would be split. For every person on her side, another would see her as the enemy. Maybe the FLO had a sixth sense for such things, or had seen the furore in its foetal stage. Because here it was.

Vicious Facebookers accused Libby of knowing exactly what her husband had been up to – *She knew, course she did, probably didn't want to lose the house.* Some even said she was involved – *Washed his clothing I bet, and used the knife to cut potatoes the next day.* Even some who accepted her innocence labelled her stupid for being oblivious – *He comes in covered in blood and she doesn't notice?*

If the phone had been her own, she would have smashed it against a wall.

Joanne Yeowell's family had given the standard quotes about loss and sorrow, about hoping her killer would get what he deserved. However, one of their clan had been more vocal. A reporter had spoken to Joanne's uncle, a man called Mike Voyzey, from his prison cell, and the story was already in various digital newspapers.

Seemingly unfazed by the prospect of a reprimand, Voyzey had called from a stashed mobile and had no qualms about admitting this. The story described Voyzey as the black sheep of the Yeowell family. While his brother made riches, Voyzey fell into drugs and crime, and a decade ago got twelve years for manslaughter. Voyzey had seen none of that money and none of his family. They wrote him off. His rich brother, Joanne's father, Devin, paid him to officially change his surname, to further distance him from his relatives.

However, being the black sheep of the family didn't mean Voyzey wasn't hollowed out by the murder of a niece he had no contact with. He made that very clear. She listened to his unauthorised prison interview and couldn't miss the venom in his voice as he spoke about Joel.

Libby could read no more. Jesus, her life had turned to mush unbelievably quickly. This hellish new world she'd been teleported into wasn't even twelve hours old yet. God knew what the next fifty years would bring.

Internet gossip had been running fast through the gears all night, and had reached a fever pitch by the time the police held a press conference at 10am. The chief superintendent running the show confirmed the discovery of Joanne Yeowell's naked body, wrapped in a thick polythene dust sheet, in woods alongside Pacific Isle Golf Course.

According to the preliminary post-mortem report, Joanne's death was due to significant neck injuries, but that was all the chief super would disclose. He said that Joel Mytton, a thirty-five-year-old Sheffield man, had been arrested in connection with the murder and charged, and would have been attending court later that morning.

Except he couldn't. Joel had died in custody last night and an unnamed police officer had been arrested for murder. This statement, of course, prompted a blizzard of questions, but the policeman refused to divulge any more information until the investigation had been completed. The scarcity of details prompted speculation, fuelled by the blossoming rumours that Joel had been involved with an organised crime group.

Had he been killed by members of his gang, to keep him silent? Was Joanne's murder connected to this gang? The officer refused to comment, but surely he knew this ran the risk of people using his silence as confirmation of any and all theories?

There would be no murder charge against Joel now. He pointed out that criminal prosecutions could not be pursued against the dead even with an outstanding charge, as per the court of appeal in the case of Turk versus Regina in 2017. He was careful to stress that the media should not use the existing charge as evidence of guilt when reporting the story.

He then undermined his own words by adding that the evidence backed up 'a decision to charge and that, with a living suspect, we would have pursued it.' He said that Joanne's family, under the Right to Review scheme, could request an examination of the CPS's decision not to continue with proceedings. To Libby's mind it sounded like the police were saying Joel was definitely a murderer, but, hey, our hands are tied.

The superintendent finished by asking for Joanne's family to be left alone to grieve and answered none of the questions fired at him.

Libby hadn't thought about Joel's family, but they, too, had been suffering. In Birmingham, where he'd been born, various relatives had faced reporters on their doorsteps, but had refused to comment and had shut themselves away. His parents had suffered the worst and been forced to flee on an impromptu holiday, but they'd left one comment in their wake: *We don't see our son and we cut him off years ago.* Not exactly true, but Libby understood their wish to distance themselves, blood or not.

It pained her to wonder how they were feeling right now, knowing he was dead and that nobody was sympathetic. She would have to visit them at some point.

As for her own family... For one brief moment that upset her, she was glad both her parents were dead. But that didn't make them immune, as she found out a little later, when she borrowed the chaperone's mobile again to call Emery. Libby had expected Emery to talk about Joel's death, but instead her sister launched into a moan about calls from cranks and reporters. She said people were outside her house right now, begging for an interview. 'They come right up to my window,' she said. 'How can this be legal?'

'Are there no police there?' Libby asked.

'There's a car outside, sure, but just two cops, and they're doing nothing to stop it.'

Libby felt her pain. 'Keep the door locked.'

'I have. Look, Libby, someone has vandalised the burger van. Graffiti. But I washed it off. And they... Mum and Dad's headstone has been smashed.'

'What?'

'Yeah. The police released the cemetery as a crime scene earlier, and people just flocked in. That's what I heard. One of these scumbag reporters showed me a picture of the grave. Smashed up. Fucking animals. Everyone hates us.'

Libby knew she had to try to calm her sister. 'No. Not everyone. Bad voices are the loudest, that's all.'

'I guess. This is still a damn nightmare.'

'I'm sorry about this, Emery. I brought this on us.'

'How? You didn't kill that girl. Although...'

Libby knew what was coming. 'I didn't know about this, Emery.'

'Did you not have an inkling something was up?'

'No, no, no. How can you ask me that?'

'It was just... it was just surprising he managed to hide such a thing from you. You were his wife.'

'He managed it because he's a monster. I didn't know anything until I worked it out. It upsets me that you think that. I expected it from the rest of the country, but not my own sister.'

Emery fell silent. Libby wanted to know how her sister felt about Joel's murder, but asking now seemed wrong. She said she'd talk later and hung up.

TWENTY-TWO

Franz woke early and made breakfast for his children, wife, and her mother. When he brought eggs on toast to Lacy, she was awake and sitting up in bed, and knitting again.

'Did you find out yet who sent that officer to kill Joel Mytton?' she asked.

'It's still early, Lacy. I have people out trying to find answers.'

'If it was Voyzey, he'll want to know why his niece was killed. We don't need a man like that coming after us.'

'I'll get more people on it.' *Some* would have been the correct word, not *more*. The latter applied only if people were already on the job, which wasn't the case. He hadn't tasked a single soul with finding out who had sent the superintendent to Joel's cell. Because it didn't matter. If Joel had blabbed to the police, Franz would already be in handcuffs. So he hadn't and now couldn't. As for Voyzey, well, even if he was involved, Franz wasn't worried about some Jabba The Hut-looking jailbird down south.

'And the wife,' Lacy said. 'She might know something she shouldn't. Maybe someone should have a word.'

He smiled. Always the maybes. Years ago Lacy had liked to put herself front and centre, in the thick of his business, and often tried to tell him what to do. But then she got her hair fucked up by a salon one day and, enraged, ordered him to burn the place to the ground. She soon regretted her outburst when one of the staff, staying late, died in the fire. Since that day she'd never given directives. Just her 'maybes'. Weirdly, he found it cute.

'I'll get people on the wife, too,' he said.

'Just a word, mind. If you hurt her or scare her too much, she might moan to the police.'

'Sure.'

'Just a warning to keep quiet. That would be best. One man can do it. No scary team.'

'Will do, babe.'

'Oh, I'm not saying to do it. It's just a suggestion. And it should be on her doorstep. No need to snatch her. Too risky. That's what I'd do.'

He held back a grin. 'Aye-aye.'

He had no intention of going after the wife. Her husband had just been exposed as a sadistic killer and wrecked her life. If telling tales about gangster involvement in a kidnap plot could lessen the impact, maybe even rescue Joel's stinking character, then she would have done it already. So she knew nothing about Franz. He was in the clear.

Which meant back to business as usual. He headed out to Go Go Kartz. As the owner, he didn't have a specific role but liked to muck in. He especially liked to talk to the parents as they watched their kids fly round the track. It was nice to converse with people who didn't know his alter-ego, didn't fear him, or want something from him. His wasn't an adventurous lifestyle these days, but he was older and wiser now and that was how it was supposed to be.

It got his mind off things to a degree, but always in the back were niggling worries that Joel's death wouldn't be the end of things. There were already whispers that Joel had been involved with high-level criminals. The police would dig more, probably hoping to find accomplices. Franz wasn't out of the woods yet.

At 10am the police held a press conference and announced Joel's murder the night before – by a police officer. Charges couldn't be brought against Joel, for he couldn't defend himself in court, but the police were not closing the murder case. Franz expected it. The wheels of justice hated not having someone to convict. SYP and the CPS needed someone in the dock to spit at, if only to appease a mega-rich and grieving father who had the clout to do them political damage.

Franz was more intrigued by media speculation that Joel might have killed other women. Police forces around the country were delving into unsolved murders. Franz figured it was just desperation, but he couldn't fully shrug it off. After all, Joel's killer had visited him to chat about a dead woman. He hoped the bastard hadn't been slicing girls up left and right.

Franz continued to scour the news here and there and learned of an impromptu press conference called for 1pm. Word had gotten out that Joel had written a confession and trolls were up in keyboards, so this was probably about that. This revelation worried Franz a little, although his hands were still uncuffed. At 1pm, he excused himself and hid in his office to watch the show.

The confession was read out by the same chief superintendent from before. Word for word, but with no explanation of how it was acquired. It painted Joel in a pretty good light considering a dead woman was the result. Franz bought it to a degree. The Joel he knew definitely might have turned lethal if he'd been threatened with a weapon. But an accident? A little cotton wool padding there. But Franz couldn't have been happier, for the confession contained nothing about a kidnap or accomplices.

It caused a stir on social media. People wanted Joel convicted by his own words. Someone pointed out that the Criminal Justice Act 2003 had abolished hearsay exceptions, meaning dying declarations could be used in court. One newspaper listed a set of famous historical deathbed confessions, including Oliver Cromwell's claim that he falsified accusations of treason against Anne Boleyn so that King Henry the Eighth could get rid of her.

The ganglord found himself drawn to the final four words of Joel's confession:

I am so sorry.

An apology from Joel? To the police, to the public? Hell no. That was the sort of thing you said to a loved one who'd be ashamed of your actions. Like a wife.

Maybe he told her everything. Husbands do that.

Franz's own wife's words, now returning hard and strong. Joel had talked to his wife in the police station, which shouldn't have been allowed, and then suddenly he'd released a bullshit confession. Had Joel lied to his wife along with the rest of the world?

Franz didn't buy it. Joel had loved this woman enough to keep her in his life, but secreted away. She meant the world to him, and what she thought of him would be important enough to sway his actions. A wife could easier forgive a failed kidnap death than a cold-blooded rape-murder. And a wife might force her husband to invent a squeaky-clean, terrible-accident story in order to salvage some pride.

Franz now accepted the truth with a heaviness in his gut. Dangerous secrets should have been banished to oblivion when Joel's heart stopped pumping... but now it appeared that this information had transferred to Libby Mytton.

Franz slipped away and drove somewhere quiet in order to make a phone call. It was to a man who knew a man called Alain. The former came back a minute later with a number for Alain.

'I have a job for you,' Franz said when the call was answered.

'I can spare a day or two,' Alain said.

'How quick can you get here?'

'Twenty minutes.'

'You're in England already? Did you not leave after the last job?'

'Unless I planned to come by rocket, then yes, I'm here. As for why I'm still local, that's not something for you to worry about.'

They arranged to meet half an hour later at Locke Parke. Each had performed anti-surveillance manoeuvres just in case the police were tailing them. Franz had police officers who'd alert him if there was a surveillance team and hadn't heard from them; but being careful cost nothing. Alain was not a man he should be seen with.

Alain wore a flexible grey suit, as usual. He was forty-two, four inches below Franz's six feet, and today had no wig covering his bald head. There was no fake nose or fake beard, either. For the first time ever, he saw Alain in something close to his true form. Appearance was the only thing he knew about the guy.

His inert appearance made him good at getting people to trust him. But when he couldn't, when he faced adversity, he was unflappable. People had shot at him, tried to stab him, chased him, and Franz bet Alain's heart rate had never got ten above normal. It meant Alain could be acerbic because he didn't mind getting it fired right back at him.

The two men sat on the steps leading up to the bronze

statue of Joseph Locke. Sightseers were about, but none looked like undercover officers.

'How are things?' Franz said. 'No disguise?'

Alain paused. He seemed to be thinking of a certain response. Then he shrugged. 'Got something for me?'

Straight to the point. 'Something for today, if I can arrange it.'

'Not too early. I have prior business until this evening. Tell me.'

'You remember a man of mine called Joel?'

'Seriously?'

Franz conceded the point. Alain was a mystery, but he was really good at what he did. He always thoroughly researched his employers. Franz had used him various times over the last five years, at many thousands of pounds a pop. At their first meeting, Alain had presented him with a document detailing everything he knew about Franz's business and colleagues. Which was a lot more than the police knew. It was a way of saying: do not underestimate or trick me.

'I do,' Alain said in response to the query about knowing of Joel. 'Very much a news feature at the moment.'

'So you know. And you know he's got a wife?'

'Not surprised. I mean that *you* didn't know. If you outlaw that sort of thing, people are going to go behind your back. I knew about her from the start.'

This was a revelation. But not a surprise. 'You knew she existed way back? And didn't tell me?'

'I do the job I'm paid for, no more or less. Is this what you want from me? To find out who else in your employ has a wife or a husband?'

Given his grin, Alain didn't believe that was the case at all. Franz said, 'Joel's wife visited him at the police station. He might have told her things she shouldn't know. I want to know what those things are. But I don't know where she is yet. My officer on the inside is trying to find out where they've hidden her.'

A man of action like Alain hated having nothing to do with his hands. When he couldn't buzz around, he gave his fingers cigarettes. He lit one now. 'Oh yes. Shame about that kidnap plan going belly-up. That could have been a big payday. But what do you need from me? What's my job?'

Franz frowned. 'I just told you. I want to know what she knows about me.'

'That's not a task. That's a conclusion. What's my job?'

Franz sighed. Was Alain larking about? 'Okay, nice and simple. Your job is to put Libby Mytton in front of me so I can ask her questions.'

TWENTY-THREE

'Just make sure my name is never connected to this.'

After giving this order to the detective superintendent, fresh from his killing of Joel, Voyzey had found the ability to relax. He'd managed good sleep and was in high spirits when he woke the next morning. So was his cellmate, but that was because fry-ups had been returned to the breakfast menu after a hiatus due to that old excuse about budgets running amok.

Voyzey's good mood didn't last long. Killing Joel had been like taking paracetamol: soon the effects wore off and the pain returned. Joanne's murderer was gone, feeling no pain or guilt of his own, but her family still ached and would for a long, long time.

At 10am, a prisoner brought a radio to him, so he could hear a live press conference hosted by the police. Everybody – bar one fool – in the nearby cells kept the noise down while he listened. That fool soon regretted his noisemaking.

And Voyzey regretted listening to the conference. Poor Joanne, found dead on a golf course, wrapped in a dust sheet. Neck injuries were mentioned, which probably meant a slashed throat. The thought of it made Voyzey's skin crawl. The police said that her killer, now dead himself by murder, wouldn't face trial for this crime. That the Yeowell family would not get justice.

'Already got it,' Voyzey said to himself. But did he believe it?

At 1pm, the police held another conference and this time read from a confession written by the killer the night before. Voyzey found a transcript of it online. He didn't buy that bastard Mytton's claims for a damn nanosecond. He knew criminals, knew monsters, and the tricks they played. This fucker had carefully created a dot-to-dot confession that would give the cops an answer for whatever they found during Joanne's autopsy.

She undressed to have sex with him? Bullshit to cover the fact that he'd stripped her. She had rough sex with some other guy just before heading to the graveyard? A neat way of explaining damage to her vagina. Her body bounced around in the van? A lie to explain bruising to other parts of her body.

The vile bastard had raped and murdered her, yet was trying to shove bullshit about an unfortunate accident and subsequent panic down people's throats. Voyzey wished the man was still alive so he could be killed again, this time slowly. He couldn't shake an image of Joanne pleading for her life as Mytton abused her.

A reporter talking about deathbed confessions mentioned that Oliver Cromwell had made a dying declaration before perishing from malaria, in which he'd admitted setting up the King's wife. Voyzey already knew the story: years later Cromwell was exhumed and posthumously executed by hanging. Apparently his head now somewhere under Sidney Sussex College in Cambridge.

Voyzey stopped watching the press conference before it was finished, having heard enough already. It was almost association time. When the doors were opened, Voyzey made his way to the top tier, aided by his cellmate, Nando. His knees hurt the entire way and the stairs almost killed him. But he had to do this.

He entered the cell of a man doing life for killing his wife's new boyfriend. The top floor was single-occupancy, so there was no cellmate. The man quickly got to his feet, worried about why a gangster like Voyzey wanted to see him. 'Relax,' Voyzey said, shrugging off Nando's helping arm and approaching the window under his own power.

The cell was on the north side of the prison, with a view over the main entrance. He could see over the perimeter wall and down the access lane, to the main road. At the junction were trees that partially blocked his view, but with his head in the correct spot he could see what he wanted.

On the far side of the dual carriageway, about 200 metres away, was a red-brick square block of flats with orange balconies. Galinwind Court, if he remembered correctly. A handful of prisoners had families living there for easy visiting. In the middle of the top floor was a balcony with a flower box attached to the railing.

He started to feel dizzy so sat on the lower bunk, forcing the occupant to vacate it. Since he never got stopped and searched on the wings, Voyzey had brought his mobile. He made a call while Nando stood at the door to keep watch.

'Joel Mytton,' Voyzey said to the man who answered. 'I want his body when he's buried. They'll dump that fucker in an unmarked grave and tell no one bar the family, so you'll need to do some detective work. When you've got it, let me know on this number.'

That done, he tried to stand to look out the window again. But his legs wouldn't have it and he waved away help. Instead, he imagined the top floor flat across the way. If a posthumous hanging was good for Oliver Cromwell, it would suit the bastard who killed Joanne. Voyzey planned to string Joel fucking

Mytton from that balcony. And Voyzey would stare at him, in the flesh. That would go some way to easing his pain. He would have to get a pair of binoculars smuggled in during the next Canteen Day.

The very thought of it was also enough of an analgesic to make the next few hours spin by fast. But soon the throb returned, and with it more anger. Something had been niggling at him, but now he knew what it was. Sitting on the toilet back in his own cell, he pulled out his mobile phone and loaded up Mytton's written statement.

The ganglord found himself drawn to the first four words of Joel's confession:

You never knew this...

That line, in reference to Mytton's enjoying alone time at graveyards, wasn't for the police. Of course they wouldn't know of this hobby. They wouldn't know his favourite colour, what meat he liked on Sunday roasts, or anything fucking else about him. *You never knew this* was the kind of declaration that preceded a surprising revelation. That meant it had been aimed, not at judgemental strangers across the world, but at the single person who knew Mytton the best.

His wife. The bastard had been giving his beloved woman the answers she needed.

How much did she know? The confession seemed to hint that she hadn't had a clue about the murder. Why had he concocted it right after meeting with her? Because she had convinced him to come clean?

Bullshit. The bitch wife had coached him on what to say in order to dampen his guilt. She had arranged a meeting with her damn husband to make sure he got his story straight and didn't sink them both.

Voyzey had no proof of this, but he let the theory off the leash, and soon it had set up roots. Now he was convinced:

Libby Mytton had not only known before his arrest that her husband murdered Joanne... she had also condoned it.

Wait. She called the police on him.

'Only because he became so whacked in the head that she knew she was next,' Voyzey said aloud. 'She knew what he'd done to Joanne Yeowell and didn't care.'

Voyzey had become a learned man from his time in prison, with nothing to do but read to expand his mind. He knew about an English law expert from the 18th century called William Blackstone, who had invented the Blackstone Ratio. He was quoted as saying, *It is better that ten guilty persons escape than that one innocent suffer.* The beyond-reasonable doubt principle, borne of the Ratio, was the cornerstone of the legal system and the only honourable way to operate.

Fuck that. He was driven by Voyzey's Ratio: *It is better that a thousand innocents die than that one guilty bastard takes another breath.* Libby Mytton might be innocent, and she might not. It wasn't worth the risk of letting her off the hook.

She was out there, living life, happy, and sure in her fucking warped mind that she was safe. She was going to be dead wrong. Literally.

TWENTY-FOUR

At around 8.30pm that night, Monroe visited Libby at the Premier Inn with news. The police had finished with her house. It had been released back to her. She could go home finally. Sick of a babysitter, she had sent the other detective home before midday, but had been cooped up in the hotel room alone since. The rooms either side of her had been taken, which she was thankful for, although she hadn't heard a peep out of the guests.

'Home.' She said the word aloud to test how it felt. It still sounded wrong, but she had reassessed things since deciding never to go back to that building. Joel had washed bloodied clothing in their kitchen. He might have sat in the living room and planned his crime. But nobody had died there. She had inner strength and needed a pipeline into it now. The best way to try to move on was to try to make things normal again. That was certainly possible now that Joel was dead. No lengthy trial.

But if she abandoned every aspect of her existing life, she might always feel like... a fugitive – that was the word that popped into her head. Like she was running. Well, she would not crawl under a rock and die.

'Yes,' she told Monroe. 'I want to go home.'

'Are you sure you want to right now? You could give it a few days.'

'You said there's no media hanging around my house now.'

'True. But that's because they know we've got you somewhere else. If you go home now and they find out–'

'I don't care. I'm sorry for cutting you off. I just want to get back to my life.'

'There's other people to consider. Joel was involved with...'

Libby knew, of course. She'd heard the rumours about Joel having ties to an organised crime group. People had been oozing from the woodwork to sell their stories of being victimised by him, or assaulted by him, or even of being his co-conspirator in robberies and muggings and drug deals. There was no concrete evidence as yet and Monroe had stressed this point, but Libby didn't care. She wouldn't doubt a damn thing that emerged about Joel's shady past. How could she after what he'd done?

If there were criminals out there who might target her, so what? Join the damn queue. And so it was. She was leaving this place.

TWENTY-FIVE

At the same time that Libby was preparing to leave the hotel, Franz and his wife were at a barbeque hosted by a neighbour. One good thing about having Lacy's mother staying with them was that she could babysit. Also present at the barbeque was the young couple from across the road. Nice enough people, if not for what they did for a living. Which wasn't sales, as they'd claimed. They'd been living on the street for two months and had tried various times to be friendly, including at this weekly get-together. Franz had forced himself to be polite back.

Tonight, though, he'd had a bit too much to drink and couldn't fight an urge for some fun. Being strait-laced all the time was a chore and sometimes he reminisced about the old days, when he'd enjoyed nothing more than a good rumble. He approached the male neighbour, waited for a chance to hop into the conversation, and said, 'So how's work?'

The male – John – said, 'Good, good.'

'So where is it you work again?'

'From home. I do sales.'

'I know, I know. But which company?'

John paused. And was saved when his *wife* appeared. The

other neighbour, who'd been chatting to John, departed. Alone with the couple in a corner of the backyard, Franz said, 'So are you two actually fu... fun, having fun tonight?'

Actually fucking yet? he'd nearly said. It made him laugh.

Back when Franz was building a name and an empire, the cops had enjoyed a little game of harassment. Gym, pub, golf course, birthday party, Asda, it didn't matter: in would walk a gaggle of police officers to confront him. Sometimes it was just to threaten him off-the-record, or to cause embarrassment in front of his friends and neighbours, but often there had been arrests that they knew would go nowhere. If they couldn't give him thirty years for murder, six hours for mistaken identity would have to suffice. All part of the persecution.

That was back in the old days, though. Now, he was no longer a low-level thug on the rise. He was at the top of the pile, on a throne. The most powerful underworld figures couldn't be worn down by the police breathing down their necks, and random raids at 3am would never reap a bounty. People like Franz were many degrees separated from the crimes they committed and there was scant chance of establishing links.

Many people had undertaken civil prosecutions against him and all had fallen flat: his gang's structure was so confusingly intricate that it was impossible to pinpoint an ultimate culprit. And such prosecutions worked on the fifty-one per cent test, a balance of probabilities. If some poor upstanding fellow couldn't even bleed him for compensatory damages, what chance was there for a criminal prosecution with its beyond-reasonable-doubt standard? Add to the mix a team of no-nonsense, highly paid solicitors ready to slap the police with injunctions and civil claims, and the result was an enemy who backed off.

After a couple of years sans hassle, Franz had felt secure enough to finally buy a real place of his own where he could raise his kids and find true new friends. He'd lived right here for five winters now, free from door knocks by law enforcement personnel.

The police, though, were dogged hounds.

Franz had officers on the inside who knew when detectives and specialist squads were keeping tabs on him. Two months ago he got wind of their latest endeavour. A couple of detectives were pulled in from some faraway force – so they weren't known faces – and inserted into a for-rent house over the road. These pretending-to-be-married cleanskins did nothing but rot in their home all day, watching him with their cameras and microphones and writing down everything single thing he did.

But he never did a thing and never allowed his criminal employees to come within throwing distance of his home. Franz found the police's wild optimism cute at times, and their desperation pitiful.

'Yes, we're having fun,' said the lady, Mary, in response to his question. They both looked a little perturbed because Franz had never approached them before. Good detectives they might be, but their acting skills were lacking.

Franz wanted to play with them some more, maybe even admit that he was onto them, but his phone rang. His secret encrypted one. He excused himself and walked to a quieter part of the yard to take it. He could feel the cleanskins' eyes on his back. An OCG head slinking off for a late-night phone call? What they wouldn't have given to know who he was talking to!

It was his peeler from Woodseats station, and he had some good and bad news.

The bad: 'I've heard your name mentioned.'

Curious. The media had talked a lot about Joel's gang involvement, but nobody knew anything definitive that tied him to Franz's OCG or any big players within it. Blue uniforms as yet hadn't decided he might be worth interviewing about Joanne

Yeowell, and none of his neighbours were giving him suspicious stares. So far, so good.

But no more. For the first time, his name had been uttered. It could have been the start of things going downhill. But now he had the woman in his sights. If he could find out what she knew, and what she might have told the police, he could begin damage control before things ran away from him.

And if it was too late for that and she'd already told them enough to sink him? Well, it would count for naught if Libby Mytton was unable to give her testimony in court.

He ended the call and got hold of Alain, and imparted the good news. 'We found her at a Premier Inn. But you don't need to take her from there. She's going home tonight. But watch the house for a bit first because there might be police with her. Wait till they've gone, of course. Just a suggestion.'

'Wasn't about to go storming a place full of police officers. I'm an exterminator, but not the Terminator.'

Franz didn't know what that meant. 'You need me to give you the address?'

'Don't be a silly-billy, dear,' Alain said, and hung up.

A little more relaxed now the ball was rolling faster, Franz slotted away his phone. He noticed the cleanskins still staring and headed over to them. He had a smile and it was genuine. He'd realised his 'suggestion' to Alain had mirrored his wife's little foible.

The female cleanskin, Mary, said, 'Important call?'

'Very,' Franz replied.

'Anything that would interest us?' her fake husband added, trying to strip his tone of acute desperation.

No should have been the answer, but Franz had been short of fast-lane fun for too long. So he said, 'Very much so,' and was unable to hold in his laughter.

TWENTY-SIX

Monroe drove Libby home. Anxiety heaped upon itself the closer they got to her street, but when they made the turn, Libby felt it all drain away. The last time she'd been here, so had a curious herd. But they'd had their fill, it would appear, and departed. Her road was quiet. A few people walked here and there, but that was standard and none of them was gawking at her house. There was a single police car outside the property, but otherwise everything looked just as it had before hell was unleashed.

Monroe parked behind the police car and Libby waited while she went to chat to them. She absent-mindedly stroked a new, cheap mobile Monroe had supplied.

The DC was soon back, and with good news. 'No activity for hours. A few faces stopping to stare, but that's it. I guess nobody was expecting you back just yet. You want to go in the back way?'

'You mean sneak in? So nobody knows I'm here?'

'Yes. If word spreads that you're here, this place could become popular again.'

It didn't take much thought. 'No. I won't hide like a burglar.'

'Shall I come in with you?'

Libby shook her head. 'Thank you, but no. In fact, could you remove the police car? I think it brings attention.'

Monroe objected, but Libby doubled down. She wanted to try to get back to normal as best as possible, and a police presence would make her feel... exposed. It was the only way she could describe it. Public and media interest in the Joanne Yeowell affair hadn't evaporated, but it had clearly diminished somewhat. Libby would take the risk that the street wouldn't suddenly become a hotbed of activity. Murder tales were at their most intriguing when there was a killer to hunt or punish... neither of which applied here.

Monroe and the police car were gone a couple of minutes later. Libby was on her doorstep, key in hand and looking up and down the street. A couple of faces were at windows, but nobody came outside. Yet. She went inside.

The house felt cold, and not just because of the November chill. Her first job was to look around the entire property. The police had searched everything, not knowing in which nook or cranny they might find a clue. She already knew they had taken all of Joel's tools, especially the Stanley knife suspected of being the murder weapon, and every item of his clothing. Evidence that was now unnecessary. She had found it easier than expected to come to terms with his death, but little reminders like this, which might not cease bombarding her for many weeks, were hard to ignore.

The space where his clothing and other gear had been in drawers and wardrobes gave her a funny feeling. For the first time, she truly understood that she was a single woman now. She wondered how long she would wait to tell a new lover, if she ever had the will to find one, about her ex.

Whatever mess the forensics team had made during their hunt for evidence had been rectified, but she saw clear indications of that search. She felt violated, but maybe that was a good thing. It seemed to hint that she still felt like this was home.

She pottered about for two hours, cleaning this, rearranging that, all of it designed to help her relax. This was home, after all. At one point she heard voices outside, heard her name and Joel's mentioned. No doubt a couple of morbid people intrigued by the infamous house. She didn't go look and put the TV on loud to cover the sound of any repeat event.

She expected reporters or neighbours to knock the door, but none had come by as midnight struck. Either it was too late, or the police had done a good job of hiding the fact that she was back home. Maybe something fresh and explosive had hit the news and wiped her from the headlines. She refused to go near the internet because she didn't want to hear yet more vitriol about herself.

Perhaps, instead, the police had had a devilish time keeping attackers at bay. She even had a peek through the bedroom curtains, half expecting to see a wall of cops holding back a sea of locals who waved torches and pitchforks. But the street was serene.

She hoped it would stay that way.

TWENTY-SEVEN

Half a mile from Libby's house, a Ford with two guys was parked in a supermarket car park. The occupants were tall, in their twenties, similar in height and appearance, with long faces and shoulder-length, wavy brown hair. Given that they also wore matching green bomber jackets, they'd often been mistaken for brothers. They managed a gym in London and were amateur boxers.

The passenger's fighter nickname was 'Hawk' because his name was Dale Hawkins. The driver, who played on his phone, was 'Tempest' Tony Berkshire. He had a healing inch-long cut below his left eye, which he now fiddled with.

Hawk grabbed his friend's hand, which had also become a habit. 'Stop picking at it. Leave it to heal. How many more times do I have to tell you?'

'Whatever. Why are we still here? Are we not kicking in the door and getting the bitch?'

Hawk sighed. Tempest was a good kid, but his head was gone. Too many full-contact sparring sessions and questionable boxing matches against superior opponents. Sometimes he sounded punch-drunk – a sign of brain damage. And he was often hasty and impatient, which was another red flag. 'We can't do it yet. We don't know if the police are coming to see her. Let's just watch for another hour.'

'We've waited all day.'

This was true. With no means of finding Libby's hiding spot, Voyzey had sent this pair to watch her house. They couldn't just sit outside the property for hours and risk raising suspicions. So, earlier, they had driven by to plant something. On TV, they had seen the road when it was a hotbed of activity, with cops and crime-scene technicians and gawkers.

Today all of that was gone. The house had been released back to Libby and people seemed to have shifted their focus to other news. Nobody was around and there wasn't even crime-scene tape. The place looked like nothing newsworthy had happened here at all.

Hawk had hidden a trail camera in the garden hedge of a house across the street from Libby's home. Camouflaged, weatherproof and with night vision, the device allowed the men to monitor the property from a distance. It was motion activated and Hawk got a notification on his phone when it started recording.

Just minutes ago, they had watched Libby return home in the company of detectives, although she hadn't entered the property with the target. Hawk had made a call to Voyzey's fixer, who relayed the message to the top dog.

Voyzey was having his once-weekly, late-night shower and sitting on a stool while the water bounced off him. His cellmate, Nando, had helped him travel and was waiting by the door. He also had Voyzey's phone and handed it over when it rang. A nearby guard heard it, stuck his head in, saw someone whose activities should be ignored, and did just that.

Voyzey loved the update from Hawk. 'Perfect. Tell them to

bag her up and get her down here. Right now. And give Hawk this number so I can talk to him direct from now on.'

Nando made it happen. When Hawk took the call, he was a little perturbed, believing they should watch the house a bit longer first. Tempest, on the other hand, was eager for action. Reluctantly, he gave his partner permission to drive to Libby's house.

Once there, Hawk retrieved his camera and directed Tempest down a lane between two properties. It delivered them to the area with the twin rows of garages at the rear of the houses. There was no way onward, though, so he turned the vehicle and pointed its nose at their single escape route. He shut off the engine and headlights. The only illumination came from the houses some thirty metres to either side of them, but most of that was blocked by the twin rows of garages.

'I don't like this,' Hawk said.

'The dark?'

'The fact that we're trapped if someone comes down here. Let's get it done. In you go.'

'I thought we're waiting to make sure no cops are in the house.'

'I'm not even sure how we'd do that. Just go hide in the backyard. I don't like hanging about here. I'll drive round the block for ten minutes. Make sure you're out by then.'

Tempest argued no further and got out of the car. The final part of him to exit was his left leg, which Hawk grabbed. 'Hey, you know what to do, right? I mean what not to do.'

'Do grab, don't kill.'

'That's it. You bring her out here, and I mean right away. No touching her.'

'I have to bring her out using telekinesis?'

'Don't joke, Tempest. If the door's unlocked, go slow. If it's locked, boot it and move quick.'

'Blitz attack. Love it.'

'Don't love it too much. Blitz only if you can't get in without creating a racket. Good luck. Get going.'

Hawk slid into the driver's seat as his comrade vanished into the dark. He started the engine. As the car turned right to enter the lane that would take him onto the street, he had to stamp the brakes. Another car, which had just turned in, did the same with just three feet between their bumpers. Shit, his headlights. Hawk flicked them on.

Hiding his face by pretending to scratch his nose, Hawk worked with the other driver to slowly guide their cars past each other in the tight space. And then he was by, and moving faster, and out, and gone. He hoped the other driver hadn't noted the car's registration.

Because after tonight the police were going to badly want it.

The man called Alain, who'd been hired by Franz, cruised past the Mytton house for a look at the lair of a for-kicks killer, which was a different animal to his own kind. He'd expected protestors, for Libby Mytton hadn't exactly been accorded the kind of sympathy he'd expected for the wife of an accused murderer.

But the street was quiet. He had to check the map to make sure there wasn't another street by this name. You wouldn't have known that earlier that day the authorities had combed the house to find evidence. Public interest was fickle and short-lived and he knew this from experience. He'd created many news stories in years gone by.

He knew the area from Google Maps, so made the turn down a sloped lane between two homes, to access the garages at the rear. But as soon as he entered, he had to slam on the brakes.

A resident's vehicle was on the way out. Its headlights flicked on.

Alain fiddled with his rear-view mirror, so his hand would block sight of his face, as the two drivers inched past each other on the thin lane. Once he was at the garages, he drove to the end and turned around, then got out. The area was pitch black, silent, the perfect setting. But he didn't trust it. It was a dead-end and he had no idea who might block him in. It could be the police. He couldn't assume that blue line defenders weren't keeping Libby under surveillance, especially if there had been threats against her.

Google Maps had shown him another street running parallel. He could park there, sneak past a house and hop the fence at the back of the rear yard, into this area, and his car would be safe. He headed there. He parked outside a house whose windows were all dark.

In the boot was his suitcase, inside of which were various disguises.

Into the glove box he put his gun, a pocket pistol called the KelTec P11, designed for concealed carrying. He'd had it since 2019, the year it was discontinued, and normally it accompanied him everywhere, just in case. For the same reason, he now chose to leave it behind. He felt naked without it, but he wanted to be able to talk his way out if he ended up surrounded by police officers.

He considered turning off his phone because a call, and a bright light, at the wrong time could ruin things. But he was never out of reach and decided to take the risk.

Finally, he looked at his disguises suitcase... and rejected it again. No, he would stick with his promise to avoid playing a role for this mission. A couple of weeks ago he'd had some news – more like a development – that had forced him to remain in the country, and which would alter the course of his life.

During their meeting at Locke Park, Franz had asked: why no disguise. The answer, which he'd almost admitted to the ganglord, was that Alain planned to get out of the game. Yeah, that old movie trope. Well, even hitmen had to have one last job. And leaving his au naturel appearance on cameras and in people's minds and in police databases would force his hand. With a burned real identity, he could never again risk another jet-setting criminal adventure. In fact, that in mind... He tore off and shredded his latex gloves.

Two minutes later he was back by the garages, and in search of the Mytton back gate. He found it not only unlocked but wide open. That was enough to give him a smile.

Which he lost when he entered the yard and saw the back door of the house also wide open.

TWENTY-EIGHT

Libby had just finished her bath and wrapped herself in a robe. She sat on the bed and plugged in her hairdryer – and that was when she heard a mighty crash from downstairs. At first she wondered if it was a collapse of dirty pots and pans on the unit by the sink, left from the day when her life fell apart.

She knew that wasn't the answer at all just a second later, when footsteps thundered up the stairs. Someone had just booted in her back door.

She froze as a tall man appeared in her doorway. Green jacket, blue jeans, and a mask that creased as he smiled. It was obvious this wasn't a random burglary. This was about Joanne Yeowell for sure. He would have looked dangerous to Libby even without the item in his hand. A knife.

'Please don't hurt me,' she moaned. 'I've done nothing.'

'That's right,' he said, moving closer. He stopped at the foot of her bed, with the doorway, her escape portal, behind him, out of reach. It might as well have been a mirage. 'You did nothing. Nothing as your man raped and killed girls. We know there's others.'

For a brief moment, she'd hoped this man was here for

goodies and no more. This was so much worse. He was going to give her 'neck injuries', just like poor Joanne Yeowell. It was going to be the first of a thousand attacks across the coming years, all because of a man now beyond reproach.

'No, that's not true,' she said. 'Please. I got the police–'

'Only because your bloke got so whacked in the head that you were next. You knew what he'd done to Joanne Yeowell. Maybe you even picked her for him. Was that what happened?'

'No, no. Please.'

'Sure it is. You like the pussy, too. I bet you and him drove around that night, pointing out the girls, assessing them. And you saw Joanne and said, "Yep, she'll do. That lovely brunette there." And you sicced him on her. *Fetch, boy!*'

'No. Please.' Her voice trailed off on the final word: she knew it was pointless to beg or plead.

'I bet you frigged off while watching him kill her. Did you tell him what to do? Slice there, stab here, that sort of shit? Did you cum when he slit her throat?'

The last of the power in her body was spent. She said nothing, just stared at him. She could change nothing now and was accepting of whatever came. It was her punishment for not seeing the monster in Joel.

'Her family is going to have your blood in revenge,' the masked man said. 'Get up. We're taking a ride. Someone has a plan to return that throat-cutting favour, so we have to go.'

He wanted her to rise, and she would, of course she would, she would do whatever he said... but she couldn't. Couldn't move a muscle, even the ones in her face that would allow her to communicate this fact.

'Get up right now, or I'll gut you right here. Leave you dead. Last chance, you slut.'

'That's no way to talk to a woman.'

At first Libby didn't understand that another voice had

spoken. And by the time she did, her assailant had already turned around to face the newcomer. Nor did she immediately fathom that he'd been injured. And by the time she did, the masked man was already out of sight, down on the ground at the foot of her bed.

In his place was another man, who bent down and, unseen by her, made stabbing movements. She heard the wet phut-phut of a blade driving into flesh and closed her eyes, even though the violence was audio only.

'Apologies for his foul mouth,' this man said when he stood up again. He was shorter than the first man, and older, perhaps in his late forties. He had a bald head and wore a grey suit, which seemed out of place for night-time break-ins.

'Most of what this bozo said was wrong,' this man continued. 'But he was right about your having to leave this place or wind up dead. More fools are coming for you. An endless stream. Your only chance is with me. No time to get dressed. Let's go.'

He held out his hand, as if she might crawl across the bed to take it. She didn't move. Couldn't move.

'You won't see the morning if you don't come. I don't care either way, I'd just rather not tell my boss I failed. No bonus for me. Let's go. Look, I just put down the bad man. You can trust me.'

She shook her head. The man delved into a jacket pocket, producing a police warrant card in a black wallet. Her eyes widened. He couldn't be police.

'Detective Inspector Alan Manvers. Now please–'

His words ceased with a thudding noise. The bald man crumpled to the ground, also out of sight, and for a bizarre second time an intruder's sudden disappearance exposed another one behind him. Was this noir farce an odd dream?

The third man was maybe in his thirties, taller than the bald man. He wore black jeans, blue jumper, and a beanie hat with tufts of brown hair poking out. In his hands was a rolling pin with a giant crack running almost the full-length – just like her own from the kitchen.

He said, 'I understand if you don't trust what I'm about to tell you. It's basically the same as that guy said. Come with me or you won't live to regret it. Bad people are coming.'

His words carried a threat, but it didn't infiltrate his tone and something in his demeanour wasn't as dark as that of the other two men. He didn't ooze the same menace, despite being in her home unannounced in the dead of night, with a weapon. He stood there, waiting, hand outstretched towards her.

Before she could pause to think, Libby found herself reaching for that hand.

TWENTY-NINE

It took Alain a few seconds to get his bearings, remember where he was, and fathom that he'd been bested by someone. And the woman, Alain's property, was gone along with him. There was blood on the side of his head. But he was alive, which meant he was able to fight another day, and how could anyone complain about that?

He grabbed a towel from the bathroom and walked – no rush – from the house. And then returned when he realised he didn't have his wallet. Oh yes, he'd been flashing his fake policeman's ID when someone whacked him. He found it lying atop the man he'd killed in the Mytton bedroom, but sweetly there was no blood on it. Maybe the police would assume Joel had killed the man and somehow they'd missed the body during their searches of the house. Alain smiled at the joke.

Outside again, he paused to listen to his environment. No sounds that suggested the neighbours were alert to a commotion at the sinister property. So he could afford a little time to work on himself before contacting Franz.

Back in his car, he drove to a remote place where he wouldn't be seen with his interior light on. Using the rear-view mirror and his phone, he inspected his head. There was an inch-long laceration above the ear, which was a real good spot to target to knock someone unconscious. It wasn't lost on him that wearing a wig would have prevented the laceration, if not unconsciousness. Bad choice, but he could laugh at his stupidity.

He used a first-aid kit to clean and suture the wound, before applying concealer from his disguise bag. He convinced himself it didn't count as cloaking his identity. Job done, he got his spare suit from the boot and dressed inside the car. That done, he thought of his next move.

Tricked, beaten, robbed: perhaps he should be a bit annoyed at that? Maybe later, though, because right now he had an awkward phone call to make.

Although he had buffers between himself and whichever crime he'd authorised, it always helped to have a good alibi. This was, in part, why Franz had been happy to attend the barbeque, and why, once it was over, he was now in his driveway, tinkering under the bonnet of his car to present himself to viewers. When Alain called, Franz got behind the wheel for privacy.

'I was too late,' Alain said. 'I arrived up just as a car was leaving. Libby and another man were inside it. Someone else got to her, Franz.'

'She had help?'

'No. She didn't seem to go willingly. She was kidnapped. I went inside the house and there's a dead guy in the bedroom. So there were two men and she managed to kill one.'

Franz had to get him to repeat everything, because it sounded unreal. 'So someone else is after her?'

'It would appear so. Send your cleaners to the house because the body can't stay there.'

Franz had to get Alain to repeat that, too. Then he said, 'Okay. So who sent those men. Who took her?'

'I'm sure you'll need only one guess.'

Alain was right. There was only one man who could and would have tried to kidnap Libby Mytton. Mike Voyzey.

THIRTY

When Hawk returned to the garages, he didn't see Tempest waiting. They were a good duet because of their contrasting characters, even if some people thought of them as a trope straight out of a cheesy gangster movie. Hawk was the smart one, the guy who did all the talking, the chap who was reliable for problem-solving. Tempest was the engineer's tool. He enjoyed the black-ops, but maybe a little too much. Hawk was worried that Tempest might have seen fit to help himself to some of Libby Mytton's biology, despite orders not to.

He was impatient, but chose to give his partner another ten minutes. After driving around to burn the time, he revisited the garages and found no change. Round the block he went yet again, this time with clenched teeth. If Tempest had raped Libby Mytton, they could deal with that. Not so if she'd fought and he'd gone too far and she was dead. Voyzey couldn't torture a corpse.

Back on Mytton's street, he parked close to the house and pulled out his phone. He had to risk making a call. But Tempest didn't answer.

Hawk drove to the garages and turned the car so it was

facing the exit. He made his way to the Mytton gate, and through. The back door was wide open, a lit kitchen beyond. When he entered that room, he immediately felt something was off. It was too quiet and had a remote feeling to it. He didn't know what that meant, but he didn't like it. He moved quickly now, certain he wasn't going to be confronted.

When he entered the main bedroom, he froze. Tempest was dead on the carpet, gashed in the neck, blood everywhere. Hawk sat on the floor, staring, thinking. How the hell had Libby Mytton managed to do this? Knowing she was a target, she must have kept a knife nearby.

Voyzey was dead against hiring men who sexually abused victims, but sometimes they slipped through the cracks. Like Tempest, who had a history of rapes, including two performed during home invasions. Facing a terrified, submissive woman was home turf and he must have gotten complacent. In his comfort zone, he had let his guard down, allowing Libby to strike. Dickhead.

And now look. Hawk would have to tell Tempest's grandmother, who'd brought him up since he was five. And she had real bad dementia, so he'd probably have to give her the bad news every day until–

Again he froze, this time not at a sight but a noise. Downstairs. The scuffle of feet. Someone was here. In the next moment, he heard a male voice: 'Leave that shit. Take it on the way out.'

More than one person. He knew they were coming upstairs. Quiet but quick, he slid under the bed. Soon, the owners of the voice and the feet appeared in the doorway. Hawk's position allowed him only to see legs clad in dark trousers and feet in boots. Three men. Shit.

'Anyone know this tosspot?' one said.

Murmurs of *no*. Someone said, 'I'll take his mugshot,' and

bent down to get a close-up of Tempest's face with a phone camera.

'Reckon he came from London or they know people up here?'

'Fuck knows. The boss might know from this photo.'

A fourth man entered the room and said, 'Lads, shall we get a table up here for a conference? Or maybe get on with getting rid of this guy?'

These were guys used to cleaning crime scenes, Hawk realised. Nobody was disgusted or seemed like a fish out of water. They worked fast and efficiently to encase the body in a black plastic tarp they'd brought. As they rolled the body onto the wrapping, Tempest's face turned towards the bed. Seeing the blind eyes, Hawk felt his rage building. The people manhandling his best friend talked about a recent football match, clearly unperturbed by their work.

When he was wrapped up, three men carried Tempest out of the room. One guy remained behind, in the doorway, and opened up with a fire extinguisher. He sprayed white foam everywhere, as if trying to repaint the whole room. A direct jet was aimed at the bloodied carpet where Tempest had lain, which forced spray under the bed. Hawk shut his eyes and held his breath as he turned into a snowman. He prayed he wouldn't cough. And he prayed these people weren't about to burn the house down and cook him.

Crime scene neutralised, the man left with his empty extinguisher. Breathing as little as possible, Hawk waited until he heard a vehicle leaving the area. Wet from the foam, he fled the house and, in his car, made a call.

In his cell, Voyzey listened carefully to the story being hollered down the line. It was a wild tale, but he trusted Hawk. When he was asked if he knew who might have sent the cleaners, only one name sprang to mind. Joel Mytton had worked for Franz, one of South Yorkshire's biggest criminals. A guy who had the clout to mount a rescue of his former employee's wife.

THIRTY-ONE

Franz was in bed, trying to sleep. Impossible. Voyzey surely wanted Libby Mytton to kill her because his bloodlust wasn't satisfied after whacking Joel. But would he question her first? If so, what would she tell him about Franz's operations? Enough to make Voyzey think he could muscle in? Or would the bastard pass that information to the police?

Worse, she might spill the beans about the plot to kidnap Joanne, which would start a gang war and drag him back into the old way of life. He didn't want to have to start arranging security for his family. He'd hoped he was past all that malarky. He had to hope that his people could find her before it was too late. But time was running out.

Someone knocked on his door, then posted something. This late, with what was going on, there was no way it was an innocent delivery. Franz got up and opened his phone so he could see the feed from his doorbell camera. No one there. He looked out the window, careful to leave the light off and present little of his body for a sniper. He saw nobody in his garden and no strange vehicles on the street.

Still, he sent an empty message to a number in his phonebook. It was alarm call and it would bring a dozen people to his home, ready for action. He headed out of the bedroom and turned on the downstairs hallway light, so he could see what had been shoved through his door. It wasn't a flaming rag. Closer inspection told him it was a mobile phone with a piece of paper held against it by an elastic band. He went down the stairs.

He'd been right to be concerned. The piece of paper was a Polaroid photograph. He recognised the face of one of his sex workers. She looked like the one he'd sent on an errand with the peeler who worked at Woodseats. Now she was dead in a hole in the ground. So, Voyzey had gotten to the peeler and was sending Franz a warning. He wasn't sure why.

Franz cancelled the alarm call but requested a man to sit in a car outside his house, just in case. Then he checked the delivered phone. It was cheap plastic thing that had no sent or received messages or calls and no names in the phonebook. He realised he was supposed to use it to field a call, and it rang in his hand at exactly that moment.

Franz walked into the downstairs bathroom, where he'd have privacy even if someone else in the house woke.

'Do you know who I am?' said the caller.

'I do,' Franz replied. He couldn't believe it. 'You saved me a phone call.'

'So you've heard of me? I should be flattered to be so special.'

'Don't be. People like you are ten a penny, Voyzey. I've dealt with dozens like you. And yes, I know your kind very well. You're known as a bad man because you're in prison and you have nothing to lose. And you love that people know it. You need it. In your world, reputation is everything and the only reputation that matters is toughness, violence, viciousness. You operate fast and loud and you do it front and centre, visible to all, because people need to see you flex. If they see a smidgen of weakness, you'll be eaten alive.'

'My turn,' Voyzey said. 'You also thrive on your reputation. But your world is wrapped in cotton wool. Out there, being a nice and beneficial member of society is the key to success. But that's not you, so you have to play a role. You have to lie to everyone and disguise yourself, all to fool people into thinking you're something you're not. You have to operate from the shadows, always worried that the truth will come out. Your core is the same as mine, Franz. But I don't have to pretend otherwise.'

Franz heard a creak from upstairs, meaning someone had gotten up. Not good.

'People like us, we're just solitary fellows,' Voyzey continued. 'We need people to do our bidding. The darker the soul, the better, right? There's a limit, though, and you don't seem to have stuck to it. You hire rapists and women murderers.'

'One anomaly, Voyzey.' That wasn't quite true, was it? Joel wasn't the only guy he'd hired who'd enjoyed making women suffer. A couple of years ago there had been someone called Quinn, a real sick psycho. Franz had caught that guy and he was now dead and buried. 'Seems to me that you got your revenge, Voyzey. I hope you don't think I had knowledge of what happened to your niece.'

'You wouldn't be breathing if I knew that for sure.'

More noises upstairs. Franz heard Lacy call his name. He covered the phone and yelled that he'd be up in a moment. He decided to get straight to the point. 'What do you want?' he asked, but he had a sneaky suspicion.

'What I want is something you've got, Franz.'

And here it was. Voyzey wanted revenge, but blood wasn't currency. One of Voyzey's men had been taken down at the Mytton house, so it was obvious that Franz had sent people there and wanted Libby. The inmate would give her up in exchange for something worthwhile, and that would help soothe his injured soul.

'And what would that be?' Franz said.

'You owe me his damn wife, and I want paying.'

Franz paused. 'Excuse me?'

'Don't play fucking games. You're protecting her. I don't think she's worth it. Not worth having your people killed left, right and centre. I want her. She's involved in my Joanne's death.'

Franz realised that Voyzey's threats and his aggression were bullshit, intended to throw his enemy off the scent. Voyzey couldn't win a gang war against him and surely knew it. Better to act innocent and hope to convince Franz that... what, some other bad guy had kidnapped her?

But to expect this cheap trick to work was to treat Franz like a fool, and it irritated him. He had held his tongue and shown this man respect because he'd lost a family member, but that could go to hell now. So could a sweet little deal to get him to hand Libby over.

'Cut the crap, Voyzey. Your people took her and we both know it. How about you give her to me and it'll be your people who get to keep their hearts pumping?'

'Don't lie to me, Franz. I got to Joel in a police station, and I got to your house. You might think you're an untouchable hotshot, but you're not surrounded by goons all day and night. It might be a grenade through your letter box next time.'

Franz clutched his phone so hard he heard something on it crack. 'But you are surrounded by goons all day. Locked in a box with them, and you can't pay them all to be on your side. I only have to outbid you with one lunatic in there and it's game over. Where is she?'

'Don't play me for a fucking idiot, Franz. I'm surrounded by walls, and you have no clout in here, even if you think you do. There's only five hundred men in here, and half of them wouldn't touch me and the rest can't get close. But there's a million in your city that I can get to, and they could take you out in a hundred different places at any time of the day. That's how people like us go down, Franz. We bleed out at the hands of faceless nobodies for a payday.'

'No blaze of glory. No star-studded send-off. A sub-chapter rather than an epilogue. I totally agree. But I'd choose to die at my own home rather than in a prison cell any day of the week.'

'I want her, tonight, Franz. Don't push me. I'm going to call you in half an hour, and you'd better have her wrapped and ready for delivery.'

Voyzey sounded too sincere, too angry, for a man playing a role. Something seemed off. 'Okay,' Franz said after consideration. 'I'll give her to you, but only because I've already questioned her and got what I needed. She's in a bad way, though, and might not survive.'

'I don't care. She's mine! Write this address down. Have your men take her there, and don't fucking try to trick me.'

Voyzey gave him the address. Franz had to sit on the toilet before disbelief made him collapse. The fat bastard didn't have Libby Mytton.

'Voyzey, listen to me carefully. I'm giving you my word now. I don't have Libby Mytton. I thought you had her. If you don't believe me, I'll have your head cut off tonight. I promise you I didn't take her.'

The violent threat, mixed in there with a touch of pleading, did the trick. Voyzey was clearly stunned because he stumbled over his words before finally getting a sentence out. 'Someone took that woman out of her house, Franz. I know it wasn't me. And if it wasn't you, then who the fuck was it?'

Franz took a deep breath. 'It seems there's a third player out there, and he also wants Libby Mytton for some reason.'

PART 3

THIRTY-TWO

'You're staring,' the man said. He watched the road as he drove, not Libby. She realised he must have felt her eyes burning into his head.

There was trepidation, but she wasn't scared. He'd saved her, but she had no clue for how long. Or even if this wasn't a big trick. Finally, she asked the million-dollar question. 'Who are you?'

'One of Joel's friends. I'm sorry that he's dead.'

Emery hadn't mentioned Joel since his death. Police had, but as people dealing with Joanne Yeowell's murder and with her grieving family, none of them had used the word *sorry*. It meant a lot to receive sympathy, even if it came from a total stranger. She had begun to think that nobody really cared for her own pain, as if she deserved none for marrying a man who later turned killer.

'Are you a builder?' she asked. 'Someone on his team? I thought I knew them all.'

'I'm from way back.' He flashed a wallet at her and she saw a driver's licence through a clear plastic window. Roy Floode.

He was forty-two. It might be the whacked night, but she didn't recall that name ever leaving Joel's lips.

'Way back? You mean his gang life, don't you? So that's true? Joel was part of a gang?'

'Yes. We were best friends until I got out.'

'But he never did? He was still involved with people like that? That lifestyle? And somehow I never knew about it?'

'He was very secretive,' Roy said. He then explained that he and Joel had been enforcers, which meant they did violent work. If someone needed a bloody warning or interrogating, or a building needing burning to the ground, Joel and Roy were the guys sent. They worked for someone called Franz, who was a real big player in the underworld in the north of England.

Gangsters, burned buildings, interrogations. A different world. How on earth had Joel managed to hide it all from her? 'Did this Franz send you to help me?'

'No. In fact, he's after you, too. He thinks you know too much about his business because of Joel. Joel kept you a secret from the people on that side of his life.'

'Why?'

'Safety. People in our business are always under threat. You're a real good bargaining chip.'

'But you knew about me?'

He did because Joel shared that secret with his best friend. 'But we'll get to that. Look, we need to get you somewhere safe.'

'My sister's house. She can–'

'She can't keep you safe. They know about her and she's probably under surveillance.'

After they had run to Roy's car, he had made her cower low in the passenger seat to avoid eyes. Now she sat up. 'What? So she might be in danger, too. We have to contact her.'

'Not right now. We're dealing with Voyzey and Franz. Two big gangsters, both of them after you. We can't do a damn thing about your sister right now. She's safe until the moment you contact her, and then you're both dead.'

Her heart thudded. 'What do you mean?'

'If they do something to Emery, you have no reason to return. If they keep her under surveillance, you might walk into their trap. Just as you were planning to do.'

'So what do we do?'

'For tonight, we just hide. I know a place down south, but it's too risky to make the drive tonight in case we attract attention. We'll get a hotel for tonight. But not in Sheffield. Too hot. Just be strong, as you have been so far.'

Strong? Discovering her husband was a murderer changed something vital inside her. Everything was moving at breakneck speed and she was on autopilot, unable to fully absorb reality. Once the delayed shock finally hit, it would probably have the impact of a meteor. She didn't think she was strong at all.

She asked no more questions, even though she burned to. There were a million of them, but they were jumbled into an unintelligible mass. Her brain felt numb. She would get answers when Roy was ready to impart them.

She put her hands into her bathrobe's pockets, and there felt her mobile phone, which she'd been using in the bath. When she plucked it out, Roy snatched it. 'No phones, Libby. It can be traced.'

'Let me have it,' she pled. 'I need to phone my sister if she's in danger.'

'You can't,' he barked. 'This phone number is compromised.' Roy released the steering wheel so he could use both hands to snap the phone in half right before her eyes. He worked the two pieces back and forth until they came apart, then extracted the SIM card and destroyed that, too. Wide-eyed, she watched him lob the detritus out his window.

'No one has that number,' she said. 'No one can trace that phone.'

'We don't know that. We can't risk it. Libby, you need to understand that you're in danger. Voyzey and Franz have access to all sorts of people. If you phone for help, if you contact anyone from your life, the wrong people will know, and they'll find you. Let's just ride out this night and let me think.'

His words were stern enough to sluice away her brain's foggy haze, and she managed clear thought for a moment. Long enough to grasp the danger enveloping her. She couldn't forget that Roy had just rescued her from a pair of men who broke into her house.

'Can you keep me safe?' she asked.

He gave a reassuring smile that failed its mission. 'I'll do my damned best.'

They drove for a short time in silence. She looked up from her lap after a long while to find they were on a desolate road cutting between a massive steelworks and a wastewater treatment plant. The tarmac was dead straight, with no side streets, no way out except onwards – past a horde of police. There were police cars and officers in high-vis jackets everywhere, as if a major incident had unfolded.

'Vehicle checkpoint,' Roy said.

Perfect, she realised. In all the haste and confusion, she hadn't considered the police. *Now we'll be safe. The police will take care of me and–*

Roy turned left, into a tree-enshrouded driveway leading to a gated entrance into the steelworks. The tarmac was pitted and trash-filled, the gate battered and rusted and chained shut. This was not an operative entryway. Roy stopped the car just inches from the gate, so it was out of sight from the checkpoint fifty metres down the main road. He turned off the engine. The trees crowding the driveway cast a deep gloom and she could barely see Roy's face.

'What are we doing?' she asked.

'We can't get past the police,' he said. 'We'll wait them out. If they see us turn around, we'll look like we're avoiding them and they'll come after us.'

For the umpteenth time tonight, her mind swirled with confusion. 'I don't get it. Why don't we just tell the police?'

Roy put a hand on her arm. 'We can't. This is bigger than you think. We can't go to the police. It's why I came alone, Libby.'

This was all becoming too much. 'Are you saying the police are in on it?'

'Voyzey and Franz have coppers at their beck and call–'

'But not all of those people up there.'

'It only takes one, Libby. You have to trust me. You heard that a copper killed Joel in his cell, right?'

She took a deep breath. She had tried not to think about that, and for a time had been successful. But Roy was right. If one of the enemy could get to Joel in a police station, Libby's chances of survival in custody were slim.

'But what do we do? We can't run forever.'

'No. For tonight we'll just stay away, hide. And tomorrow we'll come up with a plan to get you home.'

Her brittle psyche wouldn't cope with more terror. There was a massive energy dump. 'I trust you,' she said, suddenly exhausted. 'I just want to sleep now.'

She put the radio on and found a station playing soft music. She needed the background music. She settled back in her seat and closed her eyes, for nothing bad could get into the darkness she herself created.

Roy said, 'I'm sorry.'

'It's okay. It's not your fault I'm fragile china.'

'You're not. Joel once said you have sturdy resolve when your back is against the wall. But that's not what I meant. I mean this. I'm sorry that we're here.'

'It's fine.'

She heard a sob and opened her eyes to find Roy wiping tears from his face. It didn't seem real at first, and she had to touch his face to see if the tears were tangible. When her fingers became wet, she knew she hadn't imagined it. Roy was crying.

'Hey, no, don't be upset,' she said. Those words felt alien because for so long now she had been the one in need of compassion. And he was a stranger. 'You saved me.'

Roy thumped his thigh. 'I messed this all up. I didn't have this worked out. I made Joel a promise and I should have been ready. I should have gotten ready as soon I knew there was a threat against you, but I wasn't ready.'

She put her hand on his thigh, to prevent him whacking it again. It worked. 'No, it's really okay. You saved me. I'm here and safe because of you.'

'But look at where we are. I should have you in a safe house somewhere, nice and warm. Not stuck out here with me. I should have had people in place for this. An infrastructure. A plan for you. But I'm an idiot, and weak, and we're flying by the seat of my pants because I wasn't prepared.'

She could think of no response other than the same lie: 'It's okay. We're okay. But what do you mean by a promise? To Joel?'

'I was Joel's best friend. We looked out for each other. The boss, Franz, he didn't want his people getting married...'

Franz didn't like employees with families, he said. Partners and children could dilute their commitment to him, but they could also be used by enemies. A man's wife or daughter could be placed under harmful threat, or a custodial sentence could part them. A guy facing such a problem might be willing to talk and give up the boss, or even kill him.

'Joel met you and fell in love,' Roy continued. 'But he was deep in with Franz, unable to get out. So he hid the truth. I don't know how he managed it, but he kept you a secret.'

This was hard to hear. She had assumed that Joel had gotten into crime after meeting her. But he'd already been involved. Crime was there first. That made *her* Joel's dirty little secret, not the other way round. For three years. She could hardly believe it. Joel had lived two separate lives and somehow they'd never converged. Until now. If he hadn't killed a girl, hadn't had his face plastered across the news, the truth might never have come out.

'But you knew about me?' she said.

'I was out of the game by then. Down south, new life. But we were still best friends. Yes, he told me everything. He talked about you a lot. Constantly. That right there. It's a dog bite you got when you were six.'

He touched a tiny scar on the back of her right hand. Then he pointed to her left earlobe, where there was a small red birthmark. 'As a teenager, you used to wear a flower earring to cover that mark. Am I wrong, Alice?'

As a child she had been a giant fan of *Alice's Adventures in Wonderland*. She had told kids in her class at school that she had a middle name, Alice, when she had none. She stared at Roy, hardly able to believe it. He'd just stated three facts that he shouldn't know. Some people from her past were aware of the dog bite and her fake name... but Joel was the only person she had ever told about her birthmark anxiety.

Roy saw that he had astonished her. 'Joel and I were close, Libby. We didn't have any secrets.'

Really? 'So did you know he could do something like this? Murder a girl?'

Roy rubbed his face. 'I guess he did keep one thing from me after all.'

THIRTY-THREE

Franz had coppers with their ears to the ground who would alert him if Libby contacted the police. She'd had plenty of time to do that, yet hadn't. There was no police activity at her house, and there sure would have been if she'd told her tale. Best guess: the man who'd helped her escape knew the tricks of the trade and didn't trust the police. Smart bastard, whoever he was.

It meant Voyzey and Franz had time to hunt them down. They decided to combine forces and use people already out in the field to sustain the momentum. One man from each side.

'Who gets her when she's captured?' Voyzey said. 'You're only worried about what she can tell the cops. I think my situation is more important, don't you?'

Franz didn't. He killed for gain or to solve a problem. Never revenge. It was for weak souls. 'Sure. So I'll have her questioned, then you can take her for... whatever you want. That suit you?'

It did, with a condition. 'I get to say where we take her. And my people will be in charge when yours interrogate her.'

Franz agreed and they set the ball rolling. Each kingpin sent one of his men to the northeast corner of a twenty-four-hour Tesco car park. This late the store was surprisingly busy, but that faraway corner of the car park was desolate. Two cars arrived at roughly the same time and the drivers emerged to size each other up.

'Hawk, right? You look like the other guy,' Alain said. 'Brothers?'

Other guy? Hawk clenched his teeth. He stepped closer to the stranger. 'As good as. Are you the tosspot who killed him?'

The wise choice here was to deny the charge lest it cause serious friction. But doing so would pin the blame on Libby Mytton, and this brash fool might do something unrepairable once they had her.

Besides, such a lie was only for the fragile and repentant. 'The very one. He was out of his depth, like you. And I'm here to be your waterwings.'

Muscles in Hawk's jaw throbbed. 'When this is over, I'll make you regret killing him.'

Unable to control another man's man, Franz had told Alain to take charge. 'Just try not to get yourself killed first. Now, one rule. I run this show, okay?'

Aware of his own restrictions, Voyzey had ordered his man to take no shit. So Hawk said, 'You're running nothing, dead man. We work together until the woman is found, and then we go our separate ways. Your way is going to be six feet under.'

'I may have just defecated in my pants out of abject terror. We're using my car.'

Hawk was okay with that. They got in. Alain, behind the wheel, said, 'Here's the plan. We go watch the sister's house to see if Ms Mytton turns up. If we can work together, everybody gets what they want.'

Voyzey had no intention of upholding his half of the bargain with Franz. He had told Hawk to take the girl once they had her, and to drop Franz's man in the dirt if he tried to stop it. Other men would be hovering nearby to offer aid if needed. It went without saying that this change of plan was to be kept secret. But fuck that. This bastard had killed Tempest.

'She goes to Voyzey,' Hawk said. 'No arguments. He lost a niece, so that trumps whatever your boss wants with her. I'm taking her and there's fuck-all you can do about it. Make no hassle and I might spare your life. That's just a *might*, mind.'

Franz had told Alain to dump this guy once they had Ms Mytton. But to give him no indication of the intent to deceive, of course. Alain decided he didn't like that statute because Hawk was a royal pain in the arse. He faked a yawn. 'You're a cure for insomnia, my friend. Enjoy your last night on earth and don't waste it insulting people.'

'I'll enjoy ripping your tongue out, you piece of shit.'

Alain pulled his keys from his pocket. 'Make some calls to loved ones. Clear the air so they don't feel bad when you're gone.'

'You still got the knife you killed Tempest with? I'm going to use that on you. Same cut.'

Alain fished in the glove box and handed Hawk a pad and pen. When he saw his new partner's puzzled expression, Alain said, 'For you to write your will, in case you haven't already.'

'Just fucking drive. You're boring me.'

'This is going to be such a fun partnership.'

Alain started the engine and set off. As the car left the car park, Hawk glanced in his wing mirror and saw a blue Ford Transit pull away from the kerb some way back and follow. It was known as the Tumbleweed Wagon and was based on the rolling jails of the American Wild West – the team leader was a fan – that would wander the lands, picking up prisoners from small towns for transportation to prison. With barred sides, the wagons would draw crowds intent on staring at the prisoners.

Not so with this vehicle, which had no cargo bay windows and a metal bulkhead separating that compartment from the cabin. Once Hawk had found Libby Mytton, the Tumbleweeds would snatch her and transport her to London to play whatever endgame Voyzey had in mind.

A few minutes into their drive, Hawk glanced in his wing mirror and saw the Tumbleweed van take a turn and vanish. He knew why. Voyzey suspected that his enemy would also try to snatch Libby when the point men found her, so he'd told his Tumbleweeds to keep an eye out for another van. Underworld rumours told of a Go Squad, men who could be called upon by Franz for action at a moment's notice. He figured they were the cleaners who had removed Tempest's dead body from the Mytton house.

Putting his faith in Hawk to deliver Libby Mytton, Voyzey had decided to use the Tumbleweeds to draw Franz's people away, should they appear, and lead them on a merry little chase. Hawk saw the Go Squad's van take the same turn to follow the Tumbleweeds, as planned. Obviously their orders were to stay with Voyzey's hit team and neutralise them if they got heavy-handed. Good, because he didn't need escorts, or want them. When it was time to carry out a death sentence on Alain, Hawk planned to be the sole executioner.

He glanced at Alain, noting that the man was also watching his wing mirror.

THIRTY-FOUR

Soon the police checkpoint broke up and cars blew by the driveway where Roy and Libby were parked. The world was silent again.

'Give me a sec,' Roy said. He exited the car and moved to the end of the driveway, to peek left and right. He was back behind the wheel seconds later. 'All clear. Let's go. We'll get you some clothing.'

He found a twenty-four-hour Asda just half a mile away and parked. When Libby tried to get out of the car, he put up a hand. 'No, you can't. You're a known face. We can't risk it. People will stop you in there. And it won't look right if you go in in a dressing gown. Tell me your clothing sizes.'

He had a fair point. She gave him the information he needed and he ran to the store. He was back in eight minutes, with a blue pullover, and jeans, socks and training shoes. She wanted to dress in the back seat while he stood away, but he wasn't willing to delay their time here. The best he could do was to turn the rear-view mirror so he couldn't see, and she got changed while he drove. Once done, he told her to clamber over into the front.

Libby sank into her own thoughts and paid no attention to where they were going. When she left her dreamworld and re-entered the real one, she saw it was very dark beyond the car windows. It felt like deep space, the car their rocket blasting through it without friction.

It was the countryside, she realised. And the lack of a sense of movement meant they were parked. The darkness wasn't all-consuming, though. On Roy's side of the car was a lit-up house whose long driveway they were parked at the end of. Past the house were the black, blocky shapes of farm buildings.

Roy himself was counting money. She knew why. A cheap wooden sign staked into the earth at the mouth of the driveway advertised a Ford Focus 52-plate for £500.

'Where are we?' she asked.

He jumped at her voice. 'Hey, gorgeous. You slept.'

She did? 'Are you buying that car?'

'Hopefully.' The cash in his hand was part of a bigger haul in a paper bag on his lap. He slotted the bag into his coat pocket. From another he extracted a pair of surgical masks and two pairs of sunglasses. 'Best if the owner doesn't recognise you.'

She understood. She put the mask and glasses on, as did Roy. The car then turned down the driveway and parked behind the tractor, out of sight of the road.

'Say nothing,' he told her. As he shut off the engine, a handsome young man in dirty coveralls exited the house and waved. Roy buzzed his window down.

'You after the Ford?' the man said. He sounded Welsh.

'Sure am, but there's a catch. The soon-to-be ex-wife is trying to nail me. I'd like her to not know about the car for at least a week, until after she's bled me dry. So I need to delay transferring it to me. I'll come back in a week to sign the logbook.'

The farmer eyed them both suspiciously. 'Sounds dodgy, mate. Not sure I want a part of it.'

'Don't worry about it. So, the sign back there advertising the Focus – couldn't tell if that was a five or an eight.'

The farmer gave a barely perceptible smile. 'An eight.'

'Eight hundred it is.'

Roy had that exact amount ready, so he'd planned this trick all along. The farmer took the cash, but before he handed over the keys, he pulled out his phone. 'Mind if I get a snap of your ID? Just–'

'–in case we rob a bank in this car and the police knock on your door,' Roy finished for him. 'Don't worry, I'll swap out the licence plates.'

It took the farmer a couple of seconds to decide this stranger in the mask was joking. But he insisted on the photo, so Roy presented his driver's licence to the camera. After that, the farmer wrote a receipt for the sale and handed over the keys.

When the farmer was gone, Roy said, 'Libby, you drive the Ford and follow me.'

She tailed Roy's car for half a mile, until they reached a small wood on the right. They parked and Roy approached her window, telling her to wait. She watched him drive his car deep into the woods, until it got stuck. After spending a minute concealing it with branches, Roy got behind the wheel of their new purchase and Libby climbed into the passenger seat.

'It'll probably be found tomorrow morning,' he said. 'But we'll be well away by then.'

Well away? She had hoped this nightmare would be over, naught but a memory, come morning.

THIRTY-FIVE

The 2011 Census listed the civil parish of Wavewell as having a population of 909. The settlement was named after a Saxon chieftain called Wauve – it was in the Domesday Book as Wauveuelle. The church had a crooked spire due to sunlight mostly heating the lead on one side, and every May the locals...

Libby didn't really care about the words coming from Roy's mouth, just the fact that they did. She found his voice relaxing and soon felt drowsy. Her nerves had been buzzing like a faulty electrical outlet and he had helped to calm her.

Soon he pulled the car to a stop. They were on a rise with flat fields on the left. To the right, the land slipped sharply downwards, and at the bottom sat the village, perhaps a quarter of a mile away. Out here in the middle of nowhere, it was impossible to miss, even at night – or especially so since it was the only source of light.

From this raised position she could see the whole village laid out, shaped like a crucifix. Or a flat-pack box. The latter in mind, Libby saw the village as a kind of pop-up book. The crooked church spire was level with her eyes, which made for a strange sensation of floating. She imagined that spire being crooked from folding away into its box incorrectly. It made her smile.

'It looks dead,' she said. A bad choice of word. The smile vanished.

'It's nearly midnight,' Roy replied. 'Maybe there's some devil worshipping going on, but otherwise everyone will be settled down. And that means we're going to have trouble getting into the hotel. It's there, look. Down the road with the bridge.'

She saw it. Off the main drag was a tarmac lane that bored through a field and navigated a small stone arch bridge over a dried stream. At the end of the lane, sitting all alone, was a white stone building in a garden enclosed by tall hedges. There was a gravel car park behind it.

Roy said, 'Doors were locked at eleven, so guests can't get back in. That seems unfair, especially if you pay for just one night.'

'So what do we do?'

'Cash opens doors. At least I had the foresight to get that part right.'

His self-admonishment proved he was still upset that she had been dragged through the night on a half-second's notice with no real plan in place. She patted his shoulder. 'It's okay. I can sleep in the car.'

'No way.'

He drove to a right turn about fifty metres ahead. This new road snaked down the hill and into the village. First, they entered a residential area of two-storey semis, which struck Libby as similar to any urban street back in Sheffield. After that, they passed bungalows and cottages mixed in with trinket shops and tea rooms. There were also some surprising properties, like a massage parlour and a skateboard shop.

Few souls were about this late, but the handful they saw

paid close attention to the car. Tourist spot or not, the locals seemed wary of strangers, especially at night.

Soon they reached the side lane, which ran between a library and a convenience store. The street sign – Buffalo Lane – must have been commissioned by an urban planner on drugs, for it was spiked into the top of a phone box on the corner. They turned down and within a few seconds were out of the village and heading along the tarmac track that cut through a field.

The stone bridge had parapets that were nothing but three-inch-high lines of single bricks, which was no real method of preventing careless drivers from needing crane-based recovery. Roy guided the car across it slowly.

Soon, they passed the hotel and stopped in the makeshift car park. The entrance to the hotel's grounds was a lychgate in the perimeter hedge. A sign named the hotel: Country Rooms. That kind of did what it said on the tin.

Roy got out and went round the front of the property. About five minutes later, Libby heard a noise from the vicinity of the back gate. It opened and Roy stood there, beckoning her. When she went to him, he took her hand and, bent low like kids, they headed down a paved path slicing through a neat lawn with chairs and tables and a small stage on one side. The area was dark, silent, immensely eerie.

The back door of the hotel was wide open. Roy stopped before they got there. 'I told the owner I was delayed getting here,' he said. 'He thinks my assistant messed up the reservation. I paid twice the price of a room, cash. He specifically told me no guests.'

'So I can't come in?'

'I said to him, it's midnight, mate. What do you think I'll do, find a girl and sneak her in the back door?'

He'd been building up to that joke, she realised. She was meant to laugh. Perhaps another time.

They headed through a sunroom, then a dining room, and entered the lobby. All three zones were empty and dark. The owner must have gone back to bed. They tiptoed up the wide stairs–

–'Watch this step, it creaks'–

–and onto the first floor. Libby was reminded of the time when she was seventeen and her first real boyfriend had sneaked her into his home. Through the kitchen, then the living room, where his parents watched TV with their backs to them, and upstairs, to his room. Tonight was twice as scary and not a fraction as hip.

Roy had already unlocked the suite. He virtually pushed her inside and locked the door behind them. Libby let out a relieved breath. The room's brightness was liberating for her thudding heart.

The suite was spacious and archaic by design rather than age. It also had a separate bedroom, kitchen, and living room, which she hadn't expected from a small hotel in the middle of nowhere. Libby flopped onto the double bed while Roy approached the window and peeked through the curtains.

'I'll make some calls and get hold of some people tomorrow,' he said. 'Let's just settle and sleep tonight.'

'What people?'

'I know some people who can make enquiries and find out exactly what's going on. I think we need to pinpoint the bad police officers involved in hunting you. The ones working for Voyzey and Franz. We're safe here for the night. Do you need anything?'

'Yes,' she said. All running was done, at least for today, and she felt ready for answers. 'I want to know how my husband got mixed up with gangsters, and how he managed to hide it from me for years.'

THIRTY-SIX

On a commercial street one afternoon a few years ago, while working on renovating a shop, Joel had popped over the road to buy his boys a lunch from a kebab shop. As he queued, a teenager rode past on a pushbike and lobbed a stone through the window.

The owner bellowed at him and gave chase, but the kid escaped. The working day continued. When the guy in front of Joel got his turn at the counter, he told the manager that he knew people who could make sure his shop wasn't vandalised. For a price.

'No thanks' didn't go down well. The man said that here, in this rough area, it was wise to get help to avoid repeats. 'Maybe it's a dead rabbit through the door next time. Be worth thinking about.'

No thanks. The guy ordered his food and departed, but he left behind a slip of paper with a phone number – 'Call me if you change your mind.'

Joel ordered six meals and went back to the boys. An hour later, he was hard at work when a dirt bike came down the street. It stopped outside the kebab shop and the passenger leaped off. From a plastic bag he pulled a dead rabbit, guts loose and waving, and tossed it through the shop's open door. The bike and its two riders were gone seconds later.

When Joel mentioned it to his boys, one of them had a theory. A protection racket. 'You offer help, then trash a shop to show help was needed. Keep doing that until the owner agrees to pay. And the trouble magically stops.'

'Joel thought that was a cool idea,' Roy now said. 'He tried it himself. Just like that. Out of the blue. And it worked.'

Libby could barely trust her ears, even though she had recently learned that her husband was capable of murder. 'He ran a protection racket?'

'Yeah. He paid some young thugs to trash a newsagent's. The owner agreed to pay without issue, probably thinking a major gang was targeting him. But here's the thing. There *was* a major gang about to target him, but Joel got there first. It was Franz's zone and he got real pissed off at some guy operating on his patch.'

Patch. Zone. Underworld jargon. It unnerved her a little that he knew it so well. Roy had admitted that he was part of Franz's gang, but she hadn't really given it much thought. She wasn't sure she wanted to know more about his criminal life.

'Franz almost had Joel whipped within an inch of his life,' Roy continued. 'That was what normally happened if someone muscled in. But, long story short, Franz was impressed with him instead. Joel had a natural flair for leadership and manipulation, which Franz thought could benefit him. So he offered him a job. And there we go.'

'Just like that,' she said, echoing Roy's earlier words. But with added sarcasm.

'Yep. Joel became an enforcer, and I was his partner. I know it's not nice to hear.'

No shit. Libby held her disgust when she asked, 'And what sort of things did you do?'

He explained that their role was to head out to places where Franz needed action. Joel's building firm was a good excuse to travel. As the boss, he could skip out whenever he wanted, no questions asked. His men didn't mind being left to work alone because he was a bit of a micromanager, so they got an easier shift with him absent.

Meanwhile, Joel would go... do his thing. He'd be back before shift end, and home in time for tea. Libby had never had a clue that he'd been off hurting someone or destroying something when he should have been working.

It got worse. His evenings down the snooker club? Those occasions when a building job got delayed and kept him away until late in the night? The times he'd gotten a phone call and had had to immediately pop out to go fix something?

'Lies, right?' she said.

Roy nodded. 'You don't say no to Franz. What would his excuse be? Wedding anniversary celebration with the wife? Doing homework with the kids? Weren't supposed to have those things.'

'And you both hurt people?' she said, almost scowling at him.

'It's the game, Libby. But I got out in the end. Joel didn't.'

'Why?'

'Honestly? Because he liked it.'

Liked hurting people? That image didn't match the man she knew. But how could she deny Roy's claim with Joanne Yeowell's body lying in the morgue?

While Roy told her terrible secrets about her husband, they prepared for sleep. Libby didn't want the bed because trying to be comfortable seemed wrong. There was no comfort to be had. She took the quilt to one of the armchairs. Roy got a spare quilt from a cupboard and bedded down in front of the door, to block unannounced entry.

Now, his story told, they sat in silence. She wanted to sleep, but only because she wanted the new day to come. Daylight. And what news it might bring. She'd only been absent from home, from her life, for a handful of hours, but felt as if she'd been on a round-the-world trek.

But time passed and sleep didn't come. Just thoughts of Joanne, Joel, enemies. And her sister, most of all. His story of her being under surveillance was plausible, but she doubted his claim that Emery's landline was bugged. Didn't you have to get into someone's house to tap the phone?

Earlier, Roy had convinced her that she'd be caught by killers if she contacted Emery. She had been too stunned and confused to think clearly. Now her head was clearer and she saw the bigger picture. She was not the only one under threat. Emery needed protection, too. They couldn't just ignore her.

Soon, Roy was snoring. It was almost 2am. She moved closer to him. His feet were close to the door and his legs were outstretched. He'd kicked off his shoes so, in a movement like something out of a cartoon, she reached under his blanket to tickle both feet. He drew them away by bringing his knees closer to his chest. Now there was space for her to open the door far enough to slip out.

Nobody in the hallway. Nobody around downstairs. Reception was lit but desolate and silent save for a grandfather clock loudly ticking. The front door was secured by a Yale lock but no key. She was out in no time.

She started the trek up the lane that cut through the field. The world was black but she could make out the bridge way ahead, and the main road beyond it. And the little red blob of the phone box she intended to use.

She didn't care about Roy's warning about traced calls. She

could withhold the number. She had to talk to Emery, reassure her, and convince her they'd be together again, and safe, very soon.

She stopped on the bridge only long enough to look around and think what a sweet place this was. It beat the city. Right then, she promised herself that she'd get a home out in the sticks within the year. Why hadn't she ever considered this before?

The phone was in working order, so she called the operator by jabbing in 100. Reversed calls couldn't be made to mobiles, so she used Emery's landline. Her spirits rose as the call was put through, but as soon as the phone started ringing, she deflated. It was late and Emery probably wouldn't answer because she sometimes received spam calls from–

'Hello?' her sister said on the third ring. She didn't sound disturbed. With a wave of relief, Libby realised Roy had been right. Nobody had attacked or even contacted Emery. Her enemies were nearby, loaded with danger and bad intent... but just watching for the moment.

'It's me,' Libby said, forcing a calm tone beneath her words. She had to act as if nothing was wrong, for Emery had no clue her sister had had to flee in the night. 'Are you okay?'

'Sure. It's late, Libby. What do you need?'

Should she tell the truth? Emery could be sent from the house, into the arms of the police, and she would be safe. But only if the police could be trusted. Plus, if Emery wasn't actually in danger, and Roy was wrong about surveillance, then she'd panic for nothing.

'I don't need anything,' Libby said. 'Couldn't sleep. Look, I'll call you first thing in the morning. We have to discuss a tricky matter.'

'Okay. Bye. See you later.'

And that was that. Libby hung up and wanted to cry. Had she done the right thing? Two major violent gangsters were after her blood and Emery might be in the crosshairs, yet Libby just referred to it all as a *tricky matter*. It seems so abhorrent to downplay this serious problem. And it wasn't lost on her that, again, the sisters had spoken with an elephant in the room. Emery had seemed abrupt and eager to get off the phone.

Did her sister blame her for Joel's actions? Or for not having some kind of sixth sense that would have warned her away from him? Libby wondered if Emery was waiting for her to bring him up first. Should Libby have broached the subject? Perhaps she should have busted the ice between the sisters by screaming *my husband is dead!* But maybe she had no right to feel hurt by his murder, given his black soul. Would – could? – anyone offer sympathy for her agony?

Numbed, she stepped out of the phone box and stared down the main road, left and right. It was empty and silent, peaceful. The village was a very sweet place... but not home. She was now decided. Tomorrow morning she was going home. She'd get protection and stay with her sister for a while. How long could she and Roy really run anyway? She was not going to abandon everything.

Her life might not amount to much at the moment, but she wanted to keep what little was left.

THIRTY-SEVEN

'Well done,' Alain said. He lowered his pistol.

Emery hung the phone back on its wall-mounted cradle and returned to her place on the sofa. It was where she'd been sat before the phone call, and where Hawk, with a knife, was waiting.

Hours earlier, the two sworn enemies had managed to agree on something: twiddling their thumbs and watching the house of the sister was a bust. Libby might not turn up. She might make a phone call and they'd never know about it. Best to go in, be proactive, Hawk said. Alain agreed. Hawk wanted to take the lead and Alain had no objection. He was eager to see how someone from the darker, more erratic half of the criminal world operated.

The taller man's plan wasn't complicated or clever: he went round the back of the semi-detached property, booted in the flimsy back door, and rushed inside. Alain followed at a casual pace, assessing his new comrade's process. Hawk vanished through the dark kitchen, into a lit living room. Alain heard half a yell from a woman, then scuffling noises.

When Alain entered the plain living room, Emery was on

the sofa, silent and still but shivering. She wore a green dressing gown. Dumped on the floor were a book and a pair of headphones. Perhaps she'd been listening to music and hadn't heard the door being kicked in. Her terrified eyes didn't leave the knife Hawk held inches from her face as he stood before her.

Alain sat on the coffee table, just feet from Emery, and pulled out his P11. He aimed it at her guts. Hawk took a step back, willing to let his comrade take over from here.

'You have a million questions,' Alain said. 'Ask none, although I'll deal with the most important one right now. No, you won't die tonight. Not if you do everything we require.'

He loved to watch her face as he explained why she was in this predicament. The widening of her eyes. The gear-shift in her breathing. The movement of various muscles in her cheeks and neck as she slowly understood that she would save her own skin only one way: by giving up her sister's.

The three of them would wait here for Libby to call, or hopefully visit. If it was the former, Emery was required to put on 'some theatre'. Ten minutes ago she was 'chilled personified', for she had had no clue that 'Libby's World' had been rocked. 'We need you to recapture that sensation if she calls.'

'You talk like some fucker who learned English from a meth-head,' Hawk said.

Alain ignored him, so focused was he on Emery. In his world he didn't deal with many females, but interacting with them was intriguing. Some men wanted to fuck them, but he preferred this kind of power play.

'Act naturally,' he told her. 'Just like you would any other day in which your sister isn't on the run and you haven't been taken hostage. Understand?'

She nodded. He said, 'Maybe your sister will come clean about the problem she's got. But I don't believe so. I think she won't want to panic you and when she finds out you're okay, she'll pretend she is, too. So make sure to act annoyed at the lateness of the call, which would be common at such an hour if all was fine and dandy here. And then end the call quickly.'

'Stupid,' Hawk said. 'Why don't we just have her come round here, you moron? Or tell her sister where she is?'

'Because, my brainless comrade, Libby may suspect a trick. She's with a man who has some smarts and some experience. He might have warned her that her sister could be compromised. If it was me, I'd tell her to be wary of any offer to visit or disclose a location.'

'You're reading too much into it. We should just grab the phone and tell the bitch to hand herself in or the sister's head comes off.'

'At least I can read. If I was the man with her, I'd refuse to let her hand herself in. It would put both sisters in danger. But, if Libby comes on the phone and immediately tells the truth, then we might have no choice but to undertake your option. Unless that happens, we do this my way.'

Hawk gave him the finger, but no further argument.

Now, following the call from Libby, Alain checked the phone for the last number and set it into Google. He got back no result, so he checked the area code. He got the location and searched a little more. On the sofa, Hawk watched him and Emery watched the boxer – his knife, at least.

'Got her,' Alain said after a minute. 'Wavewell, a small village not too far away. And it was a landline, so they must be at a hotel. There's eight in that village. Six B&Bs and two proper ones. Let's go. Unless you want to have intercourse with this one first?'

Emery stiffened. Hawk held a hand up at her. 'Calm down, nobody's touching you. I won't let him.'

'I've had my fun with her. You're sure you don't want to partake?'

'Only from ladies who want it. Now shut your gob.'

'I'm sure you would if you knew full-well you'd get away with it. But if that's your position, then let's get her tied up and be on our way.'

Alain used tape, from a first-aid bag carried by Hawk, to bind Emery tightly to a kitchen chair and cover her mouth. He then, quietly, smashed glasses into a washing-up bowl. The chair was placed in the centre of the kitchen, surrounded by the glass.

'Try not to struggle,' Alain said. 'If you topple the chair, you'll regret it as you bleed out.'

Given the way she eyed up the field of glass around her, she would sit very still. But Hawk didn't look impressed. He voiced his worry that she'd somehow escape, or eat through the gag and scream for help.

'So what do you advise?' Alain asked him.

'We silence her properly.'

'That I advise against. We might need her for leverage.'

'But you ain't the damn guy in charge, are you?'

Emery's eyes widened as the two men argued. After a back and forth that was calm on Alain's end and heated on Hawk's part, the latter decided to take control. He pulled a coin from a pocket. 'Then let's just decide this by chance. Because you aren't listening to me and I don't take orders from you.'

'Are you Anton Chigurh?'

'What?'

'Comics are probably more your thing. Are you Two-Face from *Batman*?'

'Man, shut up. Heads we whack her, okay? Seems fair.'

Alain gave no response. Taking it as approval, Hawk flipped the coin...

Wavewell was less than twenty miles away, and they made good time. Without knowing it, he stopped on the same high road, in almost the very same spot, where Roy had parked earlier. Alain and Hawk looked down the hill, at the village laid out below.

'We wait a bit,' Alain said. 'I don't want to cruise around that place this late. People will make note.'

Hawk patted Alain's bald head. 'You mean note of how you modelled yourself on Agent 47 from the Hitman games?'

'I chose the bald head because it makes wearing wigs easier.'

'Seems to me you've got the Friar Tuck thing going on. There's stubble on the sides and back and nowt on top.' Hawk stroked his own long hair. 'How much would you give to look like me?'

'I'd have to give up chromosome four. How about you get some sleep so I can have peace?'

'Here? No hotel?'

'It's too late. We can't take someone like you into a quaint Midsomer-style village at night. They'll think you're a Grindylow and panic. We'll wait until early morning and go enquire at all the hotels and B&Bs.'

Hawk got in the back seat and stretched out. He played a game on his phone, with the sound off and the brightness low. Alain got a paperback non-fiction book from the glove box, which had a penlight bookmark.

'You click your tongue while you play,' Alain said after a few minutes. 'It's like Chinese Water Torture.'

'Good.'

They said nothing further for a few more minutes, then Hawk opened his door.

'Where are you going?' Alain asked.

'You know what they say about curious cats, right?'

'They get the cream?'

'Tosspot.' Hawk got out and stood a distance from the car. He kept his eyes on Alain as he made a phone call.

'You okay, baby?' he said when it was answered. 'Sorry I left it so late.'

'I'm fine,' a woman replied. She sounded sleepy. 'I'm used to these overnights. So you won't be back until the morning?'

'Yeah, sorry. One of the dozers is on the blink, so we're having to use shovels. We're all working into the wee hours.'

'Oh. Okay. Will you be back before midday? I was hoping you'd get some nappies on your way back. But I can ask my mum to pop to the shop if you're going to be late.'

'We'll see. I hope to be done before about ten. Love you, babe. Get back to sleep. Oh, did that bloody dryer repairman get back to you yet?'

'Love you, too, Dale. And yes, finally. He's coming at midday.'

'Midday's well awkward. Anyway, night-night, babe. Oh, hang on. What's a Grindylow?'

'I don't know, sweetie. Are you okay?'

'Always. Catch you later.'

Hawk blew his girl a kiss, put his phone away, and returned to the back seat of the car. He wasn't sleepy yet. Alain asked who he'd spoken to.

'Your mum,' Hawk snapped. 'She said her vibrator's broke off in your dad's arse.'

Alain smiled. 'Midday's a bit awkward for a dryer repairman. Couldn't he do earlier or later? It means your "babe" can't go out.'

Hawk glared at him in the rear-view. 'You lip read or something?'

'Handy trick, no?'

'Fucking don't.'

No reply from Alain. The men got on with their business in

silence. Hawk fell asleep but didn't realise it until he woke to a buzzing noise. Up front, Alain was shaving his head with a battery-operated device. He paused when he saw Hawk's grinning face behind him in the sun visor's mirror.

'Knew I'd touched a nerve,' Hawk said, laughing. 'How often do you cry yourself to sleep because you're a bald bastard?'

Alain gave him a wink and put down his device. He picked up his book again. 'I worry more about failing my mission. So try to get some sleep.'

Hawk lay down again. 'Tell me. That tosspot Joel Mytton was one of your people, right?'

Still reading, Alain said, 'I have no people. I'm independent. But I've worked for Franz often and I've come to know Mytton.'

'And you think you're clever, so tell me. Did he kill Joanne? He says it was an accident. That true? My boss doesn't think so.'

'Unsure. The police said they found Joanne Yeowell's bloodstained clothing in a bag in Joel's garage. But his confession said she stripped and put her gear aside. It sounds a little fabricated to me. But I wasn't there, so I'm no authority.'

'So you think he did it on purpose? Killed her for kicks?'

Alain gave this some thought. 'Last week if you'd said Mytton could rape and murder a woman, I would have said you were being foolish. But as of right now it's not a jolt to me. That's about the best answer I can give.'

'Think his missus knows more than she's letting on?'

'She knows more than nothing. Again, my best answer. Now, please, let me get on with my book and I promise I'll teach you how to read one day.'

'Dickhead.'

THIRTY-EIGHT

Libby managed to sleep and found herself in the bed, alone. It was 6.32am. She didn't remember getting under the covers, but she did recall a dream. Joel was alive and had been freed by the police, and he'd returned home as if expecting all to be forgiven. Now, she breathed a sigh of relief, but it appalled her. Did it mean that she was glad that he, her husband of two years and a man she'd wanted to father her baby... wasn't alive?

Roy woke as she entered the living room. She told him she needed food. He informed her that they couldn't get breakfast because it should have been ordered before 8pm last night. Libby knew because she had seen this rule written on a pamphlet on the bedside table.

'Then I'll go get a sandwich from the shop,' she said.

Roy wasn't a fan of this, but she stood her ground. He offered to go, but she shut this down, too. 'I need fresh air. And I want to do it alone.'

Roy obviously didn't like the idea, but he agreed and even gave her a £20 note from his stash. 'Get some food to go, as well.'

'Are we going to go home today?'

'I'm working on the best way to do this. I'll explain when

we're on the move. Go now and be quick, please. Don't talk to anyone, and if you have to, don't volunteer any unnecessary information. Don't tell anyone you're from Sheffield. That might tip the balance if someone thinks they know your face but can't place it.'

A fair point. 'So tell no one I'm married to a killer?'

She was kidding, but it upset her. Not the joke itself, but that she'd used present tense. Despite the dream that was fresh in her mind, she kept forgetting that Joel was dead. Was this some kind of denial? It was as if she tried to commit his death to a mental cellar but the knowledge continued to escape.

She left the room and Roy watched her do it. She felt like a kid being allowed to walk to the end of the street under a father's watchful eye. She was glad when she hit the stairs and he was out of sight.

The manager was behind the desk but dealing with a customer, so he didn't see her walk by. Outside the front door was a couple sitting in a swing chair, who said hello and nothing more. They didn't spit at her. So far so good. Then again, she was hardly Britain's most wanted fugitive. *Calm down, Libby.*

The new light of day had made her realise she had been stupid to not inform Emery of her plight. She was going to do it right now, and then call the police. Roy wanted to be a guardian angel, and that was sweet of him, but she felt he was out of his depth. And they couldn't run forever. An hour from now she planned to be face to face with Emery, and surrounded by police officers. The bad apples in the force surely numbered in single digits, so she'd be safe.

But she would not bring up Joel unless Emery was ready to discuss him. Her urge would be to scream *my husband is dead!* Even if Emery tried to shut her down, but she would hold her tongue. This morning she had a clearer head and understood better. Libby wasn't the only one hurting in the wake of Joel's evil actions. Some people got past trauma by colliding with it head-on, but others coped better with baby steps. If Emery was suffering, it wouldn't be fair to force her to make the leap until she was ready. So Libby would keep her own pain deep inside lest it aggravate her sister's misery.

She passed only two people on her way to the bridge. One was coming her way, no doubt a guest of the hotel returning from a visit to the village centre. The other was a man walking his dog who crossed the lane ahead of her. Neither did a double-take of recognition. For sure the Joanne Yeowell affair was once big news here, but interest had waned and some other story had probably become hot gossip. Unless she met a true crime junkie, she doubted she'd be exposed in this tiny village.

As she approached the end of the lane, a blue hatchback drove past along the main road and slowed down. It then backed up. The driver must have narrowly missed the half-hidden turn for the hotel. She stepped onto the grass so the car could drive past.

But the car didn't make the turn. It stopped dead in the main road, blocking the entrance to the lane. Libby saw two figures inside, but they were little more than silhouettes. They seemed to be staring down the lane, perhaps unsure if they had the right route.

Or maybe they were watching her. She stopped dead.

Just as she was about to turn back, the car moved on, past the library, out of sight. Lost tourists after all. She relaxed and continued walking. She reached the end of the lane and the phone box. It was very early but the main road was already thronged with sightseers.

As she hauled open the door of the phone box, she glanced up the road and saw the blue car stopped again. It was at the kerb, perhaps fifty metres away. The passenger door opened and a man stepped out. Her heart skipped a beat. At this distance she couldn't make out his face, but the jacket was unmistakable. Bright green.

Just like that of the man from her bedroom last night. She watched him die, so this could not be him. But the similarity suggested a connection, and that meant she was in big trouble.

THIRTY-NINE

Libby forgot the phone box and turned on her heels. She faked a casual stroll until she was round the corner of the library, but once out of sight increased speed. She didn't run because a car was coming up the lane from the hotel and she didn't want to cause alarm.

But run she did just seconds later: a glance back showed Green Jacket turning onto the lane at a jog. She'd been spotted by the phone box.

She considered flagging down the approaching car, but rejected that idea when she saw an old man behind the wheel. He would be no match for Green Jacket and couldn't save her. It was only after the car had passed that she realised she could have hopped into the vehicle and ordered the driver to blast away, fast.

She continued to run. She was fast because she wore trainers, and a bigger gap opened between pursuer and target. As she stepped onto the bridge, her foot caught on the slight incline of the arch, sending her sprawling onto her front. The bricks grazed her hands. She heard the thud of feet behind her. She got up without a glance back, but too late. Something hard hit her back and she was propelled forward, again to hit brickwork hard with her torso.

'Hold your horses there, bitch,' Green Jacket said. She got to her knees, but no further as he planted a big foot on her calf. It hurt like hell and pinned her lower leg to the stone. She looked up to see his grinning face and acne-ravaged cheeks. No mistake. This was one of the men who had been chasing her.

'You gave us the merry runaround, didn't you?' he said, wagging a disapproving finger. 'But I like the countryside, so thanks for that.'

She looked around for help. All of a sudden the land seemed darker, as if nature was conspiring with him to shield whatever was about to happen. The hotel was so, so close, but nobody was around. She could shout for help, but this man could do terrible damage before aid could reach her. The best use of her voice would be pleading.

Before she got a chance, he withdrew a knife and said, 'What happened to my friend?'

Libby knew what he meant. The man dead in her bedroom. But she could not form words for an answer.

'Did you see the bastard who did it? Short guy with a bald head. What did you see him do?'

She shook her head. It was just a reaction to her fear, but too late she realised it looked like she was refusing to answer.

'You did fucking see,' he shouted, pointing the knife at her. 'Tell me if he suffered, or I'll fucking gut you right now. I'll leave you with your head hanging over the edge of this bridge, blood dripping into the streambed. Last chance.'

He took another step back, to give her room. His heels were an inch from the single-brick parapet. It was too good to be true, and too hard to resist. Her body found energy in hope, and she got to her feet.

In the same moment, she shoved her palms into his thin

chest as hard as she could. The impact forced him to take another step back in order to retain balance, but his heel caught the parapet. There was a grunt of terror as he realised he was about to go sailing.

It happened in a half-second. One moment he was towering over her, and the next he was gone. There was a thud and a yell of pain as his gangly frame slammed into the dried streambed eight feet below.

By the time he landed, Libby was already running.

FORTY

She rushed through the hotel's entrance, panting. Done with his guest, the manager looked up from his computer and asked if she had a room. When she ignored him and bolted for the stairs, his demand for an answer was more forceful. When she blanked him for a second time and reached the stairs, he yelled for her to stop. Of course, she didn't.

She threw open the door to her room, startling Roy, who jumped off the sofa, where he'd been using his phone. 'Someone tried to grab me,' she blurted. 'Those men are here.'

'What? Here?'

'Outside. They know where we were. I don't know how. What do we do?'

'Jesus. Maybe they got a tracker on our car somehow.' He grabbed their masks and sunglasses, then Libby's arm, and pulled her from the room. When Roy reached the top of the stairs, still dragging her, he almost collided with the manager, who was coming up.

'What's going on here?' he demanded.

Roy pushed him aside and he and Libby thumped down the stairs. In the lobby, Roy tugged her towards the dining room.

They were going out the back door, she realised. Once outside, they raced across the garden out and out through the gate, into the makeshift car park. Their car was ahead.

They were ten feet from the vehicle when the blue car raced into the gravelled land. They made it into their ride, but the blue car ground to a halt directly in front it, barring their way forward. Libby now saw the driver was the bald man from her bedroom, and he'd reunited with Green Jacket.

'Don't let them get me,' she yelled. 'Reverse.'

Roy had another plan. Green Jacket opened the passenger door of the blue car and made to step out – but he ducked back inside as Roy launched his car into the door, slamming it shut. She saw the window bash Green Jacket's shoulder. She almost wished the door had cut his leg off.

Roy then reversed and cut a turn, hit first gear again, and they were away. When their wheels touched the tarmac lane, she looked back. The blue car had turned in the car park and was aiming at them. Once it reached the lane, Roy's car was thumping over the bridge. By the time the chase car crossed the dead stream, Roy's vehicle turned onto the main road.

'They're coming,' she said, breathless.

'Not for long.'

Roy turned immediately off the main road and into a garage forecourt. There was a sandwich delivery van parked near the back wall, with just enough room to permit a vehicle between the two. Roy slotted the car into the gap, neatly hiding it from view of the road.

'They won't do anything here even if they spot us,' he said.

She could only hope. They might be desperate lunatics and not worried about witnesses. Her hands were shaking. Her throat was desert dry. 'He said someone wanted to cut my throat. They were going to take me to someone.'

Roy sighed. He didn't look at her.

She grabbed his arm. 'What is it? You know something, don't you?'

'Mike Voyzey. He wants to kill you himself.'

'But he's in prison.'

'And that's where they'd take you. I heard whispers of a plan...'

Which he now imparted. She would be kidnapped and driven south, into London. Voyzey had recently wrangled his way into a job in the prison stockroom. One of his tasks was to unload deliveries of supplies for inmates. He would be there to welcome a van carrying a very special item.

'Me?' she moaned. 'They want to sneak me into prison? They can't do that!'

'Voyzey has power, and he has money. That buys guards. But you wouldn't exactly go into the prison. Voyzey will enter the van, look into your eyes, and slit your throat there and then. Your body would then be driven away and dumped.'

She was numb at the thought. How close had she come? If she hadn't pushed Green Jacket off the bridge, would she now be in the boot of the blue car, being ferried towards London? It was a terrifying scenario. She instinctively hit the car's central locking button.

'How do you know all this, Roy?'

'It's all out there if you know who to contact. I know a man who used to work for Voyzey. He knows what's going on.'

'If people know this, why can't we go to the police and tell them?'

'There's no proof, Libby. Just rumour. Voyzey covers his tracks well. Besides, I told you that we can't trust the police. We can't go to them until I can find out who's on the wrong side. I've told you this.'

She hung her head, remembering. 'I'm sorry. I'm just scared.'

'This might sound silly, but please don't be. I won't let anything happen to you, Libby. That's a promise.'

She stared at the side of the sandwich van, which displayed a large image of a woman smiling as she lifted a BLT to her face. Her happiness annoyed Libby. *But that's unfair of me,* she thought. *Sandwich woman might have the life of hell when not posing for a camera.*

After another couple of minutes, the driver of the van returned and moved his vehicle, exposing Roy's car to the main road. But she saw no blue car. They waited another couple of minutes, then Roy drove slowly from the forecourt and into traffic.

No blue car before or behind them. He increased speed to get them far from ground zero. 'Where are we going?' she asked.

'I'm not sure yet. Put these back on.'

It seemed a bit pointless in a car that was being tracked, but she pulled on the mask and the sunglasses. She covered her eyes with the mask and put her head back. Not to rest, for that was impossible. It was to try to–

'Are you okay?' Roy said.

'Yes. I'm going to blot out the universe. Hopefully I'll open my eyes to find that the last two days have been a bad dream.'

But did she really want that? She would still be sharing a bed with a sick murderer.

FORTY-ONE

'You lost them,' Hawk yelled.

'They lost us,' Alain replied, minus the other man's venom. He used the next side street to turn the car around and head back to the hotel. He parked right outside the front door, where a sign warned against such activity.

'Now what?' Hawk said. 'I doubt they left any damn clues in the hotel.'

Alain rolled his eyes. 'Listen carefully. You're the brawn, not the brains. Maybe you think you're smart because you stand out amongst the amoeba in your social circle. But believe me, my friend, you're a one-eyed man in the kingdom of the blind.'

'What the fuck does that mean?'

'It means you just proved my point. Do you remember what you said when we spotted her? "Leave this to me. Watch and learn". Remember that?'

When they'd paused earlier that morning outside the lane that led to the hotel, to help them decide if it was practical to drive down or whether they should park and take a stroll, they had spotted a woman walking towards them.

'Shit, is that her?' Hawk had said.

'I do believe so. Seems like fate,' Alain had replied. When he saw Hawk reach for the door handle, Alain stamped the accelerator and the car burst forward.

Hawk forgot the door. 'Where are you fucking going?'

'We're not going to jump out and chase her on foot. Let's see where she goes. Maybe she'll walk right past us.'

He parked about fifty metres away and they used their mirrors to watch. When the woman they were sure was Libby emerged, she paused by the phone box. 'Excellent,' Alain said. 'I'll turn around and–'

'Leave this to me,' Hawk interrupted. 'Watch and learn.' He then got out of the car. In his mirror, Alain saw Libby look this way, and then she immediately bolted.

Hawk had cursed and ran after her. Alain had looked for a break in traffic in order to turn around.

Now, Hawk gave no response to Alain's *remember that?* question. And of course not, because it was his fault she'd escaped again. Alain said, 'Can I have my turn now?'

'In the hotel? For what? You think they left clues in the room? A convenient wall map pointing out where they're off to next?'

'That would be handy. But I'll assume that's not the case and will try something else. Wait here. Can you do that?'

'Just hurry the hell up.'

'You won't go running off after any more young females?'

Hawk feigned spitting at him. 'Get all your snidey digs out now, why not. You won't get chance later when I wipe you off the face of the earth.'

Alain giggled and exited the car. He headed into the hotel, where the manager was behind the desk and had just picked up a landline handset. Alain waved his warrant card under his nose.

'Detective Inspector Alan Manvers. Two people, a man and a woman, were staying here. They just ran. You see that?'

'Yes,' the manager said. He put down the phone. 'I was just about to call your lot. Mr Smith was the name the chap gave. But he didn't say he had a woman with him. He must have sneaked her in last night. They just bolted. I haven't checked the damage to their room yet. Are they wanted? I thought something was fishy with them.'

Alain's go-to lie, used many times over the years, was that he sought armed robbers. But today he was still determined to get out of the crime trade, and that meant his caution was on simmer. He decided to offer this man something that might flag as suspicious, which was a career first. 'He walked a horse down the road while he was drunk.'

The manager looked like he'd been slapped. 'What?'

'That's an offence. Section 12 of the Licensing Act 1872. Did they show ID to get a room?'

The manager still looked bemused. 'Walked a horse while drunk. And that's a crime? What's the sentence for that?'

'Sir, time is precious. This man is armed with a Bargain Booze loyalty card so we're warning the public not to approach him with a horse. So, did they show ID?'

'Wow. This is weird. But okay. Erm, no, we don't insist on ID. But we take down car registrations in case people are abusive or they damage things.'

'Perfect,' Alain said. 'Get that for me, please.'

The manager ripped a sheet out of a notepad on his desk and handed it over. 'While you're here. You know anything about my complaint about the graffiti? I called it in about two weeks–'

'We have eighteen detectives on that right now, sir,' Alain said as he turned to leave.

Back in the car, he told Hawk what he had found. 'And now I need to call my boss. Care to step out and give me privacy?'

'How about hell no.'

Alain exited the car and stood at its rear to make his phone call. Inside, Hawk pulled out his mobile to contact his own employer.

In Sheffield, Franz had just woken and finished showering. Downstairs, wearing a towel around his waist and starting the breakfast-for-all routine, he told Alain he'd have the registration plate traced to an owner. Based on another lie-to-save-face, Franz thought Alain and Hawk had just missed Libby leaving the hotel. 'As soon as I have a name and address, I'll text you. How's it going with Voyzey's buffoon? Has he told Voyzey what we've got?'

'On the phone doing just that this very second.'

'Quite nice of us to share info like this. Because I expect Voyzey to leave us in the dirt if he finds a clue before us. Stick to your man like glue for now, but can you escape if I need you to?'

Alain laughed. 'Escape? I'm patiently awaiting the opportunity to put him out of my misery.'

The subject of the discussion, sitting five feet away, had just informed Voyzey of developments, and it had made the prisoner happy. Like Alain, Hawk had lied to his boss and claimed that Libby and her saviour had checked out of the hotel before their enemies arrived.

'Does Franz know you have the registration?' Voyzey said.

Another lie. Hawk had claimed that he'd been the one to extract the information from the hotel manager. But Alain had been within earshot. 'My bald bastard shadow is telling him right now.'

'Franz won't want to share. He'll have his man dump you as soon as he knows something concrete. Stick to him like a limpet in case they try to fuck us over.'

As for the registration: Voyzey said he'd have someone on the inside try to trace the car via Automatic Number Plate Recognition, known as ANPR. The technology allowed real-time tracking of vehicles using thousands of cameras that captured millions of plates every day. The system could even back-date searches to display a vehicle's movements in days gone by.

'As soon as we get a hit, be ready to go at a moment's notice. Alone. You'll have to put your shadow down.'

'He killed Tempest. So it'll be my bloody pleasure.'

Hawk and Alain were told, separately, to hang fire while their bosses performed the traces. Alain suggested they take in the sights of the village and grab breakfast. Hawk didn't care to ride around aimlessly, so he agreed and they found a café deeper inside Wavewell. They got a booth and a pair of English breakfasts. Hawk normally didn't touch such things, because he was often dieting and training for a fight. Alain was flexitarian and ate meat only when he needed energy and couldn't be sure when his next meal would appear.

They faced each other across the table. Hawk still yearned to tear his enemy's heart out, but needed patience. Instead, he tried to surprise the man. 'How did Brittany treat you as a kid? You've still got a fragment of the accent.'

Voyzey had told him a few rumours about the hitman called Alain, including that he'd been born in Brittany, France. Hawk wanted the bastard to be unnerved, knowing that secrecy and anonymity were important to him. But Alain simply smiled at hearing personal facts about himself, true or not. 'I still know enough of the severely endangered language to get by when I call my mother.'

'What does that mean?'

Alain laughed. 'Anyway, tell me about you. Tell me how you feel about your brother's death now? Do you feel you could have prevented it? Did you treat Tempest like the brother you lost?'

Hawk tried to hide his shock. 'How did you know that?'

'The Placerville and Humboldt Telegraph Company.'

'What?'

Alain laughed. 'I'm sorry, I did it again. Vague references that require a man like yourself to do some internet surfing. I apologise. It's my job to know people, Hawk.'

Hawk gave no response to this. Their food arrived and nobody spoke again until each man had had at least five mouthfuls. Alain went first, 'I think you're okay. Normally everybody defers to me and I hate ass-kissers. It's usually because they're scared. Nature of my work.'

'Scared because you learned how to kill at age five?'

'The postman? I heard that silly rumour, too. I like the banter you and I have. It's a welcomed change because there's too much fakery in the world. I may even let you live when this is all over. And that's honesty.'

Hawk pointed his tomato sauce-smeared knife at Alain. 'If I end up liking you, I'll put you down quick and painless. But you've got some work to do.'

FORTY-TWO

Libby and Roy drove in silence, heading west. He kept to smaller roads and never broke the speed limit. They passed by Buxton, home of the famous water, and Macclesfield, and Congleton. Soon they hit the M6 southbound just past Stoke-on-Trent. Just as Libby wondered if they were going to London, Roy took the exit for a Fresh24 service station. The car was low on petrol.

The last time she'd spoken, over ten minutes ago, she had told Roy she needed cigarettes. He said he didn't know she smoked, for Joel had never mentioned it. She told him she did, but that was a lie: she had given up three years ago. She always wondered if bad news might make her return to the habit. Answer found.

She watched Roy fill the tank then walk towards the kiosk, checking his pockets. He stopped, turned, came back. He opened the door and started searching the floor, the door pockets. Not finding what he wanted, he sat behind the wheel.

'The cash?' Libby said.

He slapped the steering wheel. 'Hotel room. Jesus.'

'Have we got no money now?'

Roy pulled out his wallet, but didn't open it. Deep in thought, he tapped the wallet against the steering wheel. Eventually he extracted a bank card. After another thoughtful pause, he headed to the kiosk to pay for the fuel.

He returned with her smokes and she quickly lit one up. Bedamned the forecourt rules about flammable liquids and naked flames. 'Thank you. You didn't want to use your card, did you?'

'No. Traceable. But I'm probably being paranoid. The people after us don't know my name.' Roy drove out of the forecourt, into the main car park for the service station, and found a bay close to the entrance. He shut the engine off and stared at her.

'What's wrong?' he said.

The first drag from the cigarette had made her woozy. But it also seemed to clear some cobwebs. 'We need to contact the police. We can't just run like this forever.'

'Not a good idea, Libby. Bad things could happen.'

'I have a sister. I have friends. I can't just abandon it all. I'm going to call the police. We can wait in the services for them. Not all of them are bad.'

'Libby, that's not–'

She opened her door. He grabbed her arm. When she protested, he yelled, 'Your sister is in protective custody. The house was attacked. You can't go back.'

Her legs suddenly felt wobbly. It was a good job she was sitting down. 'God. No. Is she okay? Tell me. How do you know?'

'I'll tell you. I didn't want to worry you. But it's right you should know now.'

She shut the car door. Roy took her hand and she let him. 'Mike Voyzey got angry that we ran,' he said. 'He sent people in to try to firebomb your house and–'

'What? Is Emery okay? I... this can't be real... I...'

'She's okay. The police found her in time.'

Words wouldn't come, although her mouth moved. Since this thing started, she had worried that someone would target Emery. Now it was real. Strangely, there was more anger than fear.

'The public knows your house was attacked,' Roy continued. 'Voyzey is making all sorts of noise about it. He's denying that he had anything to do with the fire, but he's praising the people that did it. And the public is harshly criticising you, saying you deserved it.'

The public were against her? She'd experienced that before. 'I want to see. Give me your phone.'

'I can't let you see it. Please don't try. It will only depress you.'

She couldn't move, as if gravity had increased a hundredfold. She put her face in her hands, so Roy wouldn't know if she started crying. He rubbed her shoulder. 'I made a call to a police officer who used to work for Franz. He's good for keeping his mouth shut. He said he might be able to find out where the police are keeping your sister.'

'I want to talk to her now, Roy. Now. I hate this secrecy. You should have told me.'

'I had no time. This was just half an hour ago. Look, I know you're hurt and want to see Emery–'

'Yes, right now. If she's with the police, that's good. It means we can go to her.'

'No,' Roy said. 'Remember what happened to Joel. We don't know how many dodgy coppers Franz and Voyzey have, but for sure the man who killed Joel wasn't the only one. It's too much of a risk. There will be bent officers who are waiting for us to contact Emery. We'd walk right into a trap.'

She knew he was the only one with a clear mind and tight

logic right now. Which meant he was right. She hung her head. 'I'm going to die, aren't I?'

Roy stared out the window. And gave no reply. She hoped he hadn't heard her question, because the alternative didn't bear thinking about.

FORTY-THREE

While chewing his last piece of sausage, Hawk felt his phone vibrate in his pocket. He had a look while keeping the device out of sight below the table. Alain watched him carefully.

ANPR hit. Lose your man. Call me.

He replaced the phone in his pocket and started on his final slice of bacon. 'An MRI and six weeks of consultation just to be told what I already knew. Pinched nerve. Doctor couldn't even have the decency to make a personal call.'

Alain nodded, but with a slight upturn to one corner of his mouth. Hawk figured his lie had fallen flat. So what? But a trip to the toilet hot on the heels of his text would raise flags. Hawk decide to disarm his unwanted colleague a little with some small talk. 'Hey, the sister, back at the house. You warned me not to touch her. Seems you didn't want a piece of her for yourself. You like men? Or are you married and old fashioned?'

Alain wiped his mouth with a napkin and gave Hawk a long stare while he did so. 'You said you want women only if they want you. I like the ones that scare me.'

'What?'

'An old teacher of mine. Long time ago. She's the last woman I was attracted to. Because she was a true bully.'

'And that made you want to fuck her?'

'That's a reach. But there was captivation.'

'And she was the last? That why you're a bit tapped in the head? Because you've never had your end away?'

'Perhaps we should discuss the weather. Isn't that the most popular small-talk subject?'

Hawk laughed. 'Fair enough if you don't want to talk.' He took another bite of food and got up. 'Need a shit. Order me a millionaire cake, would you?'

He felt Alain's eyes on him as he walked to the bathroom, which was empty. Hawk made the call to Voyzey.

'ANPR hits all over the place today,' his boss said. 'The car seems to be heading south and it was last spotted going through a roundabout on a road called Queensway. The only way onward is to enter the M6. There's cameras on the northbound and southbound lanes, but they haven't captured the car. It might be stopped somewhere because it's dropped off the grid.'

There was good news, though. Twenty miles back east and close to the village where they'd lost the fugitives, there was a holiday haven called Kisspenny Caravan Park. An ANPR camera close by had snapped the Ford Focus over a dozen times in the last two weeks.

'Maybe our guy has a place there,' Voyzey said.

'But they got a hotel for the night. Hey, do you know what the Humber or Humbot Telegraph Company is?'

'What? No. I reckon the man knew we might trace his registration plate. I reckon he led us on a wild goose chase and now he's changed his plates, which is why they've dropped off the grid. He thinks they're untraceable and I bet he's gone back to the caravan park. Or will do soon. I'll send some people to meet you there. Have you lost your shadow yet?'

'I'm about to,' Hawk said as he stared at the bathroom window.

With perfect timing, Alain got a text just as Hawk entered the café's bathroom. It was from Franz. He didn't even read it. With a handful of people in the café and all of them minding their own business, Alain decided to call his boss.

'Did you get my text?' Franz said.

'You got an address for me?'

'I just texted it to you. And a name. Did you not read–'

'Going now,' Alain said and hung up. He walked fast from the café and got the car. Leaving the car park meant driving past the front of the café, and he didn't slow down. When a man stepped out from around the corner of the stone building, Alain slammed on his brakes. But not quite in time. The bonnet of the car hit the man's leg, but barely hard enough to do more than fold his torso onto the bonnet.

Alain and Hawk stared at each other, and each saw a guilty face. Both had been caught fleeing. Hawk stood tall and backed away, giving the finger. Alain saluted him and drove past, onto the main road, and away.

He checked the text message for the postcode and set it into Google Maps.

Half a mile from the café, on a rural lane lined with trees, Hawk found a space to hide. By his feet was a stone he'd pulled from a crumbling wall further back along the lane. Only a handful of vehicles had blown by him so far and he didn't fancy his chances of getting what he wanted. But it came thirteen minutes into his wait.

Hawk was a motorbike guy, so he recognised the black and gold beauty as a Lexmoto LXR 125. The way the rider weaved along the single lane suggested he was out for fun rather than heading anywhere in particular. At least Hawk wouldn't make him miss some kind of appointment.

He waited until the very last moment, then heaved the stone out into the road. With perfect timing and aim, it slammed into the motorbike's front wheel. Down went the bike. It skidded twenty metres down the road with the rider tumbling right alongside it.

Hawk ran to him. The rider's biker leathers were scuffed but not torn, but one arm was bent unnaturally at the elbow. There might be road rash beneath the clothing, too. The guy was certainly in pain and moaning. Ten feet away, his bike had stalled.

Hawk said, 'Shit, dude, what the hell happened?'

'Crash. My neck. Jesus.'

Hawk grabbed the man's helmet. But gloved hands grabbed his. 'No. My neck. Don't take it off,' he wheezed.

A rule Hawk knew well. If a biker had a neck injury, don't try to remove the helmet. He did feel a tad bad when he yanked and twisted to pull the headgear free, especially when the rider squealed in agony.

Twenty seconds later, the guy was alone on the road and Hawk was tearing off into the distance on the Lexmoto.

He covered the twenty-two miles to Tansley in good time. Kisspenny Lane was easy to find. The main entrance into the caravan park was gated, but it was wide open for all and sundry to enter. Hawk rode in and along the main road. The static caravans were arranged in a neat grid. He travelled to the rear of the grounds, where there was a fine view across the fields, and parked outside an empty motorhome. He walked back to the reception building, which had a pub next door.

He sat at a table to await a call from Voyzey or the arrival of the people his boss was sending. He wondered if he'd see his targets strolling by, full of confidence that their pursuers were lost.

He saw a sign for an axe-throwing stall, so wandered over. It was open. Having a go meant giving his caravan number, but the lady in charge didn't check his name against the number he pulled out of thin air. She handed him three axes and he started lobbing.

After that, he headed to the children's play park and had a go on the zip-wire, although his feet dragged in the grass. Then he returned to the pub to buy lemonade. In all it burned an hour, and then he got the call to say his people were here.

He met them near reception. Five big brutes in a seven-seater vehicle. They had been given images of Libby to memorise. He didn't know any of them, but they knew he was in charge.

'Go park next to a motorbike down at the rear,' he said. 'Split up and go up to every caravan and peek in the windows. If you can't see someone inside, knock on. We have to find this bitch. If you see her, get her incapacitated and into your car. And call me straight away.'

'What about the guy with her?' one asked.

Voyzey hadn't given instructions about the fate of Libby's saviour. Hawk took charge of that, too. 'Leave him dead in the caravan. We'll burn it down when we leave to hide evidence.'

The search never got past its first five minutes. Voyzey called Hawk with an update. His fixer had been poring over the map and had noticed there was a service station a short way down the M6 from the roundabout where the Ford Focus had last been captured by ANPR. Voyzey told Hawk to leave the guys to search the caravan park and to head to this new location.

Hawk groaned. Service station? More guesswork. But he was paid to do as he was told.

Out in the boondocks, Alain stopped his car at the mouth of a driveway that led to a farmhouse. The map said the postcode was actually down the next turn, some 500 metres further along the road. But this was the place. He could see a tacky wooden sign staked into the earth: Ford Focus 52-plate for £500.

This was not good news. The Focus was owned by a Jamie Camber, but whoever he was, he wasn't the guy who'd rescued Libby. Camber had obviously sold them the Focus.

Alain drove down the driveway and turned his car so he could make a quick getaway. As he stepped out, the front door opened and a tall, handsome man in a tracksuit appeared. The guy waited on the step until Alain approached.

'It's the car, right?' the man called Jamie said. 'I should have moved the sign. Sold it last night.'

'It sure is about the car, my friend. I have some questions about the people you sold it to.'

He seemed curious about this, but not enough to enquire more. 'No can do, mate. I was just off to visit my girlfriend.'

Alain smiled in preparation for annoying small talk. 'Oh. Cool. Where's she live? Local?'

'Caravan park. She's got... look, pal, sorry, but I don't have time. Sorry. Car's gone.'

He closed the door. Alain stepped up to it and pulled out his fake warrant card. He was ready for his usual bullshit about seeking a wanted criminal. But it didn't appeal. He returned the warrant card to a pocket and pulled out his real wallet. He put fingers on a couple of £20 notes.

But bribery didn't appeal, either. The greasy breakfast was playing havoc with his guts and he was hovering close to the state of annoyance.

He put the wallet away and pulled out his gun. This appealed mightily.

Ten minutes later, he called Franz with news. 'The registered owner of the Focus sold it to our missing pair. He confirms he saw Libby, although he didn't know who she was. Doesn't know where they went, unfortunately.'

'You believe him? He's not involved?'

'He's not. He showed me a counterfoil for sale of the car. It just hasn't been transferred to a new owner yet. Innocent chap.'

'Then don't hurt him, okay?'

'Calm ye down. I promise that at no point in the future will I ever cause this man damage. I did get something good, though. He took a photo of our guy's driver's licence. Got a name for you now. Roy Floode. Know it?'

A pause, as was Franz's way. 'No. Address for this Floode?'

Alain gave it, as well as Roy's date of birth. The address was in Sheffield, back where all this started. Franz said he'd get some local guys to pay a visit, see if maybe there was a wife or child they could get information from.

'Meanwhile, I'll have someone check out this Roy Floode for bank accounts. Maybe we can track him if he uses a bank card. Email a photo of the licence to me.'

Franz hung up. Alain stared at the body on the living room sofa. 'Body' was the wrong term, because the man called Jamie wasn't yet dead. Breathing shallowly, bleeding from three bullet holes in the chest, but still clinging to existence for the time being. He aimed his gun at the man.

'I'd love to do the right thing and end your suffering,' he said as he put the gun away, 'but I made a promise.'

FORTY-FOUR

They sat in the car, in the services parking area, for what seemed like a long time. Roy periodically exited the vehicle to make phone calls. He'd told her he was trying to locate his police officer friend who'd formerly worked for Franz.

Libby watched the cars that arrived and left. Places like this were intriguing to Libby because people from all walks of life, all parts of Britain, congregated here, but in ignorance of each other. It was a cauldron of anonymity, and it helped her to feel… hidden.

Latest call finished, Roy got back behind the wheel. 'I know a place we can use.'

'What about your policeman friend? What about Emery?'

'He's going to make some enquiries. Meantime, he has a place we can use for a few days.'

A few days. 'I'm sick of this. I want to go home.'

'Soon, I promise. My friend knows someone in the UKPPS–'

'What's that?'

Managed by the National Crime Agency, the UK Protected People Service was a patchwork of regional police groups that offered protection to those at risk of harm. In some extreme cases it could offer people new identities, new homes, new lives.

'What? You don't think Emery needs that, do you? And me?'

'We don't know yet. Let's not get ahead of ourselves. Voyzey and Franz might have plants within the UKPPS, so we have to wait and see what my friend can find out. Hopefully Emery is with a clean team and we can arrange for you to visit her.'

Visit her sister in protective custody! Two days ago, she never would have dreamed such a sentence would apply to her. She...

There were a thousand questions begging to be answered, but she didn't even voice one. Her attention was caught by a blue car entering the area. She had seen many that resembled the one chasing them, so she had perked up each time. Tense, she watched it go by behind their vehicle and slot into a bay on her left, hidden by a BT van with a driver inside who was chomping fast food. She hadn't caught a glimpse of the driver.

'I want to talk to Emery by phone. Can your friend arrange that?'

'He's not on the protection team. He can't get close without raising suspicion. All he can do is research into the team members and make sure none of them is working for Voyzey or Franz. It might take some time. But if it comes back that they're legit, then we can make that call.'

That would have to do, although the wait would eat her alive. She looked out the window as the BT van slipped out of its bay. She watched it depart, then cast her eyes to the spot it had vacated. In a bay two beyond sat the blue car from moments ago. Now she saw the driver clearly. And her jaw literally dropped.

Suit, bald head.

'Roy.'

No answer. She looked round at him. He was deep into his phone, so she slapped his arm. 'Look.'

When she looked back at the bald man, he was staring straight at her. 'Jesus,' Roy said.

The bald man pulled a gun out of his jacket and kicked open his door. Roy started the car and stamped on the accelerator just as the bald man rushed at them with his gun raised. The Focus leaped out of the bay like a greyhound and they were away, fast. Libby ducked her head, expecting a gunshot to shatter the back window. None came so she looked back and saw the bald man jump in his own vehicle. Another car chase it would seem.

The BT van had paused at the end of the lane to await a chance to enter the slip road and exit the services. Roy cut into the oncoming lane, to pass the van.

But he immediately had to swerve wider to avoid a bike that was turning in. The vehicle blew down the thin gap between the BT van and Roy's side of the car, with maybe five inches to spare each side. But the rider's luck ended there.

Still looking back, Libby watched the blue car also enter the lane, but right into the path of the oncoming bike. There was a mighty squeal of metal as the vehicles collided. They stopped dead, but the rider retained momentum and flew over his handlebars, to slam into the windscreen of the blue car. It made Libby yell *Oh my God!*

Roy didn't care and turned left, onto the slip road, building speed. Libby felt sorrow for the biker, but mixed in there was a large dose of relief. His misfortune had been her lucky strike.

Maybe, if he hadn't glanced down to slot away his gun as he left the parking bay, Alain might have seen the bike in time to avoid it. Maybe not.

An instant after the bike thumped into his car, Alain's face slammed into the windscreen. Only seconds later, when he became aware that he was still seated, did he realise things had happened the other way round. The biker had sailed over his handlebars, into the windscreen, cracking almost every inch and ripping the whole panel out of its housing. And knocking it into Alain. The oblong window lay across the dashboard and steering wheel and against Alain's chest. The biker was half inside the car.

And unhurt. With far less shock than curiosity, Alain watched the man yank off his helmet and lob it aside.

'You're like a bad penny,' Alain said, rubbing his face to check for cuts. His hand came away blood-free.

Hawk seemed more stunned by who he faced than by the crash. 'How the fuck did you know to come here?'

Alain got out and threw his eyes around. In a bay directly across the road from him was a man who'd been about to dump fast-food wrappers in a bin, but now watched events unfolding with utter disbelief. Alain rushed over, gun leading the way. Someone offscreen screamed. Fast-food guy remained frozen as Alain stopped before him and demanded the keys to his car, a yellow 2014 Fiat Tipo whose driver's door was open.

'Ignition,' the guy said. 'I've got a baby.'

'Try nothing heroic, then.' Alain got behind the wheel of the Fiat and started it up. And then noticed a car seat with a baby in the back. Wow. The guy hadn't tried to appeal to Alain's soul, but had been worried about someone kidnapping his child. Alain wound down the window and said, 'Get the baby.'

The distraught father opened a rear door and snatched his infant child. As that door shut again, the front passenger one opened and Hawk leaped inside.

'How the fuck did you get here?' he demanded for a second time.

'Traced the man's bank card. He got petrol here. You?'

'ANPR last hit looked like they were on this motorway. I figured it was here because I'm smart. You going to shoot or get after them?'

Alain realised he still held the gun in his right hand, and it was pointed across his lap, right at Hawk's guts. Shooting had been the plan, but now it didn't appeal. He'd have a dead passenger and, given the short distance between them, blood would doubtless stain his £1,400 Hawes & Curtis stretch suit. He had no more spare clothes.

Instead, he put the weapon away and started driving in pursuit of their targets.

FORTY-FIVE

Twenty-five seconds after they left the exit ramp and hit the motorway, Libby saw a car do the same a few hundred metres back. The vehicle was just a dot at that distance, impossible to identify, and many people left service stations. Still, she worried it was the bald man.

Clearly also worried about a tail, Roy moved to the fast lane and increased speed. The dot behind them did the same. Libby hoped the driver was someone with urgency in a life that would never impact hers. Soon, she felt she had gotten that wish. The car was much closer now and she saw it was yellow, not blue. She relaxed a little.

But not for long. As the vehicle closed on them, now just twenty metres back, she saw a shiny bald head behind the wheel. His passenger looked like the guy who'd attacked her on the bridge. The same two bozos, back on the hunt.

'It's them,' she moaned. 'Go faster.'

Roy obeyed, but the yellow car was faster. The bald man veered into the middle lane and drew alongside on their left. Now there was no chance this was a mistake. When Green

Jacket saw her looking, he drew a finger across his throat. Libby locked her door and looked away.

'They're going to ram us off the road,' she shouted.

She didn't know if that was their plan, for a crash would be fatal for all concerned at ninety miles an hour, but Roy believed it and managed a burst of speed. They got far enough in front of the chase car to allow him to cut in front of it. There was a hundred metres of free road ahead until the nearest vehicle in their lane, but they'd soon eat it up.

'We can't just let them chase us all day,' she said, glancing in the mirror to see the car right on their butt. She saw a Fiat badge.

'Don't worry,' he responded. It was a useless request.

'Hold tight,' he said. She looked ahead and saw an exit and a sign for Stafford, fast approaching. Beyond it, she expected to see traffic feeding into the motorway and clogging the way ahead. But there were no vehicles entering. Roy moved into the left lane, ready to take the slip road off the motorway. But the manoeuvre was mirrored by the Fiat.

'This won't work,' she said. 'They'll just follow us and get us at traffic lights.'

Roy didn't answer. He swerved towards the slip road at the very last second, as if hoping the hatchback would be too late to copy and would blow on by down the motorway. However, the bald man had fast reactions and copied Roy's tactic immediately.

But Roy had something else in mind and instantly cut to the right again, to retake the motorway before all four wheels had even left it. The bald man didn't expect this and he was too late to correct his angle. Both cars passed dangerously close to a wedge-shaped barrier dividing the roads, one either side of it, like conjoined vehicles sliced apart by an axe. The Focus blasted down the motorway and the Fiat burned down the slip road. Libby breathed a sigh of relief.

The motorway passed over a bridge above a roundabout. Fascinated, Libby pressed her face up to the side window to watch. Below, she saw the Fiat slow down for a red traffic light at the end of the roundabout. Even better, her elevated position exposed the far side of the roundabout, where she saw the slip road that would allow the Fiat to rejoin the motorway and continue the chase. Wasn't to be. Roadworks had closed the road. It explained why she'd seen no traffic entering the motorway ahead.

Libby slumped in her seat and touched Roy's arm. 'Thank you. Well done.'

'We're not safe yet,' he said. 'But my pleasure.'

They continued along the motorway, fast. Libby had no clue where they were going, but the further the better. If they had to hire a boat and take to the seas, so be it. She promised herself that she would not die today.

FORTY-SIX

'Not good,' was Alain's response to finding the slip road shut due to roadworks. Hawk was a little less reserved and punched the dashboard five times, which was a backing beat to profane lyrics.

'Now what?' he said when he'd calmed. 'Fuck it. Just smash through.'

Alain didn't do that. He took the car past the blocked road and completed a full revolution of the roundabout. At the red light that paused vehicles so motorway traffic could enter, he didn't stop.

'Nice,' Hawk said as Alain mounted the kerb and swung hard left to cut the corner and enter the exit road. A van had to swerve out of that lane, the driver showing his concern by laying heavy on his horn. He wasn't the only traveller disturbed by seeing a Fiat Tipo heading the wrong way and directly at them. Traffic fled the lane like water shifted aside by the bow of a boat. Hawk found it hilarious.

At the end of the road, Alain cut another left turn, this time to access the motorway. The pursuit could now continue.

The traffic slowed in all three lanes, and soon stopped dead. They were in the centre lane. Libby felt her heart beat a little faster. Roy cursed.

Seeing her worry, he said, 'We're safe here.'

'I know,' she replied, but only to allay his worry. She didn't believe it for a second.

'Stop looking around like that,' he said with a faked smile. 'You look scared and people will think you're my prisoner.'

She realised she was nervous and jittery, throwing her gaze in all directions. His words calmed her a little and her thumping heart slowed. They were still a ways from the next exit and if the traffic remained locked down, their two hunters, if they chose, would enter the motorway far ahead. They wouldn't know if their targets had already gone by.

She was reminded of a time two years ago: stuck on a motorway with Joel. He had been almost frothing at the mouth with anger because of the jam. She'd ribbed him for his impatience, but now she evaluated that old scene with new eyes. Eyes that saw not a displeased driver... but a monster unveiled. Or was she being unfair with that assessment?

Joel. She did not want him in her head. She closed her eyes, put her head back, and tried to sleep. Hopefully she would dream of a life that might have been.

'Fuck.'

Alain laughed. 'You have no patience.'

Hawk sneered at him. He flicked a hand at the traffic jam ahead. All three lanes were at a standstill. 'They're gone.'

'Nobody is gone,' was Alain's reply as he slowed the Tipo to a halt behind a BMW with two kids play-fighting in the back seat. 'Look. Everybody is right here. A thousand lives paused. A hundred million real storylines on intermission.'

Hawk snorted his displeasure at the jam. Or the guy by his side. But then his attitude changed. 'Maybe they're stuck as well.' He unclipped his seatbelt and got out. Alain did the same. They were in the fast lane and on Hawk's side was a rigid box truck.

The two men got out and stared ahead, over the roofs of cars. 'You need a box to stand on?' Hawk said.

Prompted by his own joke, the boxer put a foot on the steps of the truck and hauled himself up using the wing mirror. It gave him the height to gaze across the sea of frozen vehicles.

'Looks like a spillage of something,' he said. 'Sand is my guess, so–'

'Who the fuck are you?'

Hawk hadn't even realised he was next to an open window, or a driver was staring at him. The man was fat and bearded, topless bar a sleeveless high-vis jacket. In one hand was a can of Coke. Hawk snatched it, took a sip, and dumped the can in the guy's lap. Then he leaped onto the roof of the Tipo and continued to scan the traffic jam.

The truck driver started yelling, and he laid on his horn. On the other side of the Tipo, Alain pulled and showed his P11 pistol. No more complaints.

'Got it,' Hawk said, stepping onto the Tipo's bonnet then leaping onto the road. 'Middle lane about two hundred metres. Follow me.'

Normally Alain would never have let such a wild man dictate the forward path and put him at risk... but he hadn't changed his stance about slotting this career in his rear-view. So why not spice things up a little and introduce some unpredictability? He would step in and take control when – not *if* – the fool was on the verge of making a dangerous mess of things.

Led by the boxer, the pair slipped past the front of the truck and the vehicle on its left, then turned to their right and ran along the hard shoulder.

Alain trailed Hawk as, bent low, they moved along the hard shoulder. Hawk had said the target was a couple of hundred metres away, and somewhere close to that distance he stopped and looked over the roofs of cars.

He pulled out his knife and eased between two vehicles. Alain followed. Hawk took a right into the aisle between traffic in the left and middle lanes. There he stood tall and, secrecy abandoned, bolted at full speed.

The target car was three down the line, and the big man got there in half a second. He kicked it and roared. Alain soon understood why. The vehicle was empty.

Just as Libby was about to drift off and swap the terrible real world for a sweet, imagined one, a horn in the distance snapped her eyes open.

She glanced at her wing mirror, which gave a long and uninterrupted view down the arrow-straight aisle between parked cars in the slow and middle lanes. Then the unbroken view was indeed busted: a pair of shapes crossed her path in the distance. People, two of them, moving from one lane to another.

She sat up. They had been in the jam only minutes, far from long enough for anyone to need to stretch their legs. And the shapes had moved with a suspicious urgency.

'They're here,' she said.

Roy was on his phone, checking the traffic news. He didn't

even look at her but instead cast his eyes around. 'Did you see them? Are you sure?'

She ignored his query. 'What can we do?'

She answered her own question by opening her door and slipping out. She kept her head below the roofline and scuttled to the front of the car. Roy met her there and she grabbed his arm with both hands, as if fearful of being whisked suddenly away like paper in a tornado.

'Follow me,' he said. But he pulled her as he moved away, which negated his order.

They eased between bumpers and into the central reservation, where they clambered over the concrete barrier and dropped to their knees. And started crawling along the grass on the northbound side. People in oncoming vehicles stared in bewilderment.

'Go down the slow lane, look in the cars,' Hawk said. 'See if they've made new friends.' Hawk started running along the aisle between vehicles in the middle and fast lanes, glancing left and right to see if their enemies were shacked up in someone else's vehicle. It was a fair tactic.

Alain hadn't expected the targets to be missing from their vehicle, and it felt like he'd been outmanoeuvred. Now his pride had a smudge and he no longer allowed Hawk to take charge. He saw a pair of young women in the car behind the target vehicle. They were enjoying the show, and that told a story. He pulled out his P11 and, without a care for who saw, aimed it at the windscreen.

'If you would be so kind, ladies, please point out where they went,' he shouted over the blare of rushing traffic on his left.

Not realising they were part of whatever they had

previously found funny, the two women dumped their smiles in a nanosecond. Both jabbed fingers towards the northbound lanes.

Thanking the women with a wink, Alain leaped the barrier. As if its driver suspected the bald, suited man was on a suicide mission, a Range Rover thundering down the fast lane swerved into the middle one with a blare of its horn. Alain looked both ways and immediately locked onto his prize. Libby and her benefactor were sixty or so metres away, crawling in the loose stones and debris cast to the central reservation. It was quite the rib-tickling scene.

Except for the fact that, perhaps alerted by the horn, the duo were staring back at him. He wanted to yell an instruction to give up their folly, submit to their fate. Foolish, of course, and not only because they'd never hear him.

But what did it hurt to try? So he wagged a come-here finger. It was no surprise when the pair got to their feet and started running. Alain burst into a sprint.

'There!' Hawk yelled. Much closer to the targets, the lanky fool vaulted the barrier and landed in the chase way ahead of Alain.

'Stop fucking running,' Hawk yelled at the fleeing pair. Then, 'What the fuck?' as a man in a suit and almost a foot shorter cruised past him. It made Alain smile despite everything at stake.

Surprisingly, it was the shorter man who closed the distance between them rapidly. Neither of the bastards seemed to be slowing down, however. Not trusting her own gas tank, Libby threw caution to the wind and turned into the oncoming

THE THREAT

blizzard of northbound traffic. And she did so with Roy's hand still locked in her own.

Forced into a lane of speeding vehicles, he yelled in shock. But Libby hadn't acted with recklessness and had timed her manoeuvre well: they stepped into a wide space formed because of the presence of a slow flatbed truck that had no business in the fast lane.

Somehow, they found another gap in the next lane, and then again, and by the grace of something celestial managed to plant shoe rubber on the hard shoulder without provoking a single blare of a horn. Here Roy took the lead and stepped over the metal crash barrier. But Libby remained on the other side, halting them in place with their connected arms bridging the railing.

'Car,' she said, pointing with her free hand. There was a lay-by a couple of hundred metres away. In it, a solitary vehicle. Seeing this, Roy stepped back over the barrier and they started running again.

Frogger. That was what his targets' risky tactic reminded Alain of. It was a classic arcade game from the eighties in which players guided a frog across a busy road with forward and sideways hops. He'd played it as a kid, back when hobbies and downtime were things that mattered. The thought made him smile even as he realised Libby and her saviour had heightened their chances of escape by crossing the northbound section of motorway.

But they had paused on the hard shoulder long enough to allowed him to close the distance, and now he ran alongside them with three lanes of speeding metal in between. He pulled and aimed his P11, and tried to get the sights on the man called

Roy Floode. He aimed low, for a non-lethal but highly incapacitating shot. This man had given Alain a lacerated head that made shaving awkward, so he was due a reprimand. With him downed, Libby would certainly give up the battle.

However, he couldn't get a shot fixed. He was reminded of another old pastime: the shooting range. But here it was inversed: instead of running man targets whizzing past stationary obstacles, the former seemed fixed in place as he paced them, and the latter – vehicles – blitzed by, ruining his aim.

Seconds later, he glanced ahead of the fleeing pair and realised why they hadn't disappeared into the woods. They were going for a car in a lay-by. Alain stopped and aimed. He fired, but heard the bullet zing off a passing vehicle.

In the next moment, the couple were in the car. The owner must have been taking a dump because he ran from the trees, shouting. His instruction to vacate his ride was rightly ignored.

Off to Alain's right, over on the hard shoulder, he saw Hawk. He had wisely found passage across the road, but it had burned enough time to neuter him. The car burst from the lay-by before he got there.

It joined traffic by causing a car to brake hard and the driver to lay on the horn. Alain was unsure what to do. It was a horrible feeling rarely experienced. In something close to desperation, he looked ahead of the escaping car, to find a suitable vehicle to shoot and hopefully cause a traffic jam. But the sheer fact that it was a desperate move made him discard it.

The car, and the targets, were gone seconds later, swept away in the metal river. Across the road, in the lay-by, Hawk threw up his hands in despair. He ignored the owner of the stolen car, who was demanding answers. Alain looked for a chance to cross and soon got it.

'Why didn't you shoot her?' Hawk said as Alain got safely onto the central reservation.

'I couldn't risk killing her.'

'Then you...' Here the owner of the stolen car interjected, was reprimanded and slapped by Hawk, and the boxer continued his line: '...then you could have shot the parasite with her.'

Alain considered this. 'That's a skewed diagnosis of him. Rather than a parasite, he's a symbiote. He's not manipulating her. They exist together as one, by choice.'

Hawk laughed at him. 'It was just a word I used for him. I'll swap it for "dickhead". Not everything needs fucking dissecting.'

'Except me. I'm sure you'd love to dissect me.'

Hawk looked at the passing traffic and the vehicles locked down on the other side of the barrier, from which myriad people stared in wonder. 'Maybe later. How about right now we just get out of here before the cops come?'

'It appears that not everything you say is useless junk.'

Hawk flipped the bird, then the two men ran from the lay-by and were swallowed by the woods.

FORTY-SEVEN

Roy left the motorway at the next exit, then took some turns off the main roads to get them deep into the countryside. Libby, lost in despair, numbed by their near miss, didn't even notice the world around her until the car stopped. She was surprised to see they were parked on a residential street. She blinked hard, like someone coming out of a dream.

'Where are we?'

'Housing estate in a place called Cafferton. And as for why...' He pointed at a house across the road. In the driveway was a red 55-plate Peugeot 206 for sale for £900. She understood. They couldn't continue in a stolen car. 'Have we got the money for it?' she asked.

'I'll have to do a bank transfer. But I'll offer more if they only want cash.'

Libby waited in the Kia while Roy rapped on the front door. It was answered by a man and both of them spent a few minutes walking around the 206. The deal was done quickly. A bank transfer for the keys. Roy got in his new car, but it didn't move for a few minutes. She saw him on the phone.

When he was done, he drove the 206 alongside the Kia and

waved a finger, instructing Libby to follow him. He led her to a nearby pub car park. It was three-quarters full. He waited outside but directed her in. She parked the Kia and abandoned it with the keys still in the ignition, then transferred into their new vehicle.

'I just got a call from my friend. You know, the police officer?' he said as they left the estate. 'He believes there's a UKPPS agent who's working for Voyzey, and he's part of Emery's protection unit.'

'What? Is she in danger?'

'No, at least not yet. They're waiting for you to contact the police, so they can put you in touch with your sister. Then the call will be traced.'

Traced calls. Might that, instead of a tracked car, have been how the men chasing them found the hotel in Wavewell? She had called Emery from a phone box. Was it her fault?

'My officer also found us an old safe house that's empty,' Roy continued. 'That's where we're going now. He'll work out a way to get on Emery's protection unit, then he'll arrange for you and her to have a secret phone call. And after that he'll work on a way of exposing all of the officers on Voyzey's and Franz's payroll. With luck, we can get you home to Emery soon.'

This was great news, but she was worried about the time frame. 'Will this be today? Maybe tomorrow?'

'He's not certain. Tomorrow he thought, but maybe by the day after. I have to be honest and say I don't know how long this will take.'

Will we survive that long? she almost blurted out. Instead, she just nodded. Given that her husband had tried to kill her and other men were attempting to do likewise, Libby felt lucky to have survived so long. She would try to be patient, knowing that she might already be dead if luck hadn't held her hand.

'I want to keep you safe, Libby, and I think the only way is to stick together. But I won't force you to stay with me. I've kept you almost as a hostage so far and I hate myself for it.'

His sincerity hurt her. So much so, in fact, that she forgot about the people after them, and focused on him. He'd been through a lot. Clearly he was still upset about having uprooted her from her safe life. 'You were just trying to help. It's okay. You've kept me alive. I want to stay with you.'

'Good. And I promise to keep you safe forever. But I have to take charge, Libby. Perhaps even get bossy. We have to do this my way. And there's only one thing we can do, like I said earlier. There's still extreme danger out there.'

He was right. So far she had been an obstacle to her own safety. Calling Emery had been an almost lethal mistake, and one he had warned her against. Recently, distress and panic and sorrow seemed to define her personality, leaving no room for common sense. He knew what was best for her. She didn't. 'Okay. You're right. You take charge.'

'You have to be willing to do exactly as I ask. Nobody can know where we are until this thing is cleared up. We're going off the grid. A deep hide. You know what that means?'

'I think so. Away from everyone. We can't show our faces. Somewhere remote. It's the right thing to do.'

'We've been risking our lives by travelling the streets, by staying in that hotel. We have to stay indoors. Stay away from everyone. We have to act as if the whole outside world is radioactive. And everyone out there is a plague-riddled zombie. Can you do that?'

She would not die today or the next. Voyzey's goons were not going to take her. He was not going to satisfy his bloated desire for vengeance by spilling her blood. 'I can, and I will. I promise.'

'Are you ready to disappear right now? Give up everything,

for as long as it takes to expose the people after you? Even if it's a month?'

Ready to? It was all she wanted now, if it meant she could live. 'Yes.'

He touched her shoulder and gave a smile. 'Then let's go. Let's vanish off the face of the earth.'

FORTY-EIGHT

Once out of the woods, Alain and Hawk crossed a field and found a main road with a bus shelter. Here they paused. Hawk pulled out his phone to call Voyzey, while Alain got in contact with Franz's deputy. The man was officially the second-in-command and set to take control of the firm if the boss died or left, but he didn't relish the thought. He was a man quite happy to work the front line and get his hands dirty.

Although he had memorised the registration of the stolen Kia, Alain opted not to relay it to Franz's deputy. He'd have to explain how he got it, which would mean admitting another failure to capture the Mytton woman. And the car would likely be abandoned long before its location got traced.

Instead, Alain told a tale: got to the service station, saw no sign of the targets. It was a lie he and Hawk had agreed upon, to save face. 'Don't bother tracing the Focus again. Because that we did find. Abandoned.'

'Any worth in having people come down there to try to get a look at CCTV?'

'For their new vehicle? No. There's no cameras near where they abandoned the car and we don't know if they hitchhiked or took a walk. Did you send people to check out Floode's address in Sheffield?'

'Bogus,' the deputy said. 'Street is real, but there's no number 25.'

Curious. 'Our man is careful. I need a car at my location. How long?'

'Give me an hour. Any preference?'

'Anything but a Fiat Tipo. Nothing that looks similar, and nothing yellow. A saloon would be nice.'

Alain hung up. Hawk, having finished his own call to Voyzey to relay the same fib, said, 'Now what? We just wait? I heard you ask for a car.'

'We wait. Right here at this bus stop, so we don't stand out.'

Hawk sighed and sat on the bench. 'I think I hate the countryside.'

'I don't. It beats the megalopolis. I've had my fill. It's nice to be able to see more than a hundred metres without being in the sky.'

'You might get to die out here. I'm still working on that.'

'Looking forward to it,' Alain replied with a smile.

The two men said nothing for almost an hour. A blue Volkswagen 2019 plate Passat cruised down the road and stopped at the bus stop. Behind it was a motorbike. Hawk wanted the bike, but Alain said no. 'We might have to do a lot of sitting around. And I'm sure you don't want my arms around you.'

The bike and its two occupants vanished. Alain and Hawk went for the driver's door at the same time. Hawk got there first, but Alain held the door shut.

'You're not in charge, dickhead,' Hawk said. 'I'm driving. Move your hand or lose it.'

Alain smiled. 'I thought we'd established our roles here, Hawk? I'm the jet-setting playboy. You live in the dirt. Your world is a small collection of trash-littered streets, your social circle entirely composed of offscourings, all of it wrapped in a miasma of debauchery. Did you forget?'

'Silly me, you cheeky cunt. Haven't forked out any of your riches on a bloody hair transplant yet, have you?'

'It's on the list right behind a Patek Phillipe Grandmaster Chime. My point is that you're a stranger in a strange land out here. It's not wise for you to try to make decisions or work the controls.'

Hawk laughed and threw his hands up, frustrated. 'You talk some baloney, pal. I'll enjoy shoving my shit-stained undercrackers down your throat.'

'One more for the list, it would seem.'

He stomped around the car and got in the passenger seat. Once Alain was behind the wheel, Hawk asked what their 'next move is, O grandmaster?'

'We can do nothing but wait on standby until we get word from Franz.'

Hawk didn't like what he'd just heard. 'This is horse shit. I don't do dawdling well.'

'Neither do I, but what choice do we have? Libby Mytton is gone as of right now. But she'll make a mistake just like before. And then we'll have her.'

PART 4

FORTY-NINE

'We're close.'

She looked up from her lap. It was the first time either of them had spoken in a while. And the first time she'd glanced out the windows in ages.

They were on a winding country road, heading to a village that a sign they passed called Cullerton. That meaningless word aside, she had no idea where they were, and didn't ask. The time was just after ten in the morning.

Before they reached the village, Roy pulled into a lay-by. Libby asked if everything was okay.

'Yes,' he said. 'This safe house is, well, safe. But getting you there is a problem. We can't risk someone seeing you in the car.'

'Shall I lay down in the back?'

'No. I hate to do this... but can you go in the boot?'

She just stared at him, looking for something in his face that indicated a joke. It wasn't there. 'Are you serious?'

'We have to drive through the village, along the main road. A lot of houses and stores with flats above. If you're seen–'

'I've got my mask. Nobody will know it's me.'

'No, but if the locals see two people in this car, then they'll expect to see you out and about round the village. We can't have that.'

'Then I'll stay in the house for a few days.'

He shook his head. 'In a place like this, tongues wag. New arrivals pique interest. People will want to meet us. But all they'll see is me out when I'm buying supplies. They'll wonder where you are. They might want to pop round to see us.'

'So you just say I'm ill or busy.'

Another headshake. 'That wouldn't work. People would get suspicious and–'

'You mean they might think you killed your wife if I was never seen again?' It was part joke and part frustration.

But Roy gave a sincere nod, proving that the dead spouse theory was exactly his worry. 'If they don't know about you, they can't miss you,' he said.

He had an answer for everything, even if she didn't like it. He wouldn't be swayed. And maybe he was right. She had to remind herself that he was the smart one, the one who knew best, and the one in charge.

Reluctantly, she climbed into the boot and he shut the lid, entombing her in darkness. But it was the safest option.

Roy started driving. After just a minute or two, he took a left and she heard the crunch of gravel. There was a bump, then it felt as if they were travelling down a shallow, winding slope. Soon the car stopped and she heard him exit. The boot opened.

'I am so sorry,' he said.

She clambered out with the gusto of someone who'd spent days locked up. 'Let's hope nobody saw me climb in there.'

They were in a large clearing that straddled a brook. The back end of the open area was a sheer cliff face five metres high, over which water loudly tumbled into the brook. On this side of the water was a two-storey cottage with its flank facing the brook and its rear yard running up to the cliff. The scene was picturesque enough to feature in a snow globe, but it was lost on someone banished here. She felt nothing.

Roy took her hand. 'Let's go see inside.'

She pulled her hand free. Just before the waterfall was a wooden bridge, which she walked onto. She stared at the cascading water, which rained a fine mist of wetness onto the wood and over her. Roy stood at the end of the bridge and asked if she was okay.

'I am. This is just a bit overwhelming still. You go in. I'll be there in a second.'

'You can't be seen out here. There's a walking trail nearby.'

'There's no one around. Anyway, they might think I'm a hiker, too. I just need some solitude, please.'

'Things have escalated, Libby. Come on in. This is too dangerous.'

There was an urgency in his tone that she didn't like, so she followed him to the front door of the cottage. The step was fashioned from house bricks and one was a little loose. He lifted it out.

'Damn. There should be a key here.'

'Where did you find this place?'

'I told you. My police officer friend. It belongs to his parents. There should have been a key here. Let's go round back and check.'

She followed him into the rear yard, which had fake potted plants and outdoor furniture and a fire pit. The back door was the stable kind, with a split to allow the top half to open. The upper section had two long glass windows. The door was locked.

'I'm going to have to bust it open,' Roy said.

She watched him do it. He wrapped his fist in his jacket and punched through one of the glass windows. He stuck an arm through. The upper half was secured to its partner by a bolt. In seconds he had the top half open.

The bottom half had a mortise lock and there was no key. Roy climbed over the half-door and helped her do the same.

Once her feet were on the floor, she pulled Roy close and hugged him. It was not for comfort, though. She felt so many overwhelming emotions that she just wanted to vent, and she did it by squeezing him as hard as she could.

'Oh, I'm jealous of your husband,' he said, laughing.

So was she, but for a different reason. Now he was in agony no longer. He was free of suffering, while she was left to pay for his actions. She envied his death. In that moment she, too, wanted to die.

FIFTY

After they looked around the place, which was fully furnished and even had tinned foods in the cupboards – no phone, though. A shelf in the kitchen was loaded with bottles of alcohol that looked rare and expensive. Libby headed to the back door, meaning to go sit in the yard to think. This was all too much, too surreal and unreal. If she read about all this happening to someone else, she'd dismiss it as over-the-top.

Roy blocked her path. 'No, we can't go out. Walkers might see us. Please.'

It seemed like overkill, but she had no will to argue. She had to acknowledge that her mind was fuzzy and she couldn't think properly. Roy was looking out for her and she had to trust him to do what was right.

She headed into the living room and absent-mindedly looked through novels on a bookcase. Roy followed her. He said, 'I'm going to go hide the car now. I need you to stay here.'

'Okay.'

'Here's the thing, though. I can't trust you at the moment, Libby.'

She turned to him. 'What do you mean?'

'You're confused and desperate. You might do something silly. Or you might get seen at one of the windows.'

Confused was correct. She had no idea where this conversation was headed. 'I'm lost.'

'I need to hide you, Libby. Follow me.'

In the hallway he whipped away a rug to expose a trapdoor. She hoped she was dreaming. 'You want me to hide in the cellar?'

'It's just for an hour or so.'

She reminded herself that she was just a passenger on this terror rollercoaster. Roy was the pilot and he knew what he was doing. She told him to wait a second and walked to the kitchen, where she grabbed a bottle of alcohol off the shelf. It was a black product called Justino's Madeira Boal and said 10 YEARS OLD on the label. The dustiness of the bottle said it might be twice that age by now. She only cared that the alcohol volume was 19 per cent. She hadn't had a drink for a few weeks, but desired one more than anything right now.

When she returned to Roy, he opened the trapdoor. He apologised for this 'necessary' turn of events. She gave no reply and walked down old wooden steps, into a dingy room. Roy pulled a tatty cord to kickstart a weak yellow bulb.

The cellar was like her mind: damp, stinking, cold. It seemed to be exactly what she deserved. By one wall was a mound of boxes whose tops were covered by a tarpaulin. Against another there was an old washing machine and tall fridge with a heavy duty wooden workbench between them. Three rolled rugs stood in a corner, next to what looked like a couple of seats from a vehicle. Roy dragged over a kitchen chair from a set stacked in an alcove. She didn't sit.

'I'm sorry about this,' he said.

'Maybe you're right. I can't be trusted not to run screaming down the road.'

Was she being truthful or sarcastic? She wasn't sure, but Roy opted for the latter – or maybe that was her flummoxed head misreading everything. 'Later, if you prove you won't do something silly, we won't have to take such drastic measures.'

She opened the bottle of Boal. 'Just go. And be quick, please.'

Without another word, Roy left. He shut the trapdoor behind him and she heard his footsteps crossing the kitchen floor.

FIFTY-ONE

When Roy returned, he told her there was news. But it was not good. On his phone, he showed her a video on a YouTube channel called *Crime Time News*. The production value wasn't great. The research was better. The creators had been very busy in such a short amount of time.

The documentary featured interviews, re-enactments, and archival footage, all to voiceover narration. It started with Joel's arrest, using mobile phone video taken from the back bedroom of a house on their street.

Libby was stunned to see footage of herself, sitting against the garage door, feet scrabbling in the gravel to keep her weight against the metal and prevent Joel's escape. Along came the man walking his dog, to add his weight. The meaty clangs of Joel trying to bash his way out were clearly audible. So was the voice of the woman filming it all as she gave a running commentary. She seemed to find it all amusing.

Then the police came. Three cars, six officers. Dog Walker fled the scene. One officer escorted Libby away, watched by the camera, as others barred the door. She was surprised to see how wobbly she was on her feet.

When the officers were ready, they opened the garage door and pounced on Joel. Libby was spellbound, having never seen footage of his arrest. She expected him to fight like a trapped animal, expressing the rage she'd encountered that night. But he went quietly.

Here the narrator said, 'The woman who took this video could not have realised she had just witnessed the arrest of a man wanted for the most high-profile murder in recent years. No one could have expected their neighbour to be guilty of such a crime. Joel Mytton was, apparently, a normal man...'

The programme cut to footage taken on her street, with neighbours and in some cases friends being interviewed. 'He seemed so normal,' said Mr Jones, a man Libby knew. He lived about ten doors down and had once borrowed their lawnmower. 'Last man on earth I would have thought could do such a thing. Still traumatic. Still hard to believe. Dead now, but he never got a trial. So we don't know for sure, do we?'

'I never saw Mr Mytton angry,' said an old lady who lived across the road. Libby used to wave at her if she was gardening out front. 'He was always polite, always willing to help with odd jobs. We all liked him and his wife. I find this truly shocking. I guess it just shows you never know people inside.'

'Decent dude and all,' was the diagnosis from their next-door neighbour, Darren. 'Apart from what he did, I mean. Was into the tennis and snooker and all. We had some laughs. Did he hide the bad side? Or turn it on like a switch? Gonna put me a wary eye on everyone from now on.'

Also interviewed were some of Joel's workmates, and the man who ran the corner shop, and the landlord of Bowlers, which was the pub that Joel's building firm had been renovating when Joanne Yeowell died. Each person had something nice to say about her husband. Each professed astonishment at discovering he was a killer.

But how did the world learn that Joel Mytton was a murderer? Not by the traditional methods of hard police work. He was exposed by his own wife, Libby...

The narrator gave a brief biography of her to a slideshow of photographs, which the creators had obviously gotten from her friends. It included soundbites from some of those so-called friends, and even a video of Joel and her at a birthday party. The backstabbers.

The programme then returned to the garages. It was clearly sometime later because the police had cordoned off the area and turned it into a major crime scene. Investigators in white coveralls were all over her garage like flies.

Night one, just an hour or so after the shit hit the fan, yet word had clearly spread. Now myriad people were at the scene and recording it on their phones. She saw shots from the end of the alleyway, over garden fences, and more from bedroom windows. Each videographer liked to talk, sometimes to the camera and sometimes to other people.

'That was Joel Mytton from down the road. He's been a naughty boy.'

'This has got to be something big. Look at all those cops. They don't close off an area this big unless it's murder. I bet there's a body in there.'

'This was to do with that missing woman. Gotta be. Crime-scene vans, twenty CSI and cops. Has to be. He killed her. Had to have.'

A narrator spoke. 'Mrs Mytton told police she had no clue her husband had a dark heart, until the day when she trapped him. But others weren't so fooled...'

The video cut to more vox pops from neighbours. The woman living right next door to Libby said, 'There was always something about him. Something chilling. I couldn't put my finger on it. But I never liked bumping into him at night. He felt cold to be near.'

One of Joel's former employees, fired for bogus sick days, chimed in with, 'He was always a perverted bastard. I'd see him staring at women, licking his lips. And the way he used to hold a Stanley knife. Trance-like, like he was imagining slicing someone up. Don't know what took the cops so long to realise.'

While the owner of the local corner shop always felt Joel was a nice customer, his teenaged daughter was another story. 'I hated serving him,' she said as she stacked a shelf in the shop. 'He was so creepy. He had dark eyes, almost black. You could see the evil in them. I sensed he had no soul. Even the dog hated him. Uuugh, he makes me shiver.'

So who was Joel Mytton and what drove him to murder?

Up next was a segment that truly transfixed Libby. The show's creators had travelled to Birmingham, where Joel was born. They visited the house where he grew up, his old school, and a youth centre where he hung out with pals. They spoke to childhood friends, teachers, and former dirt-biking colleagues – this was a pastime Joel had long given up by the time Libby met him. She was angry but also impressed by how much the creators had managed to achieve in such a short time.

The segment was very matter-of-fact, without prejudice, and no different to how they might have biographed a movie star. Those interviewed kept the tone, with not a single one of the people from his past claiming to have spied the monster of the future. It seemed that everybody, bar two, was willing to talk. Those two, of course, were Joel's mum and dad. Given that parents are instrumental in shaping a child's personality, Libby wasn't surprised they refused.

When the documentary turned to the subject of Joel's connections to organised crime, Libby grabbed Roy's phone and shut off the video. She couldn't face more terrible revelations about the man she'd married.

In the last few minutes, she had learned new things about her husband. She realised they had never really spoken about his childhood in all their years together. She had never seen a picture of his school, or his parents when they were young. She hadn't known much about the crew he rode dirt bikes with. Didn't know he'd got a head injury when he jumped off a garden shed at the age of eight. Didn't know what pets he'd had, what childhood dreams, or who gave him his first kiss.

She didn't really know her husband at all, did she? Had he tricked her? Was she naïve? Or was he simply a man who didn't like to look backwards?

While upsetting, she did find a little solace in this. It meant she could convince herself that she had done nothing wrong by not fathoming the character deep inside him. Earlier she had beat herself up for being ignorant to his lethal personality. Now she saw things differently. The beast that was Joel had been veiled before all and sundry.

She was on her knees on the floor, with no memory of having sunk to them. Roy stood tall over her, staring down. She said, 'Did you ever see something in Joel? Something that said he was a monster?'

'Yes,' was his immediate reply. 'Everybody in the firm did. I'm surprised you didn't.'

A memory surfaced. Emery, making the same claim. Did everybody think the same way? Did the world suspect she'd known about her husband's murderous mind? 'I didn't. I...'

'The world doesn't believe you, Libby. More importantly, neither does the Crown Prosecution Service. I just heard that they have authorised South Yorkshire Police to charge you with assisting an offender.'

She started to shake uncontrollably. 'What? So the police are after me?'

Roy's iron-solid front seemed to buckle and he knelt before her, his voice now soothing. 'Calm down, Libby. Yes, there's an arrest warrant out. You're on their wanted website right now. Assisting an offender for murder has a maximum sentence of ten years. The public is crying out for that. But I don't know if you'll get such a lengthy sentence. Possible, I have to admit.'

She grabbed his hand and squeezed hard. 'But I told the police about Joel. I got him arrested. I didn't help him.'

'I know. I believe you. But I'm the only one. The only one who believes you, Libby. The public is baying for your arrest. They know you're missing now and they think you ran to avoid the police. They think you're guilty. The police must know something I don't.'

'What? So you *do* think I'm guilty in some way?'

'I don't know anything for sure. But it doesn't matter. I'm here to help you, and I'm the only one who can.'

She was reminded of the man who broke into her house and confronted her in her own bedroom. His accusations. *Yep, she'll do. That lovely brunette there. And you sicced him on her. Fetch, boy!* Did everybody, friends and neighbours included, believe this? Was no human being amongst the billions on the planet on her side.

'Do you want my help?' Roy said, his timing perfect. He, and he alone, was on her side.

'Yes,' she said, almost breathless. 'I want your help, Please.'

'Then I want something from you. We're all alone here, and we have to be for quite some time. You understand that, don't you?'

She nodded.

He said, 'Remember back in the hotel, when we played cards?' She didn't, but she nodded. 'We played cards together because we had no one else to play with. It was just us. If I *need* to play cards, and the only other person with me knows how to play, then we should play, shouldn't we?'

She didn't know what he meant, but she nodded again.

He leaned close. She thought he was going to whisper in her ear, but his lips touched hers. The kiss lasted half a second before she turned her head away.

Now he sounded upset. 'I need the touch of a woman, Libby. But how can I find one? I'm here with you and we can't leave this house.'

At first she misread what he said. She was dulled, hazy, delirious, and she thought he wanted her to help him find a partner despite the Sword of Damocles hanging over them. But his next words erased all confusion.

'It's just you and me here, alone. I want you. I find you so attractive. This has been so hard for me. Doing this. Running with you. Leaving my life behind. Abandoning everything so I could save you. Abandoning women and sex.'

He turned her head and leaned in to kiss her again. This time she didn't veer away, but she closed her mouth to prevent it. 'It's so hard being near you and unable to touch you, Libby. This hurts me. Hurts me badly.'

'What do you want?' she asked. She had a gut feeling, but she couldn't trust her own brain's logic right now.

'Sex, Libby. I need it. We're locked up here alone, so you're the only woman I could possibly have it with.'

That was her gut feeling, but hearing his words confirm it was still a whack to the psyche. 'I can't. I–'

'Then I'm gone, Libby. I've sacrificed a lot for you, with nothing in return. My own life is in danger because I saved you. I also aided a criminal. I gave you everything, and you won't give anything in return. It's the least you can do to repay me for saving your life. If you can't do this one little thing, I'm going to have to leave you. And try to get my own life back.'

Aided a criminal? Was she a criminal? 'Please don't leave.'

The third time he kissed her, she let him. Perhaps she should give him sex just to ease his suffering? After all, it was only bodily contact. A little bit of her energy could give him the happiness he was entitled to. And she couldn't let him leave her here all alone.

She returned his kiss, and he took this as her willingness to do whatever he wanted. He was right, she felt. He took her hand, and she knew it was so he could lead her upstairs. To the bedroom, where happiness was made. He deserved this little thing for saving her life. It was the right thing to do, even if she was too muddled to fully understand that.

FIFTY-TWO

During their phone call, Voyzey had accused Franz of having to operate from the shadows in order to keep his respectable image clean. The man wasn't wrong. Franz had kids now and they needed a dad who wasn't a jailbird – or dead. And they needed to be proud of him. The role of a decent, hardworking businessman provided a measure of fortification against getting arrested or whacked.

But sometimes it was tough. He often thought about the old days, when he'd been a free man and able to let himself go wild. And it was common for him to miss those good times. How often had he wanted to join his Go Squad on a mission? Or had wanted to bury an annoying Go Go Karts customer instead of just barring them? Just last week he'd had to write to the council about teenagers riding motorbikes in the field behind his house, when all he'd wanted to do was round them up and pull some fingernails.

And hadn't he felt a little jealous of Joel, who had managed to live a life at both ends of the scale and keep them separate?

So, he decided to take the plunge and get in on the action. It was only a meeting to give department heads some orders and should have been done by conference call, but he decided to arrange a get-together. He chose to have it in a room above a gym, where his people often held card games.

It was a risk to present himself at this location. The police would think it was Christmas if they had the place under surveillance and saw ten serious criminals arrive, along with the boss. But today he liked the idea of risky shenanigans.

'Anyone know why I brought you here?' he began after quieting his men down. Half had chairs and the others stood or sat on the floor or against walls.

'To hand out bonuses?' one said.

'Maybe, to the first man to find what I want.'

And what he wanted? Libby Mytton found and brought to him. Alain was on the case, but he was out in the field and had a babysitter and so far was proving to be...

'Well, a failure. Him and the man he's with are twiddling their thumbs, waiting for a green light and a location. My Go Squad is doing nothing, too, just following Voyzey's van full of men around while those guys also do the thumb-twiddling.'

'Don't let Alain hear you say that.'

'But that's the case. Everybody is waiting for a eureka moment and nobody is making headway, which means *I'm* going to have to throw more manpower into finding Libby Mytton. So I want you lot out there, ears to the ground, that sort of thing. Find information. Find Libby and this man called Roy Floode.'

He told them how he'd come by that name: the man's driving licence. He also gave his men the location of where Floode's bank card was last used. He wanted his department heads to send bodies out there to quietly ask questions.

Someone said: 'Hey, do we believe that stuff about Joel and

that woman he killed? That there was rape and torture and that he kept her head?'

Only a handful of people knew that Franz had tasked Joel with kidnapping the woman, not a single one of them was present at this meeting. Franz would play naïve. 'Joel went rogue. I don't know why he killed some woman. I don't have a clue what you people do when off the clock. But you're not exactly saints. And don't believe what you read in the damn press. He didn't keep her head or even cut it off. Where the hell did you read that?'

There were more questions but Franz shut them down. 'Back on topic,' he ordered. 'Libby Mytton and Roy Floode: find them.'

'What's this Roy Floode guy look like?'

Good point. Franz remembered that he'd asked Alain to send him a picture of the man's driving licence. He got out his phone and checked his emails. There it was. He opened the image and handed his phone to the nearest man. It was passed round the room while Franz listed some rules. Send only your most loyal men into the search. Collect Floode right alongside Libby, in case he also knew about Franz's inner workings. Harm neither if possible. Don't use guns in public. And don't–

'Hey, this looks like whatshisface,' someone cut in. He was staring at Franz's phone. 'Him who was on the team couple of years back. Remember that fucker? Tried that side wheelie and crashed his car.'

The guy who'd just passed him the device snatched it back. 'Piss off. He had a beard, didn't he?'

'You can shave a bloody beard off. That's him. Used to be one of us.'

Franz stormed over to the two men and grabbed his phone. He tuned out his men, who were now very intrigued that a former employee might have run away with another employee's wife. He had a real close look at Floode's photograph, and he mentally painted a beard on the clean-shaven face.

Holy shit. It was that guy all right. Libby was shacked up with someone who used to be part of the OCG. Joel's old friend.

But how could that be possible when...

FIFTY-THREE

When Libby was seventeen and first had sex with a boy introduced to her by a friend, it was a magical experience. Although not for him, apparently, because he told his friends that she lay beneath him like a sack of potatoes. She hated that analogy, but it returned to her mind now.

She lay on the bed and Roy climbed on top of her. He did all the work. She couldn't help but think of herself as a sack of potatoes, and she knew she should do something to please him. But she couldn't. How could she when sex was the furthest thing from her mind?

Roy said things he believed were sweet and made noises relevant to the sex act, but she knew he wasn't happy. Not afterwards, at least. When he was done, he leapt off her as if she had just turned white hot.

'Are you okay?' she asked. She pulled the quilt over her.

He fully dressed before replying. 'I thought I meant more to you.'

She should console him, but she had a sudden urge to say something sarcastic. She bit it down. Sex at such a time seemed illogical and outlandish to her, but maybe it was different for men – or this man, at least. He might use sex to combat grief the way she would often use comedy programmes. She should say something nice. She couldn't think of anything.

He took his phone and left the room, which gave her time to dress alone. She was at the window when he returned. She said, 'Do you think they have problems in their life?'

Roy saw her pointing finger and rushed over. Outside, walking across the bridge, was an old couple with a dog. Roy grabbed her arm and pulled her aside. He shut the curtains.

'Don't let anyone see,' he hissed. 'This is a guest house. If there's guests, the locals will gossip. I told you that.'

'I'm sorry. I didn't think.'

He sighed, but it was not from disappointment. Something else. He took something from his pocket and moved to the thick radiator. She heard clicking but his body blocked her view. However, when he moved aside, she saw what he'd attached to the radiator.

A pair of handcuffs.

He grabbed her arm. 'Sit down by the radiator.'

'No,' she said. She knew he meant to chain her up. 'What's wrong?'

'I'm sorry, but it has to be this way. You can't run.'

'But why? What's happened? What have I done?'

He didn't answer and forced her onto her knees. She fought back, but he was stronger, and inevitably the opened cuff was snapped onto her wrist. Roy backed away and sat on the bed. She got some resolve back now the fight was lost. 'Okay. So now I'm chained. So tell me what the hell is going on.'

'It's bad news, Libby. It–'

'Is it Emery? Has something happened to her?'

'It will upset you and I can't have you suddenly trying to run back to Sheffield. I don't know if I can stop it. Our only chance of survival is to stay hidden. This is now our home. It might be for a long time.'

She didn't miss that he'd ignored the question about her sister. She asked again and demanded to talk to her.

'You can't. You just can't.'

She tugged hard at the chain binding her to the radiator. In a cartoon, it would grow a mouth and guffaw at her attempt. No hysterical strength for her. 'Tell me,' she yelled. 'You have to let me talk to my sister. Now.'

'You can't,' Roy repeated, but this time he hung his head. 'Ever again.'

What are you saying? The words formed in her head, but they were trapped there. Her voice was silent. A chasm opened in that ocean floor, and she was tumbling deeper after all.

'I'm sorry, Libby. But Emery is already dead.'

FIFTY-FOUR

'You look angry,' Roy said.

She shook her hand to rattle the cuffs holding her to the radiator in the bedroom. 'Let me out.'

'I can't just yet. You'll run. That's too dangerous. You need some time to get used to this.'

'To my sister's death? How much time do you think? Two hours? Four?'

She saw him getting worked up. 'Use your brain. Too dangerous.'

It had been just one hour since he'd delivered the news, which was that Emery had been dead all along, ever since the night Libby had escaped. All of his tales about an escape from a burning house and protective custody – lies designed to Libby from mentally disintegrating.

Libby had said he must be wrong: *I spoke to her. I called her that night. She was fine!*

Then they were already there, Roy had said. That's how they found us in Wavewell. And they killed her. They killed her because of your phone call. They didn't need her anymore.

That had upset her most of all, knowing it might be her fault her sister was gone.

Roy had left her alone to 'grieve'. Now he was back, and she was calmer. Not by much, but enough to find some logic.

'Two people are dead, Roy. My sister. My husband. We have to do something. We can't just hide away and pretend it's not happening.'

'Shall I tell you what's happening?' he yelled. 'Killers are after you. They want you dead. The moment you show that pretty face, it'll be cut off. I can't allow that.'

She wanted to rage, to smash, but she kept that animal chained like her. 'More people will die if we hide here, Roy. Don't you care?'

'I care about you, Libby. I can save you, but you have to help me. Otherwise you're dead meat. We both are.'

Roy left her alone for another hour or so. He returned with food and alcohol. Also black, also a madeira, this bottle boasted that the drink was fifteen years old. He placed both items before her. All her rage was gone now, sluiced away by despair. Once more she had all the resolve of a beaten puppy.

'Am I a prisoner?' she asked.

'No, Libby. We're both prisoners if you want to put it like that. I told you why I've left the handcuffs on. When I can trust you not to do something stupid, I'll take them off.'

'I'm okay now. I've settled.'

'I won't bring you back home until we've found the traitors in the police. Hopefully just a few more days. Can you cope with that?'

She doubted it, but she nodded. It was the answer he wanted. She told him she needed the toilet. He unlocked her and escorted her to the bathroom. He checked the window was locked and waited outside the door.

He really didn't trust her, she understood. He thought she

was like a toddler who needed a leash so she didn't stumble into traffic. She had had time to think, though. She knew running was a bad idea. If someone in the village saw and recognised her, they'd call the police. The wrong officer could learn of this location. Too risky. Roy was right.

He left the cuffs off when they returned to the bedroom, but he sat on the side of the bed nearest the door, so she couldn't make a beeline for the outside world. But she could drink. He wanted to talk and asked her questions about her life.

She gave short answers because she didn't want small talk. She just wanted to sleep and see what the new day brought. Even though the curtains were shut, she sensed the open, dark world outside the house, and it worried her.

Later, he left the room to go have a bath. She was allowed one of her own afterwards. Then it was back to the bedroom, for more small talk. Roy was coping with all of this better than she. The clock on the wall said it was close to midnight when Roy kicked off his shoes. 'Time to sleep. I'm sorry, but I can't leave you free. Lie on the bed.'

He held up the handcuffs. She glared at them. 'I have to sleep cuffed?'

'You might have a nightmare, or a silly idea. Or sleepwalk. If I'm asleep, I can't stop you doing something bad.'

'What if I need the toilet?'

He left the room and returned with a washing-up bowl from the kitchen. She shook her head. 'Are you serious? You can't do this. I'm not an animal.'

'There's no other way. You're upset, not thinking straight. You might go halfway through the woods before you even realise it. There's the cellar if you don't want a cuff.'

'No. No cellar. You can use the cuff.'

He started to undress her, until she was fully naked. She let him. She seemed to have no control over anything now, but part

259

of her didn't care. It was safer this way, like he said. She got under the quilt.

Roy cuffed her left arm around a horizontal top bar running between the headboard posts. She would have to sleep with her hand raised, and she wouldn't be able to turn over properly, and her hand might be numb from poor circulation in the morning. She was reminded of Joel in the police station exercise yard. God, what a turn of events. Still she didn't object. Why would she when her bottle of strong wine was within reach on the bedside table?

Roy undressed and turned off the light. There was enough moonlight filtering through the curtains to show his outline as he climbed into bed. Her raised left arm was between them. 'Goodnight, babe,' he said, and leaned across to kiss her cheek.

She said nothing. She lay on her back – the only comfortable position – and stared at the dim ceiling. Roy's face was spotlighted by the bright screen of his phone as he played with it. A few moments later, the light went off as he put his phone on the bedside table. Just seconds later, he quickly rolled on top of her out of the blue.

'I'm sorry for all the bossiness,' he said.

She felt his lips touch hers.

'It was for your own good. You mean a lot to me. Everything.'

She felt his hard penis enter her.

'I love you.'

She said nothing and didn't move a muscle – except by his hand – while he had his way. Her eyes never left the ceiling.

FIFTY-FIVE

Two years ago, Franz was at the half-built building that would become Go Go Karts, watching the builders create his dream, when he was visited by a woman in tears.

She was one of his prostitutes, operating out a brothel in the centre of Sheffield, and she had run away almost two weeks earlier. Nobody walked out on Franz, so he'd put men on finding her. Ten guys, scouring the streets, knocking heads to get answers. Just the kind of job Joel Mytton had been expert at. But his team hadn't found a single clue as to the prostitute's whereabouts. Until she arrived at his workplace, no doubt to beg for forgiveness.

But that wasn't what happened. Distraught, she told a wild tale. She had been convinced to visit Quinn's house for sex, but afterwards he hadn't let her leave. In fact, he'd kept her hostage in his attic. For eleven days. She had escaped just an hour ago while Quinn was on a job.

Quinn had always struck him as 'off' when it came to women, but this story stretched belief. Franz decided he needed proof and sent his deputy to find Quinn. News came back that he was in Rotherham, collecting money from drug dealers. Rather than question Quinn, Franz sent his man to the employee's home to see if there was any evidence that someone had been imprisoned in the attic. Whatever the outcome, someone was in trouble.

The deputy had a key because everybody in Franz's employ was required to supply one for emergencies. He went upstairs to check the attic. Immediately he saw the trapdoor was busted. Up he went. Then he called Franz.

'It's bloody real,' he said. 'The attic is all boarded up like a prison. There's a grimy mattress and women's toiletries. And sex toys. And a chain with ankle irons on the walls.'

Franz liked to have the odd lunatic in his stable, for the darker jobs, but this was a step too far. 'Get some answers off Quinn. In the truck.'

The deputy dispatched a trio of meaty brutes to a safe house in Rotherham, then sent Quinn to the same address to collect money that didn't exist. As soon as Quinn got in the door, he was bundled up and hauled out to a car.

The 'truck' Franz referred to was actually just a shipping container at a container yard in Sheffield. It was owned and managed by a quartet of siblings called the Vogwills, who each had a container that had been turned into a home. The box nicknamed the 'truck' was kept kitted out as an interrogation room. Guerrilla-style, of course. No cameras or microphones, but soundproofed walls and a lot of bloodstained tools. Franz's people had been trained to no-comment when questioned by police, but here those words had never been uttered.

Quinn knew the score because he wasn't dumb. He could tell his story with or without all his fingers. He chose to remain able to double high-five people. He admitted everything to the Vogwills before even the first tool came out.

Tricking the whore into coming to his house. Keeping her locked up in an attic he'd spent four months preparing as a cell.

Numerous rapes and other forms of violence. And threats to kill her family if she refused, or wasn't wholeheartedly committed to, any sexual acts he described. The deputy was impressed by his willingness to come clean.

Franz wasn't. 'I've had it with this guy. A step too far. Take good care of him, won't you.'

The 'truck' wasn't a truck, and 'good care' didn't mean anything of the sort. The Vogwills were ordered to kill Quinn, chop him up, and dispose of the parts in a fire pit on their land. A few hours later, the deputy was visited by one of the Vogwills and given a lock of Quinn's hair tied together with an elastic band. The deputy delivered it to Franz, who put it in a jar with eleven similar items.

Even today, Franz still didn't know what drove him to want to keep such items, but would always deny that they were 'trophies'.

Today the Vogwills still ran the container yard, but they'd branched out into selling modified boxes as site cabins. Last year the youngest brother had died three seconds after realising his Porsche couldn't corner at high speed quite as well as he'd hoped. The other two brothers and one sister were scattered about the yard, tending to this or that.

Driving a van with no cabin windows, Franz's deputy visited the yard and told the first Vogwill he came across to shut the gates and call his kin together. 'Got another guy for the truck. You might have to remove some fingers because this one's stubborn.'

'Good,' said the sister. The three Vogwills walked to the 'truck' and the van followed. The trio went into the container first, and that was when five men leaped out of the van and followed them inside.

Just minutes later minutes later, the Vogwills were hanging upside down with their feet in brackets bolted to the ceiling. The container was eight and a half feet high, so their heads hung between thirty and forty inches from the metal floor. When the deputy walked in, they demanded to know what was going on.

'Time for Hangburn,' he said.

It was a game the Vogwills had invented, and they probably regretted it right now. A powerful, portable hot plate was placed underneath an inverted victim and they were asked a general knowledge question. A correct answer would see the hot plate shifted away, below the next poor soul. But a wrong answer would result in prolonged barbequing.

The first guy to get the hob was asked, 'What's the world's largest animal?'

'Elephant,' the victim said, trying to bend his body and get his head out of the rising heat.

'Nope. Blue whale.' The quizmaster consulted Google for another question. 'Who invented the telephone?'

Victim 1 got this one right and a foot kicked the hob to one side. Under his sister's head. Her long hair dangled onto the red hot plate so one of the interrogators had to hack it away. She got her question correct and the hob moved on. Victim 3 knew the capital city of Egypt and the hob returned to the first guy, who moaned about his kin having easy questions.

'Blue whale was piss easy,' the quizmaster said. 'Who was the richest man who ever lived?'

'Augustus Caesar!'

'Nope. Mansa Musa. Which country has the most–'

'It was Caesar,' Victim 1 moaned. 'Musa only had gold and people base it on what it would be worth today. There was barely a global economy and gold wasn't expensive because people couldn't use it. Nobody knew how much Musa had. Augustus Caesar was the richest.'

The quizmaster didn't buy it, but he did some more googling. A comrade complained that he didn't know his shit. Everybody started arguing. Meanwhile, Victim 1 cooked. Franz's deputy soon got frustrated and cancelled the game. Down to business. Quinn, the guy they had been tasked with dismembering and burying – remember him? Supposed to be dead and dust, but he wasn't, was he?

'No,' the deputy said. 'Instead, he's got all his limbs nicely connected and he's running around out there with a woman that Franz dearly wants to get hold of.'

The deputy called Franz with an update, and it wasn't good news. 'They let Quinn go. He promised money, and they cut him loose. He begged for his life and said he'd pay ten grand and then go vanish off the face of the earth, and that you'd never know the difference. So he paid. They let him walk. He skipped and hid under a rock somewhere. And now he's back.'

Franz paused to fully digest this news. The deputy knew not to say a word. 'All four were in on it?'

The deputy laughed, but it was lost in a scream of pain from somewhere close to him. 'Apparently Robert set it up. Just Robert. Him alone. He was supposed to kill Quinn, but Robert let him go. The others, they had no clue.'

Franz paused again. Robert. The one dead in his Porsche. The one beyond reproach. How very convenient. 'How's their acting?'

'Hard to tell because the stupid bastards are scared shitless. But they lied before.'

True. Franz felt it was similar to the Libby situation: he didn't know if he could give his trust, and assumption was too risky. 'Get rid of them.'

The deputy returned to the shipping container and gave his goons the order. They played another round of Hangburn. And then another. And more.

The winner got the heat until he expired, which didn't really seem like a first prize. But then again his kin had to hang there and watch it happen and know their turn was a-coming. So considering him to be a victor was probably a matter of opinion.

FIFTY-SIX

The bedroom was pitch black when Libby woke. Her cuffed arm felt a little numb from being held raised for so long, and her hand was cold. Beside her, Roy lay on his front with his right arm hanging over the edge of the bed. He was snoring. She had no idea of the time, but it was not morning. The alcohol had made her need the toilet badly.

She could wake him so she could be released, but he might want sex again. The washing-up bowl would have to do, then. She slipped out from under the quilt and squatted over the makeshift toilet. She could just about do this comfortably with her left arm outstretched and the cuff at the far end of the horizontal headboard bar. She peed softly so Roy wouldn't hear.

That was when she noticed a faint luminescence under the bed. She moved away from the bowl so she could get to her knees and peek under. On the far side of the bed she saw Roy's hanging arm, his hand resting on the carpet.

In that hand was his phone.

The active screen was the cause of the light. The phone displayed a MISSION FAILED, which she figured meant he'd fallen asleep while playing a game. She continued to stare at that phone. The room and all beyond faded to nothing, until that device existed alone in the universe. It was everything. She wanted it, she needed it. It felt like a lifeline after being shut away here for so long.

Her cuffed left arm locked tight before she got more than her head and shoulders under the bed. She reached out her right hand, but it fell three feet short of the phone. She backed out. Focusing on the bright screen had killed her night vision, so she blindly felt around for something to use. Her fingers touched her jeans, dumped on the floor by Roy.

She stood up next to the headboard so that her hands could work together. She tied the ends of the jeans legs into a big knot. Lying once more under the bed, she held the jeans at the waistband and tried whipping the knotted ends at Roy's phone. The shallow space made this awkward, but eventually the weighted knot hit Roy's hand. The phone slipped a little from his grasp, but the thumb and forefinger still had a connection.

She tried again, and again, and again. It seemed like she was at it for hours. Eventually, she hit the jackpot. A final strike nudged the phone free of his hand. It fell face-down, which blighted the light and turned everything black.

She lay there, panting with tension, as Roy's hand was suddenly withdrawn, out of sight. But the phone remained on the carpet. She heard Roy shift and murmur. She quickly got up and slipped back under the quilt. A bowl of pee was proof of a toilet visit should he wake and ask what she was doing. But his eyes remained closed and within seconds he was snoring again.

She looked at the bar she was cuffed to. It was connected only to the end posts, so the cuff would slide all the way to the far end. That would allow her to reach the phone. She got to her feet. The toilet excuse would take some effort to sell if he woke to find her standing on the bed. She slid the cuff to Roy's end of the bar, careful not to scrape metal against metal. The task reminded her of that old buzz wire game in which a player must float a probe from one end of a wire to the other without them touching, which would cause a loud buzzing.

That done, she grabbed the bar with both hands and raised a foot to step across Roy. When she planted that foot on the floor, she found herself in such a bizarre position, with her legs spread wide and her crotch just inches from his head. No toilet excuse would get her out of this catch.

But he was asleep. And now she could reach the phone. Still astride him, she bent down to snatch the device in her free hand. She pressed the power key to turn off the screen. All that remained was to step back over him, which was tougher than she expected without vibrating the mattress. Both feet planted together, she played buzz wire again. Once back on her side of the bed, she stepped off. Her foot landed in the washing-up bowl and a centimetre of her own pee.

She didn't care. She had the phone. She slipped under the bed. Only then did she feel safe. She opened the phone, which thankfully didn't require a passcode. She killed the game Roy had been playing and, with a shaking hand, typed in Emery's number.

It rang a bunch of times. Emery might be dead, but someone would have her phone, and that person would–

'Hello?'

That voice. No. It couldn't be...

'Emery?' she said. But surely her mind was playing tricks. The woman must be a police officer woman and she would tell Libby that–

'Look, piss on you scammers, okay? Don't ever call me again at this hour.'

Emery. It was her sister. Alive.

But Emery hung up. She must have not recognised Libby's voice and assumed she was a random caller. Before Libby could call back, she heard movement above her. Roy. In her shock, she had said her sister's name far too loud. A moment later, there was a heavy thud and the space beyond the far side of the bed was filled with a shape. Roy was right there on his hands and knees, staring into her safe zone. Right at her.

'You fucking bitch,' he yelled. An arm spiked towards her. His fingers slapped aside the phone and took it. In the next instant, he was gone. Before she could take her next breath, another thump filled the room, this time from behind her. His fingers were back, now in her hair, and dragging her out from under the bed, which he must have used to leap over her.

FIFTY-SEVEN

The night before, back at Emery's home, Hawk had flipped a coin to decide the woman's fate. He and Alain had watched the 50p piece clatter to the kitchen floor, bounce, and settle. Alain stepped up to the sink and grabbed a large knife, which he put on the floor at Hawk's feet. Emery, tied to a chair inside a moat of glass, stared at it.

'Here you go. I want no part. I think we should keep her alive, just in case.' Alain pulled out his phone. 'I'll just record the cold-blooded murder so you can't say I was involved. In case your boss thinks this is a bad idea.'

Hawk looked between the knife and the woman and the phone aimed at him, while Emery's wide, terrified eyes were locked on the sharp tip of the weapon.

'I'd suggest standing behind her if you're going to slice the throat,' Alain said. 'Blood will spray.'

Hawk thought some more, then kicked the knife away. 'Stop winding me up, you dickhead. I'm not scared to. I just think we probably should keep her alive.'

'Hey, that's a great idea. Thank God you were here to–'

'Shut your damn gob.'

Alain saluted, then used his phone to make a call to Franz. He asked for what he jokingly called an 'au pair', tasked with visiting the house to watch over Emery. 'Make sure it's not someone who likes to get touchy-feely.'

As soon as he hung up, Hawk made a call to Voyzey. He asked for the same: a 'babysitter' for the sister. When he saw Alain's furrowed brow, he said 'You people don't run this thing. Remember that.'

That done, the two men left the property. Barely half an hour later, the 'au pair' that Alain had requested turned up. As instructed, he entered through the back door, left unlocked by Alain, and found Emery in the kitchen. Au pairs are typically foreign women, and aged between seventeen and thirty. This guy had lived in Yorkshire for his entire fifty-one years, except for the odd few months here and there spent in prison.

'All right?' he said, as if he were an old friend popping by. He went straight for the kettle, careful to avoid the broken glass scattered around Emery's chair. 'Don't worry. Not the harming type, me. You want tea? Not got decaf, have you? Too late for the strong stuff.'

He made tea for them both and cleaned up the glass. He then released Emery so they could move to the living room. Emery sat on the couch and didn't touch the drink he put before her.

'Hello there,' said a voice that made them both jump. Neither had noticed a new arrival open the kitchen door and cross the kitchen, to now stand in the living room doorway. The au pair was flicking through TV channels while Emery sat in silence with her eyes in her lap.

The au pair jumped to his feet, holding the TV remote like a knife. 'Who the fuck are you?'

'Babysitter. For her. They said some other guy would be

here.' He was chubby but surely no older than twenty-five. 'There are two of us so we can do shifts.'

'Shifts? This ain't bleeding Tesco, pal.'

'But we've got to sleep, correct? Since you seem wide awake, I'll go first.' He turned to Emery. 'You mind shifting for me?'

Emery relocated to the armchair and the babysitter lay on the sofa. 'Wake me at eight in the morn.'

Unbelievably, he was snoring just three minutes later. It had been less than five since he'd appeared. The au pair returned to his mission to find something to watch on Netflix. Emery desperately tried to think of a way to get free, but bad scenarios involving failure thwarted every plan.

The babysitter indeed slept all the way until 8am, then the au pair woke him before heading upstairs for some shut-eye. Emery had managed no sleep and now absolutely couldn't. She had never been alone with this new man and she was fearful.

But he, too, ignored her. He was happy to mirror his pal and watch TV all day. The au pair woke around 4pm and the two men played cards in the living room and got to know each other. Emery felt invisible and was glad of it. They acknowledged her presence only when she needed the toilet – one escorted her to the bathroom and waited outside the door – and when the au pair made dinner for all three of them. She drifted off here and there, but only for ten or twenty minutes at a time. Each time she snapped awake, it was because of a nightmare in which both men sexually assaulted her.

That evening followed the same rhythm as the previous one. The babysitter went to sleep on the sofa around 1am and the au pair searched for sitcoms on Netflix. He was deep into *The Office* when the landline rang.

'What the hell's that?' the babysitter said, rousing from sleep.

'The phone,' the au pair said.

'Who is it?'

'Hard to tell at this juncture, pal.' To Emery, he said, 'Answer it. And remember what I told you, please. No tricks. I don't want to have to hurt you.'

'She can't answer it,' the babysitter said. 'She'll give a safe word or something.'

'We're here so she can answer the damn phone.'

'No, it's in case the sister comes by...'

The two men started to argue, so Emery saw her chance and rushed for the phone. This late, it had to be Libby. She had the phone to her ear and had said, 'Hello?' before her captors even realised. And when they did, they ceased arguing and watched.

'Emery?' said the voice on the other end. It was Libby. Emery felt her heart soar at the knowledge that her sister was alive and sounded well.

But it sank again in the next moment. The two men here, and various others, were all after Libby. Emery was desperate to talk to her sister, but knew that it was too dangerous. If the two men knew Libby was on the phone, they'd force Emery to lead her into a trap. Or they'd trace the phone Libby was using.

'Look, piss on you scammers, okay? Don't ever call me again at this hour,' Emery said, and hung up. The words burned her throat like acid, but it was the only way to keep Libby safe, wherever she was.

'So who was that?' the au pair said.

'Scam call, didn't you hear?' said the babysitter. To Emery: 'What kind was it? Tech support?'

'Something about a council tax rebate.'

'Yeah, I've had that one as well.' The babysitter lay on the sofa again. 'Just wait for us before answering the phone next time, okay?'

Emery nodded and retook her seat. The babysitter closed

his eyes. The au pair pressed play to continue watching his sitcom. Normal service was resumed.

FIFTY-EIGHT

'Why did you lie about my sister?' Libby yelled. Roy ignored the question as he dragged her downstairs, both hands clamped around her arms just under the shoulders. She tried to halt his progress, but he was too big, too strong. She stumbled over her own feet, but he prevented her from falling.

'Answer me, you bastard,' she bellowed. No response. 'Why did you lie? I need to talk to her.'

No response. They reached the hallway at the bottom of the stairs, where he jerked her to the left.

Her next words were, 'No way,' as he stopped by the cellar trapdoor.

Now she didn't resist. Her addled brain had enough wits to know he was in full control here, and she couldn't stop what he planned. Just sixty seconds after he'd caught her with his phone, she was down in the cellar in the dark, cuffed to the heavy wooden workbench, and Roy was walking for the exit.

'My sister's alive,' she screamed at him. 'I want to talk to her. I need to. We haven't discussed Joel. We can't move on until we do. I need this. Please. Why did you lie about her?'

He stopped, turned, and finally she got an answer. 'For your own good. Emery was the one thing pulling you back to Sheffield. I told you how risky it was. Do you want to die?'

'Yes,' she shouted. 'Anything to get away from you.'

He shook his head in disappointment, as if she was a dog that had peed on the carpet. 'Right now Voyzey is trying to trace the call you just made, you fool.'

'But you lied, Roy.' Her anger has subsided a little and her voice was less voluminous. 'You told me she was dead and didn't care that it would destroy me.'

'It was to stop you destroying yourself.'

'It's my life, and I can do what I want with it. You made me think my sister was dead. That was evil.'

'Evil was your husband. If you don't like where you're at, blame him. I had to make you think there was nothing to go back for. Be grateful she's alive, because she will die for real if I don't find the police traitors. Don't you get it yet, Libby? For you to be safe, we have to stay here, and no one can know it. What's happening out there is national news. Everyone knows your face. You show it, we're doomed. You make a stupid phone call and tell someone where we are, we're doomed. You'll burn everything to the ground.'

'I don't care. My sister is alive, and I want to see her. I want to go home. This is now kidnapping.'

'Call it a goddamn intervention. I'm working on making you safe. Like it or not, I'm here to help, and we're going to do this my way. Now sit here and think about how close you came to killing us both. I'll come back when you've seen sense.'

He left, slamming the cellar door behind him, leaving her alone and naked and chained.

FIFTY-NINE

The cellar had a timeless feel to it, like interstellar space, and she had no idea how long she had been here. Was it morning yet? She got a hefty clue when Roy returned after what seemed like hours, or might have been just minutes, and he carried a bowl of cereal. Morning, then. He placed the bowl on the floor in front of her.

'I'm better now,' she said. 'I can be let out.'

'Soon.'

'I won't run. Can I have some clothing? I'm cold.'

He ignored the request. 'Somehow the new car we got has been traced by ANPR. It means the police have seen our journey here. Not to this exact village, though, which is good. But they know roughly where we are. I went to the shop earlier and overheard someone talking about police being in the next village.'

Bad news for Roy was good news for her. She wished the police were here. She wanted a thousand of them in the village, checking every house and barn and bush. If she could have popped an eyeball with a bang loud enough to bring them running, she would have. She spoke softly: 'Maybe we should hand ourselves in. They're not all traitors.'

'They're asking questions, and they'll fan out to check around. They'll visit every village, every hamlet, every roadhouse. They'll probably be breathing down our necks soon.'

Again, and in the same calm tone, she tried to appeal to his common sense. 'They won't be bad cops. We can trust them. We should go to them, Roy. It's the right thing to do.'

That headshake again. 'Libby, did you learn nothing recently? There's a hundred and seventy thousand police officers in the UK. That's very good odds of finding legit ones. But it only takes one bad apple to know where we are. I can guarantee you that someone high-ranked has given orders that he's to be alerted when we're found. Even if a good cop finds us, he'll call it in, won't he?'

'I don't know.' It was the truth.

'Unless he fancies some glory and plans to unveil you like a new statue in front of the media, then yes, he'll call it in. He'll be told to wait for another set of officers to take you off his hands. And they won't be good ones.'

She didn't offer an argument. There was no point.

Roy continued. 'What we need is for the police to start tracking the car again, away from here. I need to drive to another town or village and dump it so they waste time kicking in doors there. I'll be gone a few hours.'

He left her with those words. She called out again for clothing, but he ignored her. When the cellar door shut, she pick up her breakfast bowl. She wanted to lob it hard against the wall, but that would hurt only her. She needed the food.

A few minutes later, empty bowl discarded, she heard the front door slam. She heard the car start up and the crunch of wheels on stones as it drove away. Roy, heading off on his mission. She was stuck in this dingy room for the next few hours, it seemed. She was very cold.

About ten minutes later, she heard the crunch of a car on the stone lane. She paused and held her breath so she could hear clearly. The car stopped and two doors slammed shut. Two? Next came a rapid, loud knocking on the front door.

The police?

Roy might have been right about most things, but he was also overly paranoid. Not all the police were bad. The odds were very low that the ones above her would be part of Voyzey's or Franz's teams. It was a risk she had to take in order to get back to her sister. She couldn't stay here. Roy thought of this as an intervention, but she hadn't been joking when she'd called it a straight-up kidnapping. She was his prisoner.

If she could hear the police knocking on the door, they'd damn well hear a woman screaming. So, at the top of her lungs, she yelled, *'I'm in here! I'm in the cellar. I am Libby Mytton. In the cellar.'*

SIXTY

The front door opened and slammed shut. She called out again: *'I'm Libby Mytton. In the cellar.'*

Just a second later, the cellar door thumped open. In that moment, she knew something was badly wrong. The police had found the trapdoor too quickly. And the front door had been opened, not booted in.

'You would have killed us both,' Roy said as he rushed down the steps. Her heart wanted to implode as she realised she'd been tricked. Tested.

Roy kicked away her cereal bowl and grabbed her hair, hard. He yelled into her face so vehemently that she felt spit hit her skin.

'Don't make me regret helping you, you stupid bitch. You're like a damn dog biting to avoid an injection at the vet's. I'm tempted to just save myself and toss you out, and let the fucking wolves tear you to shreds.'

'I'm sorry,' she moaned. 'I just–'

'Just nothing. Keep your fucking mouth shut. And you get no dinner for that silly shit.'

He stormed from the cellar, but before doing so he turned

off the light. When the trapdoor shut, it was so dark she might as well have been in the earth's core.

This time he was gone for hours, but he didn't leave the house. She heard him walking about in the kitchen. Sometimes flakes of wood from the joists above her rained down in tune to his heavy footsteps. She stayed silent, even though she really needed a drink. She passed the time with mental games, and memories of a world before her life turned to shit. Before Joel. She still didn't miss him and was still glad he was dead.

When her muscles needed work, she felt about on the bottom storage shelf of the workbench. There were tools and products, and she tried to guess what they were in the blackness. A tin of paint. Sandpaper. A chisel. The latter she considered trying to use to bust her cuffs. But she wouldn't get out of the cellar, and she'd forever lose what little of Roy's trust she retained.

Eventually, he returned. When he opened the trapdoor, she saw the kitchen light was on. That must mean it was getting dark, so it was at least early evening. He turned on the cellar light and tramped down the steps, no rush in him. He put a glass of water in front of her, seemed to think about saying something, and then left without a word uttered.

He got as far as the steps before stopping. He did not turn to her, but he spoke. 'You want me dead, don't you?'

'No,' she said. 'I want to go home, that's all.'

'That would be a death sentence for us both. So you *do* want me dead.' He did not wait for a response. He turned the light off, leaving her once more in abyssal plain blackness. He had seemed calmer, which was a good sign. Soon he might let her out again, if he decided she could be trusted.

It didn't happen during the rest of that day.

She managed a fitful sleep on the cold floor, ever chained to that workbench. She woke at one point and felt a blanket across her. Roy must have entered in the night and covered her. At least she was not deathly cold now. At least he still cared. He seemed to have changed since she lay beneath him. He knew she didn't want him in that way, and it had upset him. Opened a fissure between them.

When she woke a second time, it was to the sound of Roy opening the creaky trapdoor. On went the light. He plodded down the stairs and sat on the concrete floor a few feet from her.

'I've seen sense,' she said. 'Thank you for the blanket. Is it morning?'

He nodded. 'The police asked questions in the village and moved on. I went to the shop and overheard the owner telling someone that one of the officers gave him a number to call if we turn up here. Not 999, or a station number, but a mobile phone. Why would a lowly constable do that?'

She shook her head. She had no idea. But it turned out Roy wasn't after enlightenment: he sought to prove a point because he gave the answer himself.

'The officer had no plans to bring us in, that's why. He must be in the pocket of the people who want you. If the shop owner calls that number, what will happen?'

She shook her head. She knew the answer was coming.

'They'll take us away. But not to a police station. You're so naïve.'

He pulled out his phone. What he showed her was intense and barely in the realm of comprehensible. It was a WhatsApp group called Cut the Red Tape, with just three members. Its profile image was a police badge.

'It's a police group, Libby. The men are all part of the Metropolitan Police's Covert Policing Command. They deal with organised crime groups, terrorists, all the big players. They're undercover specialists in surveillance. And you're their new target, Libby. But unofficially.'

'What do you mean?'

'Maybe it's connected to the officer who killed Joel. It's not a sanctioned task. Off the books. For some reason these three officers have decided to come after you. I don't think they're connected to Voyzey or Franz. I think they believe they can claim the bounty on your head. And they're highly skilled. Look at this.'

He showed her his phone, a screenshot of an array of messages in a thread.

> ALLY445: As soon as she hands herself in, I'm set to get word.

> COPCOP1980: Can we trust they'll send the right people?

> ALLY445: I have it all set up and ready to go.

> BRUISED&CONFUSED: We'll draw her to Abbey Lane.

> COPCOP1980: For a sweet payday.

> BRUISED&CONFUSED: Getting paid for doing something fun? Can't be beaten.

'You know what drawn is?' Roy said. 'Or quartering?'

She shook her head.

'You'll be tied and dragged down Abbey Lane behind a motorbike. The tarmac will sand the flesh right off you. Grate you like cheese. And that's just for starters. Inside the cemetery, your arms and legs will be tied to four motorbikes. They'll rip you apart. Four quarters. Right on top of Joanne's grave, to honour her. That's what you've got coming if you don't think straight, Libby.'

'But I... why would the police...'

'You think we'll be arrested and taken to a police station, and that we'll be safe?' He gave a wry laugh. 'No. We'll be driven down a desolate back road, and then all of a sudden there will be an unfortunate car crash with no witnesses. When help arrives, they'll be told we escaped from the car. Gone. But there will have been no escape. We'll have been handed to Voyzey's people, or Franz's. I'll later be found dead in a ditch. You'll be found ripped apart right on top of Joanne Yeowell's grave.'

She shook her head, but couldn't form words.

'It's real, Libby. So I can't trust you yet. Not until I can get the names of all these traitors and make sure that you'll be safe. Then we can get you back to your life.'

'I want food. I need alcohol.'

Roy sneered. He clearly didn't like how she'd brushed off his pleas in favour of satisfying her belly. Without another word, he left the cellar and slammed the trapdoor. She knew he wasn't coming back for a while. At least he left the light on.

SIXTY-ONE

He was back later, with his phone. Standing in the middle of the cellar, out of her reach, he put the device on the ground.

'What are you doing?' she asked.

'I had to go somewhere else to make this call. But I have it recorded for you. This is all your fault. Just remember that. I gave it a long thought while I was gone. I tried to give you the benefit of the doubt, but... But now I know you just don't care about me.'

He pressed a button and a recorded phone call played. 'Who's this?' said a voice she recognised from an illicit prison interview. Voyzey. Her throat seemed to constrict. 'My man said you have something for me.'

Roy: Libby Mytton. You want. I have. Let's do a deal.

Voyzey: You're the bastard who keeps getting away in the nick of time. Tell me why I should deal with you? Maybe I'm close to finding you both.

Roy: I don't think so, Mr Voyzey. And I don't mean that as an insult. Things have changed. I don't want her anymore. But what I do want was safety.

Voyzey gave a pause, which Libby figured meant he was considering the offer.

Voyzey: Explain that.

Roy: I used to work for Franz. I was chased away. He thought I was dead. When he finds out I'm not, I'll be in the crosshairs. If you can keep me alive, you can have this woman.

Voyzey: I can do that deal. Where are you?

Roy: Mr Voyzey, please listen to me. I'm no threat to you. I want to do this for you.

Voyzey: Okay, fine, whatever. Where are you?

Roy: Please let me explain. Franz is your threat, not me. Joel killed your niece and he was put up to it by Franz. I know it and if you dig you'll find evidence of that. If you look into a guy of Franz's called Quinn, you'll see I'm telling the truth. That's me. My name is Quinn. I don't want anything except to be free of Franz, and you'll know that's the truth if you research me. He thinks he killed me two years ago. If you allow me to work for you, I'll be the most loyal man you have. That's all I want.

Voyzey gave this some thought, unlike with his last two utterances. Now he was taking the offer seriously.

Voyzey: And you can have it. Where are you?

Roy: I'll call you with the location in about half an hour.

A click as Roy hung up. Libby's swimming head refocused. 'You can't be serious,' she said. 'And is that your real name? Quinn? I don't understand.'

'I gave you a chance. We could have been a couple. I love you and I tried to do right by you. I saved you. You would have been dead by now if not for me. I risked my own life for you, and you spat it back in my face.'

'Please don't do this,' she pleaded. 'He'll trick you. He'll kill us both.'

'No. Just you.'

She tried to reach for him, but he was far beyond her straining fingers. He lifted his phone and dialled a number. When someone answered, he gave the address of the house.

Libby closed her eyes.

PART 5

SIXTY-TWO

Voyzey hung up the phone after the conversation with the man calling himself Quinn and gave his situation some thought.

Earlier, he had mentioned something curious to his cellmate, Nando. A guy on the top floor called Peterson had been showing some interest in Voyzey. He'd been spotted staring down from his walkway railing. It didn't really seem like much and Nando hadn't thought anything suspicious of it. But Voyzey had asked a guard about him, and learned that Peterson had a sister in South Yorkshire. Franz's domain.

'That doesn't seem like much, either,' Nando said when told. He was on the toilet and looking at his phone. Voyzey waddled over and snatched it.

'Stop playing for a minute and listen. I think he's Franz's man. Franz probably has people banged up in every prison. And this Peterson, he's one of them. He's spying on me for Franz.'

'You're doing the same. You've got someone watching Franz.'

'Which is how I know I'm right. So make sure you keep an eye on this guy, okay?'

'Sure. You're the boss.'

Voyzey snorted. 'Until there's a new highest bidder.' He looked at Nando's phone. His cellmate had been checking out a woman on Facebook. She was called Linzi Linzo and looked like a whore on her profile picture. Voyzey scrolled to find that she posted a hell of a lot, many already today, but just emojis. He didn't know what any of them meant.

'This your girlfriend?' he asked.

'Just some tart I like the look of.'

'Don't be contacting her. She's probably part of a scam.'

Nando waved this off. 'Anyway, back to you. Why are you worried about the guy upstairs, even if he is an agent of Franz's?'

It wasn't the man himself, but what he represented. He was proof that Franz either had people everywhere or knew how to recruit important ones at a moment's notice. That could be a problem. If Voyzey's men were tailed down to the house in Cullerton and Franz realised he'd been beaten to the punch, it might start a firefight. Voyzey couldn't be assured of victory in a gang war and he absolutely couldn't let Libby escape what he had planned for her.

There was only one viable path forward. Voyzey made a call to his rival to set things in motion. Franz answered quickly.

'I just heard some news,' Voyzey said. 'It appears that Libby Mytton didn't know a thing about what her husband did.'

'How? Who told you that?'

'Don't worry about it. She's not my target anymore, Franz. She can live or die and I don't give a shit. So you can have her all to yourself.'

'What kind of trick is this, Voyzey? Why would you suddenly decide she's innocent based on some guy's word?'

'No trick. Ever heard of Blackstone's Ratio? I'll let the guilty walk free rather than condemn an innocent woman. I don't have proof she's involved. I won't just punish on the off-chance that she was involved in Joanne's murder. So have fun with her. I'm pulling my men out. You're now in a one-horse race, Franz. Enjoy.'

He hung up on his fellow crimelord. He congratulated himself on his patience. Now it was time for the new plan to begin.

Just a few hundred metres from his cell, two men got out of a parked car and shot the breeze outside Galinwind Court, waiting for someone to leave the tower block so they could enter through the unlocked door. It didn't take long.

Once inside, they climbed the stairs to the top floor, where they paused to don ski masks and gloves, even though the CCTV cameras, and the woman who let them in, had already noted their faces. They stopped outside the door of number 22.

They had already been briefed and knew the flat was home to a woman whose soldier husband was away in Belize, doing jungle warfare training as part of something called BATSUB. The two men didn't know what that was or how long he'd be away. But he wasn't here today, and that was all that mattered.

'You think her man will come hunt us down for this?' one of the two said. He held a branded Amazon cardboard box, which was all anyone using the peephole would see.

'Don't be silly,' said the other, and booted the door wide as soon as it started to open.

The resident had a child, but he was a toddler and no issue. He just watched from a ball pit as the two men shoved his mother into the living room and manhandled her onto the sofa.

'Don't you hurt my baby,' she yelled, spitting blood from a lip split wide by the front door when it was kicked into her face.

One of the guys grabbed the kid and dumped him in her lap.

She was calmer after that. The other guy dropped something horseshoe-shaped on the coffee table. It looked like a foam travel pillow, but it made a solid sound when it struck the wood.

'What's that?' the woman said.

'You'll find out,' the man said. He then approached the glass balcony doors to make sure they were unlocked.

Now all they needed was the woman Voyzey planned to kill. It was a waiting game.

Meantime, Voyzey made more calls. First, to his men in the Tumbleweed Wagon. One simple order: 'Get rid of your tail and pick up the sister from her house.'

'Won't be easy,' the leader of the four-man gang said. 'The tail bit, I mean. Been on us constantly, even at the safe house.'

'Do what you have to. No limits.'

'No limits? Aw, cheers, boss.'

Next he called his man at Libby's sister's house. The babysitter had to go into another room to take the call. 'Get rid of your man,' Voyzey said.

There was fear in the babysitter's voice. 'You mean lose him?'

'No, I mean kill the sod. Right there in the house. Or he's going to stop you taking the sister. I'm sending the Tumbleweeds for her. One of them will call you when it's time. Don't fuck this up or you'll regret it.'

The babysitter was a man forced into his work because of an illicit online relationship with an underaged girl, which had been exposed by Voyzey's Stingray team.

The gangster's next call was the most important. After all, everything hinged on getting Libby in his possession. When Hawk answered the phone, Voyzey gave him an update about Libby, a postcode, and an order to go fetch her.

Hawk was pleased. Since they'd lost Libby, he had had to go

to ground. He had spent a night and part of today in a village hotel with a sworn enemy, just burning time and awaiting this update. 'Get rid of your man first, obviously,' Voyzey said.

This made Hawk even happier. 'You mean kill him?'

'No. Sorry, pal. Maybe another day. That's Franz's main man and I can't have Franz knowing he's been tricked just yet. Lose your man and leave everyone wondering, to give you a head start.'

Call done, Voyzey fished in a slit in his bed and extracted two items he'd requested. Finding them, he thought of his modified plans for Libby. Originally he had planned to have her hanged from the balcony of the top floor flat at Galinwind Court, which was visible from a certain cell in the prison. Now, she would still visit that property, but 'asphyxia due to ligature strangulation' would not be scrawled on her death certificate.

At six that morning, four inmates had been taken from their cells and escorted to the stockroom, at the back of the prison, to await a DHL van. It had reversed up to the cargo dock and its rear doors opened. To every single guest of her Majesty, this event was the highlight of the week. It was Canteen Day. The prison's one and only mass riot, some six years ago now, had been ignited by the absence of the Canteen van when it got laid up in a traffic accident.

Watched by three guards, the quartet of prisoners started unloading boxes of supplies and stacking them inside the storeroom. When it was done and the van was gone, the guards checked all the boxes to make sure nothing untoward had been hidden within. Satisfied, they mucked in with the prisoners to fill plastic carrier bags with the goodies. On each bag was taped a prisoner's name.

Two hours later, all the Canteen bags were on four carts, ready for distribution around the wings. The four inmates took one each, pushing them around and dumping bags outside cells. A song broke out as those awaiting goodies watched it happen. A guard watched each delivery man to make sure bags weren't compromised. But the guards found it to be a boring job and the prisoners were good at sleight of hand. One inmate was able to slip five different cans of food out of one bag and into others.

At ten, all cell doors were opened and prisoners scrambled for their canteens before getting locked up again. With all the fervour that prisoners loved Canteen Day, the guards hated it, and for good reason. Sure enough, within minutes, they were getting grief from inmates whose orders were wrong. All items had been chosen from a list of goods and sometimes stock was out, in which case a close alternative might be allocated. If a guy didn't mind getting Jelly Babies instead of Midget Gems, no big deal.

It was more of a problem if out of stock items were simply wiped off the list, because Canteen was also a day for settling debts. Missing Midget Gems might not worry the guy on the street, but in here, if someone was owed tuck and didn't get it, there would be hell to pay. Some guards called Canteen Day the Royal Rumble. The infirmary staff were already geared up.

However, the man missing five tins today didn't care, because he had a deal with Voyzey. The tins didn't contain food. Voyzey had a system in place to insert contraband into tins and to get them aboard the DHL van. Usually it was drugs or phones or something else outlawed for paying customers. But today two of the tins had been for him. They contained the pair of binoculars he'd wanted... and a detonator.

When Libby was dragged out onto the balcony, Voyzey would be watching through his binoculars. She would witness her sister being raped, mauled, and then lobbed off the high balcony. And then it would be her turn. Voyzey wouldn't be part of the rape, but he would play a big role in the end of Libby.

Around her neck would be a collar bomb. He'd read about their use by Columbian guerrillas, who put them on local farmers to extort money. They were easy to make and one was ready to go. It had to be this way. Libby's death would leave him thirsty if someone else's hand delivered the coup de grâce.

SIXTY-THREE

Two days earlier, Voyzey had ordered his four Tumbleweed guys to lead Franz's Go Squad on a merry chase. Game on. First, the Wagon drove around Sheffield, heading nowhere. The Go Squad began their surveillance by hanging far back, but that became too much of a headache when they constantly got stalled by traffic lights. A few hours in, they closed the gap and sometimes drove right behind the Wagon, or even alongside on dual carriageways and motorways.

The Tumbleweeds made it fun. They stopped at a café and spent a good two hours in there, knowing their rivals were cramped up in a vehicle and watching. They also took in the cinema and bowling. At night end, they got a hotel and laughed every time they glanced out the window to see their shadows camped out in a cold metal box.

Same story the next day. Another bunch of aimless journeys and various stops for food and fun, all of it to burn time. None of their enemies seemed to realise it was a goose chase, perhaps figuring the Wagon was on standby for when Libby was caught. The humour quickly went out of the game when, on the third day, the Tumbleweeds got sick of being away from home. They weren't bound to the same oppressive rules that Franz's people were. They had wives and girlfriends who missed them and, in one case, assumed her man was away cheating on her. His mates, listening in to that phone call, found it hilarious.

So the men were happy when Voyzey ordered them to lose their tail. Especially the 'no limits' part. That meant 'fill your boots'. One guy proposed an idea that got three nods of assent. They called Voyzey's fixer to get more people. He had plenty in Sheffield, awaiting the call to action.

Two hours later, the Tumbleweed Wagon drove to an Asda car park and stopped on the eastern edge. As hoped, the Go Squad took the western side to avoid being spotted. Here there was an eight-foot high berm with the River Don and a riverside path on the other side.

Perfect. Two teams of four stared at each other across eighty metres of tarmac. The Go Squad didn't see four masked men ride over the berm on BMXs and race at the van. The first two riders, on either side of the vehicle, zipped past the front doors and, without missing a beat, each man lobbed an iron bar through the window, which took out most of the glass. Hot on their tails, riders three and four blew by and a pair of Molotov cocktails tumbled through the compromised windows.

The interior of the van was suddenly aflame. The riders circled the vehicle like vultures, waiting not to eat but to put down with knives anyone who escaped the fire. But the guys inside had been so shocked and caught unawares that they panicked and didn't even try to open the doors.

When it was obvious nobody was getting out alive, the bikers vanished back over the berm. The Tumbleweed Wagon made a slow, casual exit from the area. Everybody else in the car park stopped to watch the inferno. Eleven mobile phones were extracted from pockets, but only four of those were used to dial 999. Cameras were accessed on the remaining seven devices.

SIXTY-FOUR

The babysitter was alone in the living room with Emery when he got the call. The au pair was in the kitchen, making breakfast for all three of them. The babysitter turned away to shield his phone from the woman. The man on the other end, who he didn't know, gave him a single order:

'Get her out of the house in exactly five minutes from now. Just walk her to the pavement and stand her right at the edge. We'll grab the mail on the fly.'

The line went dead. The babysitter felt his bowels loosen. Now he had to go kill the other guy, which he'd been delaying. He moved into Emery's kitchen. The au pair had sliced bacon into strips and the long knife he'd used was on the counter. The babysitter stared at it, his hands shaking. He couldn't believe today was the day. He'd long wanted to scratch a kill next to his name. But now that he was in the thick of it, inches from it, he was scared. Be careful what you wish for – wasn't that the saying? But he'd now been given a countdown, and he could delay no longer.

The au pair noticed the babysitter lurking and looked over

his shoulder. 'See if there's marjoram. That goes well on everything.'

What the babysitter wouldn't have given for a gun! But Voyzey didn't want his low-level people carrying firearms, at least not until they'd proved themselves. Maybe today would mark that milestone. After all, he'd been trusted with this job, and this kill.

'Honeymoon eggs,' the au pair said. 'It's eggs Benedict with a twist. Half an hour away. You okay with that?'

The babysitter noticed a wall-mounted rack with six rolling pins on it. They were various sizes and decorated, so probably ornamental rather than practical. When the au pair turned his back again to deal with his cooking, the babysitter picked up the largest rolling pin. Knives were better weapons, but messier. Blood wasn't his thing.

'Oh, there's no Asiago cheese,' the au pair said. 'But I prefer cheddar anyway.'

The babysitter remembered his bungee jump at Battersea Park. The fear. The thrill. The advice from his dad to avoid thinking and just take the leap, or he'd freeze. So he applied it here.

The rolling pin arced up and curved down. The babysitter wanted one strike to do the job, so he put all his might into it. Power sacrificed aim and the blow shaved down the side of the au pair's head, across the ear, and into the shoulder.

'Fuck!' the babysitter yelled, even louder than the au pair's scream of pain. The latter dropped to one knee, clutching his injured shoulder. On the way down, his hand caught a baking tray, sending parchment paper and halved croissants to the floor.

The babysitter raised the pin again and, terrified, dropped it even harder. This time he got lucky and the wood smashed into the downed man's skull. Unconscious, he sprawled across the linoleum, his cheek squashing a croissant.

Panic set in. An unconscious man would wake and want revenge. Seeing no alternative, the babysitter closed his eyes and hammered at the au pair's head, or at least where he thought it was. Half his blows hit the floor with the cracking sound, but the rest gave him the correct kind of soft thudding noise. He wanted to puke, and he did just that, but he didn't stop striking until his arm burned and his fingers lost enough power to allow the pin to slip from them.

He backed away before opening his eyes to see his work. The au pair's head was a bloody mess. The babysitter stared for what seemed a long time, looking directly at the chest to determine the rise and fall as living lungs breathed. No movement. He didn't like it. Did murder always feel like this, or did it get better with experience? He hoped he wouldn't have nightmares. This wasn't what he'd imagined.

When he'd calmed a little, he became aware of a slight movement. One corner of the fallen parchment paper was dancing. It took him a few seconds to realise there was a slight breeze entering the kitchen.

Shit. He'd stood here too long, lost in thoughts. He ran to the living room, hoping and praying he wouldn't see an empty sofa. But he did. He ran into the hallway, planning to check if the woman had gone upstairs to the toilet, and there his *oh shit* moment took place. The front door was wide open!

***

The Tumbleweed Wagon was parked further down the road, idling. It had arrived two minutes ago, as the five minute deadline was about to expire. They were awaiting sight of the babysitter and his captive. They got half of their wish.

'Shit, that's the sister, isn't it?' the driver said, in disbelief.

'We can't see from back here,' someone yelled from the enclosed cargo area.

'It's her. On her own. She's fucking escaped.'

The team leader piped up next: 'What? Where's the– Get her!'

The driver threw his van into first gear and pulled away from the kerb. The woman, wearing pyjamas, was bolting barefoot down the pavement in his direction. The distance between them closed rapidly. There was nobody else around, which was good. And she was on the same side as the sliding side door.

'Mail-on-the-fly,' he yelled to his cohorts, laughing. The sliding side door immediately rasped open.

Like Tumbleweed Wagons, mail-on-the-fly was around during the Wild West, so the team leader thought it would be fitting to adopt the same practice. The Railway Mail Service used the technique so trains wouldn't have to stop to collect bags of mail; they were simply snatched off trackside cranes as the vehicles powered past. The Tumbleweeds had never before had to hook a victim while driving by, but they'd practiced with mannequins and were sure they were up to the task.

But the woman ruined it. She spotted the van cruising towards her and veered into the road, right in front of him. The driver squashed the brakes. The sudden stop thudded his friends into the partition.

The driver put his window down as the woman ran to it, distraught, begging for help, screaming that she'd been kidnapped.

He had to stifle a smile. 'Kidnapped? Aw, that's terrible. Shit, we'll help you. Get in.'

Only now did she notice the opened sliding side door right next to her. She got half inside before seeing a couple of things that halted her: a trio of mean-looking men, and an interior remarkably dungeon-like. She tried to about-face and bolt, but hands grabbed her. In she went. Off they set.

SIXTY-FIVE

His dad, long dead, had once said, 'The hardest fight happens inside you.'

Hawk had always thought it was nonsensical bullshit until he got into boxing, then he understood. Mental determination. The will to fight on against odds. Optimism when there was no reason for it. And, most important, being able to stick to a game plan after getting it severely tested.

The latter was creating a serious battle within him right now. Voyzey had told him to dump Alain instead of killing him. But Hawk had sworn bloody revenge for Tempest, hadn't he? He'd promised Tempest's grandmother that he'd look after her sole remaining family member. What to do?

After a long night in a quaint little shithole B&B called the Pheasant Rooms, Hawk had wanted to get out, get some air. He had almost thrust his knife into Alain's throat while the bastard slept. In the morning, he had insisted on taking a drive, so they'd be ready to go if and when they got news. Luckily, Alain had stopped the car on a quiet road in order to take a piss when Hawk had gotten his phone call.

Now, driving again, Alain suggested they get more food.

That decided things for Hawk. A café was a good place to lose this asshole.

'Sure thing,' he said. 'Next one we see.' He stared at Alain. At the flesh of his throat. It would feel mighty good to slice him here, though.

The opportunity, if it had ever really been on the cards, vacated him when Alain took the next turn and they were on a commercial road. A supermarket on the left, boutique stores on the right, and people here and there. Over a dozen witnesses. The slicing would have to wait.

Thirty seconds up the road was a café called The Library, which had an optimistically large car park. Alain parked down the side of the building, away from the other cars and out of sight of the front window.

Inside, the owners had tried to justify the name by stocking shelves with books and having wallpaper depicting more of the same. The menus were in the form of old hardbacks, which was pretty cool. Paperbacks were scattered on every table and arranged on the bay window's deep sill. There were ten tables but only one was taken. That patron, a skinny female in her sixties, had a dog on a chair that was eating food from a bowl on the table. Hawk wasn't sure if that was sweet or disgusting.

Alain chose a table far from the woman and her dog and away from the window. He picked up a book. It was *The Code of the Woosters*, by P.G. Wodehouse. 'I should call you Wooster. And you can call me Jeeves.'

'That'll be some kind of insult,' Hawk replied. 'What do you do apart from read and whack people and blow your own trumpet?'

The bald bastard actually had to give that some thought. 'Maybe I should switch off more. I've been thinking about it. I want to ride the Vomit Comet. I could afford that. I do it in the car sometimes. If you drive over a hill at the right speed, you get a second of weightlessness. Let me guess. You'll make me weightless when you throw my bloodied corpse in the river?'

'Didn't say a word.'

A waitress came over and Alain ordered for them both. Alain opted for toast and jam and hash browns. He got Hawk another fried breakfast.

When she was gone, Alain stood up. 'Bathroom.'

Hawk had planned a toilet trip himself, hoping to again be able to dump this man by squeezing through a window. This was better because he could stroll out the door while the bald bastard pissed. But he pretended to be wary, so as to avoid suspicion. 'How can I trust you?'

'Because you escaped through a toilet window earlier, you think I might do the same?'

'Yeah, actually.'

Alain dumped his car keys then on the table. 'This proof enough?'

Hawk nodded. He couldn't believe his luck. Now he wouldn't have to flee on foot. 'Wash your hands before you come back to this table. And don't think of me while you're playing with your dick.'

Alain saluted and headed for a small corridor. As soon as he was gone, Hawk picked up the keys. But there he paused. He dropped the keys and grabbed a butterknife. The chance was too good to pass up. A stinking public toilet seemed a fitting deathbed for that bald bastard. It was probably the only chance Hawk would ever get if there was truth to Voyzey's claim that Alain was a jet-setting hitman.

He entered the small corridor and stopped before the door to the gents, clutching the butterknife. He was breathing hard in preparation. Nobody could see him. Bursting in, catching Alain with his back to him and his tiny dick out, and driving the blade into his heart, would be sweet, and if Hawk was fast and precise

Alain wouldn't get a chance to haul out his gun. And nobody would hear a thing.

But he didn't move. Voyzey had a point, didn't he? A secret escape was safer. A murder would upset the applecart if Hawk somehow found himself trapped in this village or the car's registration was tracked to Cullerton.

But Tempest wouldn't get justice.

Payback wouldn't be cancelled, only postponed until the mission was over. 'They say revenge is a dish best served cold anyway.'

'Was it the scampi?' said a voice behind him, which made him jump. It was the skinny old lady with the dog. She stood by the door of the ladies' restroom. 'Is that what you said? Cold? My scampi was cold the other day.'

'Yes. Scampi,' Hawk said. 'Always served cold.'

'Not sure about always. But last time mine was. But what can you do? I'm not going to Gail's Grub. They don't clean their cutlery right.'

She vanished into the restroom. The strange conversation had eroded what little remaining murderous momentum had been simmering in his gut. He returned to the table, dumped the knife and grabbed the keys to Alain's car. Ten seconds later, he was in the vehicle and pointing it at the exit.

SIXTY-SIX

Although prisoners ate breakfast in their cells, all doors were opened so they could emerge to look through the food carts as they travelled the walkways. There were three carts on Voyzey's block, one for each floor. The chap manning it was usually someone in the governor's favour, or a guy due imminent release. Today the attendant was a man called Bob, doing nine years for reckless arson. A former chiropractor, he had burned his offices to the ground for insurance while a cleaner was inside, although she survived without injury. He had helped fix the governor's bad neck, which was how he got breakfast duty.

Four years into his sentence, Bob's wife decided the waiting game wasn't for her and she had an affair. Being a man without criminal contacts, he turned to Voyzey for help. The wife got her face burned away in an acid attack on her doorstep and Bob got himself a new master.

When Bob stopped outside Voyzey's cell, he was given a present for a special inmate up on the top floor. And a note to read to the man. Bob had been in Voyzey's pocket for two years now and was no longer wet behind the ears. He waved to the upper floor, to get another cart pusher's attention. Thirty seconds later they had swapped places.

At the special inmate's cell, Bob stopped his cart and walked inside. The special inmate was solo in a cell, like all prisoners on this floor. Without even looking up from his book, the special inmate said, 'You got the skimmed milk today? That other shit gives me gut rot.'

Bob read from his note: 'When you get to hell, tell Franz hi from Voyzey.'

The special inmate was Peterson, the man deemed to be Franz's agent in the prison. Bob's threat should have made him realise he was in trouble. Whether it did or not was irrelevant, for he got no time to react. Upon the last word spoken, Bob lunged at him to give him his present. It was a sliver of sharpened metal taken from a kickboard on an old door dumped in a skip out back of the wood workshop. Voyzey wanted it delivered to the inmate's neck, again and again.

A floor below, Voyzey was given the news and smiled. Now that Franz's spy was out of the way, there was one more man to deal with.

SIXTY-SEVEN

Something felt wrong.

Franz abandoned the breakfasts he was making for his wife and her mother and, on a gut feeling, headed upstairs to look out the bedroom window. His wife was sitting up in bed, reading a J.V. Cardy book on her Kindle. She asked if he was okay.

'Sure am,' he replied. Then he caught himself. 'Actually, maybe not.'

He told her that after Voyzey had apparently backed out of the hunt for Libby, Franz had figured he was up to something. According to a report from his man in the prison, paid to keep an eye on Voyzey, the gangster had been very active on his phone since abandoning the plan.

'That might mean nothing,' she said without looking up from her book. 'He's got his fingers in a lot of pies. You're on your phone all the time, too.'

But his man had gone silent since.

'It's a prison, Franz. It's hard for people to find time to make phone calls. The guards could be around and he hasn't had time. It's happened before.'

True. But he'd just called his man at Emery's house. No answer.

'That's not a big cause for concern,' she said, still reading. 'Send someone by to have a look.'

He would. But there was also no answer from his Go Squad.

'Again, means nothing. But there's four men, so just try someone else's num–'

But Alain was also out of reach, he told her.

Now his wife forgot her book. She sat up straight. They both knew Alain's techniques well. When he was on a job for someone, that someone got priority. If Alain was driving, eating, fucking, or even killing, he'd answer a call from Franz.

'You think Voyzey is killing off your people? Some kind of double-cross?'

'Possibly. I think he still wants Libby and might know something we don't.'

She got up and came to his side, worried. 'What are you looking for out there?'

He pointed through the net curtains. 'The guy at number 18 cleared out about half an hour ago.'

Across the road and five houses down, number 18 was a property up for sale whose owners were on holiday for three weeks. After Franz and Voyzey had combined forces, a man had sneaked into that empty property. Franz had spotted him at an upstairs window with binoculars. Obviously he was one of Voyzey's people, there to watch Franz. The two crime kingpins didn't trust each other.

Lacy had been informed about the surveillance. 'Well, that's expected, right? Voyzey said he was pulling his people out.'

Franz didn't think it was so simple. 'Maybe he's gone because the shit is about to hit the fan.'

'What does that mean?'

'It means we're going to go get the kids from school. Get dressed. We're going to Barnsley.'

She knew he meant their other home, which existed for just such an emergency as this. 'What? We can't just... school... we can't...'

He glared at her. 'Do it.'

They both got dressed in record time. As they were about to leave the bedroom, they heard the sound of a fast vehicle making a sudden stop. Franz bolted to the window. A plain car was outside, stopped dead in the middle of the road. He was far from surprised to see four masked gunmen in black tracksuits leap out and run towards the house. He'd ordered such blatant daytime assaults many times.

'Attic!' he screamed at his wife as he rushed past her, into the hallway. He hauled down the ladder to the roof space. His wife was frozen to the spot, so he grabbed her and pushed her to the ladder, and forced her to climb.

As she planted a foot on the first rung, a mighty boom rang out and Franz heard the front door burst open. A half-second later, thudding footsteps were in his home.

'You're a fucking dead man,' someone yelled. 'Joanne says hi, dead man.'

Franz pushed his wife up the ladder with his head and shoulder as he climbed behind her. The gunmen were rampaging around the downstairs rooms, hunting their prey, and it gave Franz and his wife precious time. By the time the yelling intruders had turned their focus to the upper levels and had mounted the stairs, Franz was hauling his legs through the trap.

He turned to close the hatch and saw the first killer appear at the top of the stairs. They locked eyes. Franz closed the wooden trapdoor as the gunman raised a sawn-off shotgun. The door fell into its housing and this kicked in the automatic safety feature: a thick metal sheet that slammed across the square of wood like a camera shutter.

The shotgun blasted the trapdoor. Franz heard it turn to wooden shards and rain on the floor.

'Fucking metal,' someone said. A second blast hit the exposed metal cover, doing nothing but create terrible noise.

'Watch the fucking ricochet,' another voice said. 'Shoot here.'

A third blast, this time to one side of the trap. It destroyed plaster but didn't penetrate the floor. 'More fucking metal,' the shooter moaned. 'What the fuck is this place?'

'A panic room, you muppets,' Franz called out. 'Forty-five grand well spent. Always knew some brainless morons would come one day.'

'Today's that fucking day, Franz. Courtesy of Joanne Yeowell. I've been told to give you a message: welcome to Voyzey's Ratio. We're gonna burn this place to the ground and cook you inside if you don't come out. Less painful if you just give up.'

'Give me a couple of days to think about it,' Franz yelled as he moved to a table with seven monitors, each displaying feed from a different camera in the house. There was one built into the frame of the trap and he could see three gunmen, not four, down there, staring up at it. He–

'My mother!' Lacy moaned. She leaned close to one of the monitors. Now Franz saw where goon number four was. Living room. Aiming a gun at Lacy's infirm mother. Franz had overlooked her in his panic.

'That's right, we've got old bag,' yelled a new voice from below, its owner a man with a foreign accent. Clearly they'd heard Lacy's panicked two words. 'Dead if you don't come out. Come do that now. Count of five. Door still locked on five, old bag starts losing fingers.'

The table also had a control panel for the house. Franz could turn off the water and the gas and electric, in case he left a bath running or food on the hob when forced to flee. There was also a button to alert the police, and a secure landline for any other calls. And one other, special feature, reserved for those who intruded when the house was empty.

As one of the men started a countdown, Franz hit the button that would summon the police. He knew his blue line enemies would use the opportunity to have a good, long nosey about his house for crime evidence. Or maybe they'd know he was in mortal danger and just put the kettle on. But he'd never get his own people here in time. Why the hell hadn't he thought fuck-the-neighbours and posted a crew outside?

'These bastards can't risk staying here long,' he said. 'Neighbours will have heard the guns and–'

He stopped as he realised his wife wasn't by his side. When he turned, he saw her standing by the trap. Then squatting.

'Lacy, don't be stupid–'

Too late. She slapped the door release button. He ran at her, to try to save them by closing the trap again, but he was too late. Lacy suddenly threw herself backwards as a shotgun blast hit the ceiling, stripping plaster as exposing more solid metal. She crashed into Franz, halting his forward progress. By the time he'd pulled her aside, he saw the weapon poke through the trap. The proximity sensor now wouldn't allow the trap to shut even if he got to the button.

Grabbing his wife, he backed off to the far wall, as one by one the three men entered the panic room. Franz stood in front of Lacy and pointed at a wall safe to his right. 'Thirty grand, right there, chaps. All yours. Just tell Voyzey that we weren't at home.'

'We'll take that cash,' said the foreign guy, who had dark

eyes beneath his hood. 'And use it to buy Joanne flowers for her grave.'

He raised his shotgun. Franz turned, grabbed his wife, and hugged her so hard that he pulled her down to the floor when he collapsed following a blast to his back.

'Franz, it's okay, it's okay,' she moaned, feeling him clutch her still. 'Don't ever let me go. It'll be okay.'

It wasn't. She didn't know that he was already gone and his embrace was a cadaveric spasm. Intense physical and emotional stress at the moment of death had resulted in sudden depletion of adenosine triphosphate, bringing about instantaneous rigor mortis in his arms. Suicide victims had been known to die holding a gun, and murder victims clutching hair ripped from a killer's head. Franz would not release his wife for more than three hours, until a pathologist separated them.

But Lacy experienced only seconds of it. The same shotgun that had taken him away now sent her after him. Job done, two of the three men turned to leave.

'Hang on,' the third said. 'Cash.' He rushed to the wall safe.

'You ain't got code. And we ain't got time,' said the foreign guy. They could hear faint sirens.

But the guy who wanted a payday rushed to the safe and yanked the handle. The door opened with a click. The safe wasn't just empty, it wasn't even a safe. Just a door and frame attached to the blank wall. 'What the fuck?' he said.

His words smothered a click from the trapdoor, which instantly shut. The foreign guy jabbed the release button, but it did nothing.

'Idiot,' he roared.

Payday guy got with the programme. Franz had tricked them with his final breath.

SIXTY-EIGHT

When Roy – or was it Quinn? – entered the cellar again, she could see a different tone in his body language. He appeared to be feeling guilty. He looked tired and worn out, too. All this running and panic, she guessed. Or the hassle of dealing with an unreasonable prisoner. Or maybe it was the sweet thought of being pardoned by a new underworld boss.

'It's dinnertime,' he said. 'I think you've learned your lesson, right?'

'Yes. I'm sorry. I messed up. I was silly. I know you have a lot to lose, too. I'll do what you want from now on. If you need to hand me to Voyzey to save yourself, I'll accept it. Maybe he won't hurt me. And there will be no more need for running and hiding.'

He liked this new attitude. 'In that case, for my own apology to you, I will cook you a special meal. We'll eat together. We should have time before the men get here for you.'

'Upstairs?'

This part he didn't like so much. 'Not yet. Ramblers are around. They might peek through the windows.'

She knew he really meant *You might shout for help again.*

But she could wait. 'Okay. We'll eat here. I can order whatever I want?'

'Your wish is my command, babe.' Said with a smile. Did he think she was enjoying her time here?

'I would like a jacket potato with cheese and beans.'

Her choice fielded a nod. 'Sounds great. I want the same.'

'And let's make it special. Candlelit. Just you and me. But I'd like to be clothed.'

He liked this and headed off to make their meals. And to fetch her jeans and pullover – but not the training shoes. He even unlocked her so she could dress. But the handcuffs were snapped right back in place afterwards.

He left the trapdoor door open so they could speak while he pottered in the kitchen. His mood was up and jokes were made. They were like a regular couple, except for the chained-in-a-cellar part.

'Is it beans first then the cheese?' he shouted down.

'No, cheese first, so the beans melt it. And don't forget lashings of hot oil. Plus a tea towel so I can wipe my fingers.'

'You're going to eat with your hands? Philistine.'

She laughed. 'Oh, and that bottle of Stroh from the shelf. Spiced Austrian rum. I'd love that.'

'No problem, babe.'

When the food was done, he brought it down on a tray. Two steaming jacket potatoes with cheese and beans. He laid a plate before her and tossed a tea towel onto her head.

'Have fun,' he said. He then handed her the bottle of Stroh. 'Should be called Strong, not Stroh. Eighty per cent. That'll burn through you like alien acid.'

She laughed at his joke and unscrewed the top. She was one-handed, so she had to clamp the bottle between her knees to hold it. 'Salt. I'm sorry. A jacket potato has to have lots of salt.'

He smiled and got up. The moment he was out of the cellar,

she wrapped the jacket potato in the tea towel and tipped some of the rum onto the fabric. After that, she flicked the bottle like a whip, sending fluid across the cellar to coat the rolled-up rugs and the cardboard boxes under a tarpaulin.

She then tossed aside the empty bottle of Stroh, with its highly flammable 80 per cent ABV, and grabbed the candle. *Burn through me like alien acid? It'll burn indeed, you bastard.*

SIXTY-NINE

She threw the jacket potato, wrapped in a flaming tea towel, at the cardboard boxes, which immediately ignited, fast. This set fire to rum splashes on the floor. A few seconds later, Roy was back, and he got three steps down the stairs before becoming aware that his lovely candlelit dinner plans were, quite literally, going up in smoke.

'Jesus Christ. What the fuck did you do?'

He thundered over to the stack of boxes and tried to yank away the tarpaulin, which was already melting in places. However, dips and shallows containing burning pools of rum went sailing, to hit the wall and an old sofa and the rolled-up rugs. If he'd had a chance to put the fire out, he'd just blown it.

'You fucking bitch,' he yelled, before turning on his heels and heading for the stairs.

'I'll die here,' she yelled. 'Help me.'

But he was gone.

The flames now started to eat items not coated in rum, and the noise intensified. Soon there was a loud inferno and she felt the heat from fifteen feet away. The flames rose high enough to find purchase with the dried wooden ceiling joists. Soon they'd eat through the floor, and spread towards her, and consume the whole house. The light bulb was above the burning boxes and a flame shattered it. The cellar barely got darker because of the fire, but now there was no whiteness, just dancing pools of red and blue across everything.

She yanked on her cuff as hard as she could, to snap the chain, but it of course failed miserably. She screamed again for Roy, but now he was the latest in a long line of people out for revenge. He would let her burn to teach her a lesson and–

She heard his feet thudding down the stairs. He had to shield the left side of his face from the heat. She saw a key in his fingers. Even as he called her a fucking bitch, he planned to save her.

He rushed past the fire and stopped in front of her. Literally: stopped. Froze right there. She held her wrist out for him and yelled, 'Let me out.'

Still he paused. 'I should let you burn. You don't know what you've done.'

The inferno was behind him, throwing his face into shadow. She knew her own was lit bright orange. 'You can't. I mean too much to you.'

He seemed to think some more, but then one of the burning rolled-up rugs that stood upright in a corner fell. It struck the concrete with a dull whoomph, splashing flames, and this seemed to wake him up. He bent down and unlocked the handcuff. And she was free.

Or not. Roy grabbed a fistful of her pullover and dragged her towards the stairs. She knew he was not just rescuing her, but making sure she didn't escape.

The fire was growing upwards, but they had a clear run to the stairs, although the heat was intense as they hit the first step.

She felt a crackle on the right side of her face and slapped at it in case her hair or eyebrow was aflame.

Soon they were at the top, almost leaping through the trapdoor. She tripped on the final stair, but Roy's solid hold on her top prevented her from falling flat on her face. He dragged her for a second or two until she could get to her feet again. The pullover tore at the throat, the split ten inches long, but he quickly readjusted for a better grip and her hope of escape from him lived only half a second.

Joists below them gave way and a portion of the kitchen floor toppled inwards like a sinkhole. A tongue of flame shot through the chasm, followed by thick black smoke that instantly smothered a smoke alarm. A second later, a shrill beeping filled the house. It was a redundant warning.

'I'll make you fucking pay for this,' Roy screamed as he yanked her out of the kitchen, into the hallway, towards the front door. He opened it and pushed her out first. They rushed down the path. She could still hear the fire gorging itself. The kitchen window threw dancing orange light across the lawn.

'What the hell's happened?'

That voice belonged to a man with his wife. They were about sixty and were on the riverside path on matching mountain bikes. They had stopped and were staring at Libby and Roy. They had good village gossip for the next few days.

Roy ignored them and pushed her onward. Towards the couple. Libby suspected he had a wild idea to commandeer their bikes for our escape.

But he dragged her past them, and now she saw the Ford they'd bought. It seemed he didn't get rid of it after all.

'What are you doing to her?' the woman cyclist yelled. 'Why is her top torn? This isn't your home. Hey. Come back.'

That was the last thing Roy intended. They reached the car

and he grabbed the passenger side door handle. She would be bundled inside and off they'd go, her freedom once more erased.

But the car was locked.

Roy screamed with rage. She realised the keys must be in the house, gone forever. He grabbed her face and turned it towards him. 'We have to run, Libby. Please.'

In his face she saw the end of the world. A burning house, no car, two witnesses to his assault of her, one of whom she heard shout that the police were coming. Roy could not take her away unless she chose to go with him. He knew it.

And she knew it. She stared right into his eyes and said, 'I'm going home.'

'But I love you.'

'I don't love you.'

He squeezed her face harder, enough to hurt. If he'd had hysterical strength, her skull would doubtless have shattered. 'I'm a dead man now, Libby. Because of you. You won't get peace.'

'Piss off, you lunatic,' she yelled.

Roy pulled her face closer to his. 'Look into these dead man's eyes. They're going to haunt you forever. Have a good long look. You did this with your selfishness. I'm dead because of you, and that's going to kill you inside. I saved you!'

He held on to her for a second or two longer. She saw panic, fear, and the pain of her words. He seemed to be looking for similar on her face. She hoped she exhibited hate, but she would never know what she subconsciously showed him that day.

She heard a series of cracks from behind her. The heat in the kitchen caused the glass in the window to expand. Roy looked at the house over her shoulder. In the next moment, the window shattered, making the watching cyclists groan. And there were shouts from elsewhere: the fire had drawn the attention of others.

Libby saw flames reflected in Roy's eyes just before he closed them. He knew it was all over.

His hands released her face. He gave her his back. And then he was running. She fell to her knees and watched him cross the bridge over the brook, and vanish into the woods.

SEVENTY

She waited across the bridge, other side of the water, and watched the house burn. The cyclist couple sat with her and tried to get answers. She said nothing other than two words, repeated over and over: *terrible accident.*

Events took on a slideshow quality. There were three people present, then suddenly a crowd, no doubt alerted by the rising smoke and the roar of the house being consumed by fire. The newcomers too asked questions, but got no answers from Libby.

A man close to her grabbed hold of her pullover. It was a soft touch, as if she was not supposed to notice, or worry. She did both. These people didn't know her, yet a house was burning. She knew they thought she was responsible. She was, of course.

That slide vanished, to be replaced with one of firefighters tackling the blaze. She guessed she was zoning out when she blinked, her eyes remaining shut for minutes at a time.

Next, the police were there, and they zeroed in on the one fingers pointed at. If they asked her questions, she didn't recall them. Next she was in the back of an ambulance parked in the

Kwaint Cottage and Tea Rooms car park, being given a once-over.

After the next blink, she was in the rear of a moving police car, with two officers up front. She felt a bit hazy. Maybe the paramedics gave her something. Maybe it was a massive adrenaline dump. But it was good news. They were heading away from the cottage. Away from the killers coming to collect her. 'Which police force are you?' she said.

The driver, in the passenger seat, answered. 'We told you earlier. Don't you remember? Staffordshire Police.'

Staffordshire. So that was where Roy had brought her. She– A sudden flash of memory, a warning Roy had given, caused her to search for a door handle. There wasn't one that worked. 'Are you bad?'

'Bad? Us?' said the driver. She was young, sweet-looking. Libby bet this lady found it hard to soften a rowdy crowd of drinkers on a Saturday night. 'We're the good guys. You're okay now.'

Libby expected they'd say that. 'Promise?'

'Promise.'

'You're not going to crash and say I ran?'

She saw her words puzzled the officer. Right then she knew these weren't Voyzey's or Franz's people. They were good police. But she was in their car. 'Am I arrested?'

'No. You think you should be?'

She guessed the police were always suspicious. They didn't know what crimes she might have gotten up to while on the run, right? Libby didn't answer the question. She put her head back, hoping to sleep.

It seemed there was one more slide to come, for she closed her eyes and when they opened again, everything was spinning, and her whole body hurt, and she realised that Roy had been right all along.

A car crash after all.

SEVENTY-ONE

Hawk saw rising smoke before he'd even reached Cullerton, and it gave him a bad feeling. Once he'd entered the village, he heard sirens and saw a fire engine blast across the junction he was stopped at. Headed in the direction his map was sending him. Just seconds after making the turn, he had to pull into the side of the road to let another fire engine past, and two police cars and an ambulance. Not good.

Soon, he was at his destination. He'd checked it out on Google Earth. The entrance to the winding road leading to the house was at the back of a pub car park, meaning all visitors had to cross that private property. A police car blocked the entrance to the car park itself. A crowd had gathered nearby, but the cottage was below ground level and 100 metres away, so all anyone could see was black smoke.

Unable to get close, Hawk parked further up the road, still within sight of the car park, and called Voyzey. The gangster was not a patient man and was unwilling to help with a solution to the problem. 'Just get that bitch at any cost. I don't care how. I don't care if she's in police custody. The Tumbleweeds will meet up with you soon. Use them for a firefight if you need to.'

'Will do,' Hawk said, which was a damn lie. Firefight with cops? Hell no.

About half an hour later, a police car emerged from the winding path. That track led only one place: the house where a man called Quinn was holding Libby. Now he couldn't deny that the cops had been there. This was bad news.

Actually, no, it wasn't. The car was let through the cordon, out onto the main road. Hawk stared closely and saw two officers in the front and a woman in the back. He could only make out her hair, but it matched the photo of Libby he'd seen. All of a sudden she was no longer surrounded by cops and firemen and paramedics. Just two Crown servants had her, and they were taking her away from the area.

Best of all, Hawk had used his time parked here to check for local police stations, knowing he might have to avoid law enforcement if something went wrong during the capture. He'd discovered that Cullerton didn't boast one and the nearest was nine miles north, in Telford. The route there involved rural lanes. Perfect.

Hawk followed the police car out of the village, making sure he kept far enough back that he didn't give the officers a view of his registration plate. They might run it through their system if suspicious and he had no idea if Alain was a wanted man, or if the car was stolen.

Soon, they were on a country lane with a long ditch on the left side, and he saw no better opportunity for the takedown. The police car was zipping along at fifty miles an hour. He closed the distance, then indicated and made to overtake the police car. There was nothing oncoming.

When alongside it, he glanced over and saw the woman in the back seat. Just feet away, her profile lifted his spirits. Libby. There she was, finally. She had her head bowed and hadn't noticed a car pacing hers. She was about to be supremely aware of him, though.

The driver already was. She flicked a hand in a gesture that meant *get back*. On any day when they didn't have an important passenger, she might have pulled him over for his risky manoeuvre.

Hawk gave her a thumbs-up, then twisted his steering wheel violently to the left.

The nearside front corner of his vehicle caught the target hard on its offside front wheel arch, immediately shunting the vehicle from a 12 o'clock to an 11 o'clock position on the road, which angled it towards the ditch. Both drivers stamped the brakes at the same time.

Even without thinking time, the stopping distance at fifty miles an hour was thirty-eight metres. Hawk had that and a whole lot more ahead of him. The cops didn't.

SEVENTY-TWO

When Libby's eyes refocused, she saw that the front of the car was mangled. The windscreen was nothing but a hole with jagged edges, like a wild animal's open mouth. Beyond it was grass and dirt and trash. She understood that the car was at an angle, front end pressed up against the side of the ditch they'd crashed into, rear pointing to the sky. Her seatbelt was crushingly tight against her torso because gravity wanted to haul her towards that animal mouth.

The driver, who had been wearing her seatbelt, was moaning in pain and trying to wake her partner. He hadn't had his belt on and was a bleeding, contorted mess lying across the centre console. Libby shut her eyes. All it did was exacerbate her pain.

Suddenly, the driver started making terrible screams. Libby's eyes snapped open to view something she'd carry to her deathbed and maybe beyond. The man in the green jacket, one of the two who'd been hot on her tail, was at the driver's window, thrusting his hand back and forth into the car. Into the female police officer. Stabbing her, Libby knew.

Yelling, Libby reached over, to grab him and stop the

murder, but she didn't have the leverage to halt the piston-like thrust of the killer's arm. He continued to pierce the officer's body with his blade as if Libby's hand was as potent as a ghost's on his arm.

When Libby released her seatbelt, she did so without considering the car's forty-five degree angle. Unrestrained, she tumbled forward, struck her face against the driver seat's headrest, and collapsed into the footwell. By the time she'd fought to right herself, everything was quiet. She saw the female officer slumped forward against her seatbelt, almost horizontal because of the angle of the car, and dripping blood across the steering wheel and dashboard. But where was the killer who–

Libby's door opened and there he was, framed in the doorway at a Dutch angle, holding his bloodstained knife. His long hair was matted with blood and it streaked across his face and neck. A bizarre thought entered her addled mind: he didn't have permission to keep that officer's property.

'Out you come,' he hissed. 'Fucking quick.'

She didn't move, was unable to. She could barely breathe or think. The killer leaned through the doorway and grabbed her hair with both hands. The pain was terrible as he pulled with all his might and she had no choice but to help him extract her from the vehicle. When he released her, she dropped into the mud and trash and leaves in the bottom of the ditch. She saw the car's dirty undercarriage.

The killer bent over her and put the point of his knife in her ear, which hurt like hell and seemed to wake her up. 'In the car, now. Fight or try to run and I'll leave you dead right here.'

'What do you want with me?' she moaned.

He took her hair and dragged her up the embankment. Again she had to help, but twice she slipped and felt the yank in her head. It only made him bark threats and pull harder. When they were up, out, on even ground, he marched her down the road with her face aimed at the tarmac.

'I've done nothing wrong,' she shouted.

He ignored her claim. She couldn't see anything but moving road and her legs, and the journey seemed to take ages. She wondered if anyone was around, watching. And ignoring the abduction because they feared making a killer interested in them. Or because they knew who she was and felt she deserved whatever came her way.

When they got to his car, he drove a knee hard into her thigh, deadening it. 'Any tricks and you're dead.'

'My husband killed Joanne and I knew nothing about it.'

He opened the front passenger door, which had the chain of a pair of handcuffs hooked around the interior handle. 'Put them on,' he said.

She had no choice. She snapped the cuffs around both wrists, then he forced her into the car and shut the door. That was when his phone rang. The window was down, so she heard his half of the conversation even though he turned his back.

'I'm not in Cullerton anymore... Because the cops took her away, that's why... Yeah, head west along Tree Branch Lane. You come across a smashed cop car in a ditch and you're on the right track... No way. You want me to hang about at this crime scene? Grow a brain. I'll get a few miles away and call you back.'

When he hung up and got behind the wheel, she said, 'I hate my husband for what he did. I shouldn't be blamed.'

The man sounded calmer now he had her where he wanted her. 'I don't blame you. But Mr Voyzey does, and he's a bit wild and unfair and still after blood. So you're off to see him. Bad luck.'

The next moment was strange. As he turned the key to start the engine, it made a tremendous bang that made them both jump. Libby only stiffened and grunted, but the killer thudded forward into his steering wheel. She thought something in the engine had exploded.

A second bang, almost immediately after the first, made her yelp. The killer again jerked. It was followed by three more loud bangs and the killer shivered against the steering wheel on each one. And when all felt silent, there he lay, slumped forward. She saw that his back was a bloody mess and knew something terrible had happened.

SEVENTY-THREE

If asked right then if things could have turned even more confusing and bizarre, Libby would have said no. She was wrong.

Frozen with disbelief, she watched as one half of the rear seat's backrest collapsed, exposing a face, then an arm. And a hand holding a gun.

The man smiled at her as he clambered out of the boot, onto the flattened back seat. It was the bald man. This pair had been working together. It made no sense.

'Actually, it's Franz you're off to see, not Mr Voyzey. Sit tight.'

Cuffed to the door, she could do nothing else. She watched the bald man exit the rear of the car and open the driver's door. In a repeat of Green Jacket's actions to get her from the police car, the bald man cleared the driver's seat. He said she was lucky Hawk hadn't put her behind the wheel.

But Hawk wasn't dead. She heard him groan when he hit the tarmac. From her seated position on the passenger side, she couldn't see him, but she watched the bald man squat by his victim.

It obviously pained him to do so, but Hawk said, 'I heard you were a crack baby, Alain.'

Alain's hands moved. To Libby it looked like he was searching the downed man. 'It was the 1980s. Peak of the cocaine boom in France. People thought it was safe. I don't blame my mother for that.'

Hawk roared, but it was more from anger than pain. 'Just fucking do me and get it done and then piss off, you piece of shit.'

'I like you, Hawk. We had a banter that was fun. I'm not used to it. I've been too long wearing masks and playing roles. Because of that, I'm going to give you a chance. And because I shot you in the back, which is kind of unfair. So I'll leave you breathing, no matter what insults you throw at me. Maybe you'll be rescued and nursed back to full health. If you decide to come after me, I'd advise against it. But if vengeance sends you down that dangerous path, then I'll welcome the challenge. And more of that banter. Good luck with it, and I mean that.'

The bald man called Alain got in the driver's seat. He was careful not to catch Hawk when he closed the door. The car started moving away. Libby told herself not to, but she put her eyes on the wing mirror, and saw the bleeding man lying in the road. It felt wrong to leave him there, despite what he'd done.

'Where's Quinn?' Alain asked. 'Sorry. Roy Floode. That's the name he's using now.'

Quinn? Oh yes, his real name. Another mad twist that wouldn't help her brain get back on track. She could only shake her head. It was enough for Alain, who didn't ask again.

Alain pulled a phone from his pocket and turned it on. 'Just give me a moment. I had to turn this off while I was in the boot. In case you're wondering, I was there because I knew that chap back there would lead me to you.'

He pulled to the side of the road and got out to make his

call. She didn't hear a word, but she saw his frown as he spoke to someone. Two minutes later, he got back in the car, and his demeanour was different.

'I do feel for you, Ms Mytton. All that malarky with your husband. And there was an aura in your home of a couple hoping for a baby. It was never his thing, of course.'

Libby's roiling mind refocused in a flash. 'What does that mean? Never his thing.'

'Joel knew he might go to prison or be killed. It's the nature of the lifestyle he chose. It's for the best that you were sterile.'

Her husband had said that? He'd never wanted a baby? Was that why he had refused to foster or try assisted reproduction? Had he been happy to learn she was infertile?

'It's lucky you didn't have a child with your husband,' Alain continued. 'A father as a murderer. It might have turned out like me. And then bad people came for you. And you got saved by another one who ultimately meant you harm. Tough.'

It took her a second to realise he meant Roy. Quinn. She didn't want to talk, but she was eager to know if he knew Roy. It would help shift her shattered mind from Joel and babies.

'I know a lot about him. Not a man who's pleasant to women. He held someone captive for over a week once. Franz wanted him dead, but he managed to escape and go into hiding. That's where I think he's been all this time. Hiding under a rock. That fake ID of his, in the name of Roy, was only ever used once. When he bought petrol. That's not a man comfortable showing his face. Take it from someone versed in aliases.'

Libby could only nod.

'I feel silly that I didn't recognise him with you. No clear look, I guess. If I had I would have realised much earlier that he was a danger to you. I was wrong when I called him a symbiote, while Hawk hit the jackpot by referring to him as a parasite. I do feel incompetent for my error. Answer me this. How were you not aware of his true nature if you knew him through Joel.'

Libby leaned against the door because it hurt her cuffed arms less. 'I didn't, not really. Roy told me that he and Joel were good friends. Joel used to talk about me to him. We never met, though.'

'That's probably why he came for you. My guess is he thought you'd be a willing partner-in-hiding.'

She didn't care about what had come before. 'Am I going to be killed?'

'Franz wanted to interrogate you to find out what Joel told you about his business–'

'Nothing,' she pleaded. 'He told me nothing. I swear. I...'

She stopped when he angrily punched the steering wheel, sending out three honks of the horn. 'Franz is dead, so it doesn't matter.'

'So what are you going to do to me?'

'Kick you out, then drive away. You're free now, Ms Mytton. Luckily, he didn't ask for your murder. My job, instead, was to put you in front of Franz so he could ask you questions. He's now incapable. I can't complete my mission. My first failure. Go live your life.'

She looked at him for long seconds, trying to read a lie in his face. There was nothing. She had to trust him. 'I won't tell anyone about you or–'

'Oh, please tell the police the truth and mention the name Alain. It won't help them, but it might intrigue a Netflix documentary producer. Now, out you get. Start the process of getting back to being happy.'

He pulled a small key from his pocket. She knew it was for the handcuffs. He must have searched Green Jacket for it. When he leaned across her, to access the handcuffs, she felt her spirits rise. She was going to be released.

But she bit back her anticipation. 'How can I be happy with Voyzey still after me?' she said. It should have been a thought, but it came through her mouth.

'Don't...' he started, then paused, leaning across her, key just inches from the handcuffs. She had a terrible feeling he'd just changed his mind. It was confirmed when he dropped the handcuff key, sat back in his seat, and threw the car forward.

A fucking trick! To play with her mind! 'Why did you lie like that?' she screamed at him. She would have punched him if able.

He was as calm as she was enraged. 'Franz wanted to make sure Voyzey didn't get hold of you.'

She was puzzled until she saw him glance at the rear-view mirror. She looked back and saw, in the distance but closing fast, a blue van. It was the only other vehicle out here. 'Are they after me? Are they going to kill me?'

'Yes and no. I have to rescue a fragment of pride.'

What? What did that mean? Before she could yell at the infuriating bastard again, it clicked into place in her head. She knew what he'd meant. Yes, the people in the van were after her. And no, they were not going to kill her. Not if he had anything to do with it.

One of the men sent to capture her was now going to play saviour.

SEVENTY-FOUR

Libby watched out the rear window, expecting to see the van either closing on them or falling behind. But it retained the same distance. She expected that a car could outrun a van... and then she noticed Alain was in fourth gear, not fifth. He wasn't trying to outrun the chase vehicle, but to keep it close.

'What are you doing?' she shouted at him.

'Don't hold tight!' he yelled, full of glee.

The car blew over the crest of an incline in the road, and she felt her stomach lurch as she became weightless for a half-second. It made Alain laugh wildly in a way that made no sense to her. 'What's so funny?' she yelled.

Seconds after gravity was as-standard once more, he swung the steering wheel sharply left and blew through an open gateway. A sign flashed by and Libby caught only the word 'tractor'. She didn't know his plan, but she had a suspicion he wanted the van to follow them.

The van cut the same sharp turn, but not as sweetly, and she saw it rock as its flank scraped along the tall concrete gatepost. But on it came, relentless. She glanced ahead to see their path.

A wide concrete track split at a sign that pointed to the left (customer car park), and the right (shop).

Alain took the right fork, towards a long, single-storey building with wide glass windows, behind which was a showroom with farm machinery. Beyond the 'shop' was a wide open grassy space with farm and plant vehicles arranged in a row. Walking in both direction past the fronts of the machinery were casually dressed customers and staff in yellow high-vis jackets.

Some people saw the two vehicles racing at them and got clear. Others didn't move until Alain poked his gun out his window and fired two shots into the air. The booms sent cawing birds into the air and screaming humans scattering.

Alain zipped past a row of tractors and took a left turn down a gap before those blue vehicles became yellow backhoes. Libby expected to hit open field, but the car blasted down an aisle between two more rows of massive vehicles, with barely two feet each side of the car. On the left the big machines were red, on the right green.

Libby realised they were in a maze of tractors, dumpers, telehandlers, backhoes, and more. An outdoor showroom. Customers were here, too, and had to leap out of the car's path. Behind them, Libby saw the van make the same turn, but again without grace. A front wing ripped free when it caught the giant wheel of a crop sprayer.

Alain took another turn to the left, into yet another thin corridor with high diesel-driven walls. They were all loaders, the wheeled version on the left and those with tracked treads on the right. Their boom arms were raised so that opposing buckets almost touched and created a kind of roof.

And then he hit the brakes, which slammed her into the dashboard. She looked out the front windscreen to see that one of the loaders had a lowered boom and the bucket allowed no room for the passage of a car. They were trapped.

'What do we do?' she shouted. 'Please get me out of here.'

'This'll do,' Alain said as he leaped out, reloading his weapon at the same time. He slammed the door and aimed his gun back the way they'd come. She looked and saw the van enter the aisle, but again carelessly. This time it slammed diagonally into the tracked treads of a behemoth that didn't flinch.

Alan fired at the van three times, shattering the windscreen. Four armed men piled from their stalled ride at speed and vanished like cockroaches behind farm vehicles.

'Get me out,' Libby yelled, knowing the men could move about in the maze of heavy machinery and attack from all sides.

Alain didn't even look at her. He was framed in the driver's door window one second and gone the next. He'd abandoned her. She tugged hard on the cuffs, hoping to bust the door pull keeping her here. But it was solid and continuing to try might shatter her wrists. She ducked low in the seat, hoping that the four attackers would assume she'd run away with Alain.

Where is he? someone yelled.

Forget that sod. Cover me. The bitch is in the car still.

Shit. She slipped off the seat and squashed herself into the footwell. But she had no illusions that she wasn't a sitting duck.

There was a gunshot, which made her jump. Then two more, from a different direction. A bullet zinged off metal. Then a male screamed in obvious pain, but it didn't seem close. She heard running footsteps, more shouting from a distance, but no further gunshots. What the hell had happened? Who had been hit? She was terrified it was Alain, a man who had as of half an hour ago been a sworn enemy.

'The more of me there is, the less you see,' said a voice that made her yelp. She looked up to find a man at her opened window. It was Alain, and he was smiling. 'What am I?'

'Please get me...' she started, but let the sentence wither as he vanished again.

Who's that behind the thingy? someone yelled. *That you, John?*

Just like before, she heard thudding feet as one or more men ran, possibly from cover to cover amongst the big machines, then silence. More gunshots. Glass smashed somewhere. Then a voice: *She's in the passenger side still. Move in.*

You fucking move in. Where's that bald bastard?

There was another gunshot, and the zing of metal right in her ear. Someone had shot at and hit the car. Libby tried to sink even lower in the footwell.

Leave the fucker and just get to the damn car.

Someone tried, apparently. More bullets were fired. One caught its mark because there was a grunt of agony and *I'm hit, fucking hit!*

'The answer is *darkness,*' Alain said, again from right by her window. 'The more there is, the less you see. Darkness. Let's try– hang on.'

For the third time he seemingly winked out of existence, leaving her staring up at the roof of metal loader buckets. Nothing happened for ten seconds, then rinse and repeat: footsteps in the dirt, yells in the air, gunshots from seemingly all around... and an agonised scream. Libby cursed the police for not being here RIGHT NOW.

Who's fucking hit? Someone hit?

Let's just unload on the fucking car!

A second later, Alain materialised in her window. He didn't look scared or out of breath. In fact, he was grinning. 'Where does yesterday come after today?'

'Get me out of here, please!'

Gone. He seemed to be treating this like a game. When men shouted again, and one of them grunted on the tail of another gunshot, she tried to cover her ears. But that meant rising out of her hidey-hole because her hands were locked in place, and she abandoned it almost immediately.

'Please, Alain,' she yelled. 'I don't want to die.'

As if summoned by her words like a genie from a lamp, there he was. '*Dictionary* is the answer. What's got a head and a tail but no body?'

He was gone again before she could respond. She laid her head on the seat cushion and waited, shivering with terror. The following half minute played out the same as always, with men running and firing and someone shouting. Alain returned and pulled open the driver's door, the sound of which made her turn her head and–

'Peekaboo, you silly bitch.'

It wasn't Alain at the door. He'd missed an enemy, or had been dropped by this taller, younger, meaner looking man who pointed a dirty old revolver down at her face.

'Please don't kill me!' she wailed.

As for his own face: it didn't exist a half-second later. In a repeat of events in her bedroom seemingly so long ago, one man dropped to expose Alain behind him. The dead guy, minus half his head, landed in a heap half across the driver's seat. Blood coated the interior of the car and she could feel drops on her skin. Her ears were ringing from the gunshot.

Alain lowered his pistol, clearly not concerned about the man's lethal colleagues. There were none left, she knew. '*A coin,* Ms Mytton,' he said. 'Get it? A coin.'

He'd saved her, but his flippant attitude, his nonchalance in the midst of death, infuriated her. She screamed, 'This is not a fucking game, you monster!'

There was a flicker across his face, barely there in the half-second it existed. Worry? Embarrassment? Anger? She couldn't decipher it. Maybe he was puzzled that she didn't share his macabre sense of humour. He seemed like a man operating on a different wavelength to normal people. His next expression was a cocked ear.

Sirens. Police. A lot of them. In the distance, but burning rubber to get here. Alain squatted by her. 'I was just trying to distract you and keep you calm. Maybe socially I need work. Irrelevant. As I was saying before we got rudely interrupted... Don't worry about Mr Voyzey. Now go get your sister.'

And upon that statement, he performed his vanishing act one final time. But his last words hung around, echoing in her head.

Now go get your sister.

She gritted her teeth and, ignoring the pain, began yanking on the cuffs as hard as she could. The plastic door pull snapped at one end on the fifth jerk. The sound it made mimicked the noise of the ulna or radius in her left wrist breaking. But she didn't care and dampened the pain and launched herself out of the car.

With the shouting and the gunfire over, people who'd hidden for their lives started to emerge. They were like shell-shocked war survivors, moving slowly, not sure what to do. There were dead people around. Libby looked past them, through them, at the crashed van, and stumbled towards it. Seeing the cuffs on her wrists, a man stepped up to help. But she barely understood his words and his body was just a blockade, and she pushed past him.

The van had a sliding side door that rasped when she yanked it open, but that noise was smothered by her roar of pain as her shattered wrist exploded with fiery agony. But even that was forgotten when she saw the interior of the van.

The walls had been soundproofed with black panels, the floor carpeted. Sitting against the far side, with her own wrists in manacles attached to the wall, sat Emery. She wore pyjamas. Her mouth was taped, but her eyes were free to display her utter horror. Seeing Libby, she moaned against her gag.

'I'm here, it's okay,' Libby said as she clambered into the van. On her knees, she shuffled over to Emery, who started to cry, and grabbed one of the manacles. It was thick metal but secured with a spring pin – easily released if you had a pair of hands working together. Soon both of Emery's wrists were free. Emery ripped the tape from her lips and spouted thanks over and over.

In that moment, Libby felt everything change. Energy and will fled her body and she collapsed, thudding into her sister's lap and torso. She was unable to wrap her arms around her, but Emery was free and able to do so. She pulled Libby's head tight to her chest. All the breath vacated Libby and for a moment she worried there was no more strength to suck in air ever again.

But she found some to scream, '*My husband is dead!*'

'I know I know,' Emery said. 'But it'll be okay.'

'It won't. I can't do this, I can't cope, can't go on.'

'You can, you're strong, you saved me, it's going to be okay, baby. I'm here for you.'

Emery clutched her sister even tighter as tears fell and anguished moans filled the air.

SEVENTY-FIVE

The prison guards ran around like headless chickens, desperate to get to the bottom of why one of their charges lay dead in a pool of blood. They needed a culprit because that would slightly soften the shitstorm they'd be engulfed in. They didn't get one.

The police were called in, but they came with the long faces of those knowing a lost cause when they saw it. Evidence was a pipe dream. They got DNA and fingerprints at the kill site, from a bunch of guys who obviously had criminal records, but it meant nothing in a place where people were in and out of each other's rooms all the time. Every man flagged said he'd popped into the cell at some point to say hello, and nothing could prove otherwise.

When officers asked about CCTV, a guard actually laughed. The system worked and the footage quality was good, but inmates had a habit of throwing gunk to obscure the lenses of the cameras watching the tier walkways. Fixing the problem involved hauling out a ladder, just for the next guy to go and lob a handful of porridge or even faeces when backs were turned.

The killer must have been splattered in blood, but whatever clothing he'd worn was gone. As for witnesses: two guys had been having a kick-ass pool battle and apparently every single inmate out and about had been looking that way. Selective deafness was endemic in prison.

Voyzey found it all amusing, as he always did when law enforcement chased their tails. Although it was annoying that he couldn't use his phone because cells were being tossed. When a kind of calm returned to the prison and the search teams got lost, Voyzey got a guard to allow Nando out of his cell to see the chaplain.

He made no such visit, though. But he did attend the chapel, where he'd hidden his and Voyzey's phones before they killed Franz's inside man. He ignored a couple of missed calls from an unknown number and checked to see if Linzi Linzo, the woman he'd been watching on Facebook, had made a post. But she hadn't been active in hours. Oh dear. This was bad. Possibly.

He returned to his cell and gave Voyzey his phone. Nando lay on his bunk and checked again for a post from Linzi. Nothing now for three hours. Three missed posts. He stared at the ceiling and tried to summon up courage. He prayed that Linzi would write something on the dot of the next hour. Below him, Voyzey talked on the phone to someone. And he was angry. Clearly his people had failed to get hold of the Mytton woman for some reason.

But that hour came and went, and Linzi hadn't posted. Now it was undeniable. He'd hoped the time would never come. But it had. No message from whoever was posing as Linzi meant only one thing. Because it was a pre-arranged message by itself.

Franz was dead.

Go fast and don't give yourself time to think and back out, that was his motto. Nando grabbed a pen, dropped off his bunk, and stood before Voyzey, who saw the look on his face, the way he held the writing implement like a dagger, and did the maths.

'No way, Nando.' Voyzey looked to the doorway for help. There was none. 'Please don't do this.'

'Sorry, man. You got outbid.'

SEVENTY-SIX

The slideshow was back, and it was much like the previous performance.

Snap one: police filling the area, moving about between the farmyard and plant machinery, and surrounding the car and the van and the sisters, who sat between both.

Slide two: the back of an ambulance, where Libby and Emery were given a check-over – the former's second of the day.

Slide three: a cell in the back of a police van. Alone. The air had a far more intense feel this time around.

Before, there had been a fire and not much knowledge of what the hell had happened. Now the police still didn't know much, but they had far more than a burning cottage to get their heads around. Four men lay dead on the grass and two uniformed officers were deceased in a car in a ditch. Nobody was taking any chances this time. Libby was in handcuffs again, just in case she had the inclination to end more lives. She knew she couldn't be allowed around Emery – in case they worked on a story – until after the police had interviewed them both separately.

At the station, they processed her and placed her in a cell.

So, now she knew what Joel had gone through. She was fed, watered, then left to rot for ages. She slept.

When she woke, it seemed she hadn't and was dreaming. For standing in the doorway was a known face.

'Monroe?' she said.

'Hello again. Libby.'

It truly was. Detective Constable Sally Monroe, the family liaison officer attached to her during the Joanne Yeowell fiasco. She didn't know what to make of this, since FLOs dealt with suffering people. She made the enquiry.

Monroe sat by her and took her hand. 'There's a lot to unpack here. And I'm sorry you had to wait. It was deemed best if you spoke to a known face.'

Libby puffed out her cheeks. 'No one has told me much,' she said. 'I got arrested. But I didn't hurt anyone. I want to see Emery.'

'I believe you. We'll get your story out in interview shortly. I doubt you'll be charged with anything. All police forces were told to contact South Yorkshire Police if you were found. I was on standby to come to you.'

'What? All police forces? I don't understand.'

'I know. I'm sorry. Look, say no more right now. We have to do this officially, on the record. It'll be soon. And I'll be there. And afterwards, we'll get you and your sister together again.'

The interview took place about half an hour later. As promised, Monroe was present, assisting a DC from the station. Libby didn't even wait for a question and immediately unloaded everything she could remember. Throughout, the detectives said nothing. Libby stared at the camera in a corner of the room, knowing everything was being recorded – perhaps to be used as evidence against her. The story took well over an hour.

She lied only once: about the cause of the fire. She blamed a stupid accident, fearful of a charge of arson.

When she was finished, she looked at Monroe. The DC was pale, as if she'd just spied a ghost. 'Libby, there's no arrest warrant out for you, either, or public rage at you. And there's certainly no murderous police task force trying to kill you.'

Now Libby felt herself go pale. 'What do you mean? The warrant was cancelled?'

'There never was one. Libby, everything the man you knew as Roy told you was a lie.'

This didn't hit Libby with quite the thud she'd expected. Maybe nothing would faze her ever again after all she'd been through. So many lies, so much stress, all of it wrapped in violence and death. If a human psyche could come through the other side of that maelstrom intact, surely it would do so strengthened and padded.

'But there was definitely a threat,' she said. 'A man called Franz. A man called Voyzey, who is Joanne Yeowell's uncle.'

'We know. But both of those men are dead.'

She knew about Franz from Alain. 'Voyzey, too? Are you sure?'

Monroe nodded. And smiled. 'You're safe now. Nobody is after you.'

Those words gave her relief, but for mere seconds. 'Does that mean you captured Roy?'

Monroe lost her smile.

EPILOGUE

'My ex-wife saw that guy, that Quinn, in Edinburgh. That's what she said. Saw him. Was in a Greggs.'

'Flash gets about, doesn't he?' Libby said. She finished dolloping ketchup on the man's hotdog and handed it over. She said nothing further and he got the message and departed.

Libby had been freed ten hours after her arrest. Emery had been released earlier. The next day, Libby decided to get back into work. It would be good therapy, and returning to normalcy, according to Emery, was the key to getting past what had happened.

People knew her history, though, and even at work she couldn't hide away. During the lunchtime rush that first day, Libby was serving when a pair of women in the middle of the queue started whispering and watching her a little too intently. She tried to blank them, but couldn't. Soon one pulled out a phone, tapped away, and both women looked between the screen and Libby.

When it was this double act's turn for service, Libby couldn't meet their eyes. 'Hi, what can I get for you?'

One of the women had a tight blonde perm that belonged in

the 1990s. She said, 'Tell me if this name means anything to you. Joel Mytton.'

They were both staring intently, awaiting the answer. In that look, Libby saw the pair's entire previous conversation. One of the women had thought she recognised Libby and said so, but her comrade hadn't been convinced, even when shown a photo.

Libby gave a pause as she considered her response. Lie or truth?

'Did you hear me?' nineties perm said. 'Joel Mytton. Killed that Joanne Yeowell. Know him?'

Behind Libby, flipping burgers on the grill, Emery said, 'Lies are for those with something to hide.'

It was brilliant advice. Libby was suddenly sick of being treated as if she'd done something wrong. A burst of inner strength forced words out of her: 'I should know him, since we were married for years.'

'I knew it,' Perm said. Her pal just looked on in awe. 'Knew you were his wife. You changed your hair. God. Did he try to kill you?'

The guy behind the women got with the picture. 'Wow. Wait. You're the wife of that guy? That guy who chopped that woman up? Got himself chopped up in prison, didn't he?'

The news rippled down the queue at light speed. Questions came thick and fast. *How did you find out? Did he kill anyone else? Are the police going to question you? Did you see the body?* Libby felt like an alien who'd just landed in the middle of a UFO convention outside Area 51. It was too much. The inner strength fled. She wanted to do the same, but her legs refused all commands.

Emery turned from the griddle and grabbed her sister's arm, to guide her away. She filled the hatch and said, 'Calm down, you lot. We're here to serve food, not information. Anyone hungry for gossip rather than tasty burgers can do an about-face and clear off.'

The blitzkrieg continued. People talked over others and the mob fast veered in the direction of unruly. Libby, seated in the cab, tried to shut it all out, but one question seemed to bulldoze through all others and spike into her brain. Not everybody was simply curious.

How come she's not in prison as well?

Libby got up, having had enough. She pulled Emery aside and commandeered the hatch. 'Because I'm not a damn criminal. I called the police on my husband when I found out. Who said that?'

A guy in coveralls with a badge that gave his name and PJ FREIGHT put his hand up. 'How do we know you shopped him? I don't believe anything in the papers.'

Libby jabbed a finger at him. 'You're barred. Get lost. Go.'

The man swore at her, but he left the queue. Libby addressed everyone else. 'I won't talk about the case. And it's very rude to demand answers like this. We won't be serving rude customers.'

'Did he kill more than one?' asked a woman with a smug look on her face. She had already been served and was chowing down while waiting for a friend to order.

'Maybe lots,' Libby said without pause. 'Burger meat isn't cheap.'

Libby hadn't know what to expect from that line, but was relieved when a ripple of laughter passed along the queue. Another woman took Libby's joke as permission to break the rule. 'You can talk about certain things. Not evidence and stuff. Feelings, for instance. If I asked something and got an answer, I might just buy extra.'

Libby tapped the menu and grinned. 'Lunchtime XL Special. One question for every purchase.'

Beside her, Emery looked impressed. 'What happened to the wilting flower I knew?'

Never again, Libby vowed to herself. She scanned the faces in the crowd and something changed. Not amongst the people, but inside her own head. Way back, she had tried to comfort Emery with a claim: *Bad voices are the loudest, that's all.* Despite being advice from her own mouth, she had been unable to apply it to herself and had continued to believe that the whole world hated her and blamed her for what Joel had done. Until that very moment. Suddenly, she no longer saw disapproving glares, but curious ones.

In the four days since it all ended, Libby had treated the whole affair like something to be embraced, not avoided. She had answered every question thrown at her, as long as the one asking bought a Lunchtime XL Special.

Someone wanted to know: *How did the police find out about everything?*

The entire sorry tale was out there for those who cared to research. The police had released information, but gaps in the story had been plugged by dogged journalists and the friends and family of some of the dead and the incarcerated. Libby was happy to tell her side of the tale, but with care: there was still a major police investigation underway, with criminal charges on the horizon for key players still drawing breath, and she had been warned not to jeopardise it. Libby wasn't one of the accused, thankfully.

Emery had been held hostage in her own house for two days, but she had escaped when one captor killed the other. To then be snared by more evil men. Only after they were found alive and well did police attend the sisters' homes and find obvious crime scenes. Amazingly, nobody had visited the properties in the interim. No reporters, no police, no true crime fans or vigilantes. How the story might have changed if someone had found Libby missing much earlier.

Why the sudden interruption to public interest in her? She remembered, back in her house on the night she'd fled, making a joke about something 'new and explosive' wiping her from the headlines.

In a sense, this had indeed happened. Dog walker, the man who helped her trap Joel in the garage, had re-emerged from the shadows to tell his story.

Just as Monroe had hinted, Dog Walker – real name of Jake Anderson – was a criminal, with a history of assault and burglary. Two years ago, he bought £3,000 of goods from a catalogue and vanished without paying. He had hidden after the story broke because his creditors were on the hunt.

As Libby was bathing that seemingly long-ago night, Anderson contacted a newspaper to tell his tale. His reason for this was not gain, but to help Libby. He was quoted as saying, 'It's mad that people are stomping on that woman. Her bloke was wild in that garage. He would have striped us both. She was scared shitless. Jesus, so was I. How about we leave her alone, eh? She probably ran to get away from all that crap. Can't you people go find another celebrity who touched up women twenty years ago?'

As someone directly involved and suddenly eager to talk, media focus shifted away from Libby. The timing couldn't have been more awkward.

How many people got killed?

Franz and his wife were dead in his house, although his mother-in-law was alive and well. Police had attended and found three gunmen trapped in a safe room. They had been sent by Voyzey, but he was dead so they had abandoned their right to remain silent and sang like canaries. They had named a missing fourth gunman who had fled the scene.

And Voyzey's death? Unsolved, but police believed Franz had paid his cellmate to perform the kill. Also dead was another prisoner with ties to South Yorkshire, but not to Franz. A case of mistaken identity.

There were other deaths attributable to the Joanne Yeowell fiasco. Dale 'Hawk' Hawkins, who hadn't survived his bullet wounds. His friend, 'Tempest' Tony Berkshire, although police had only his blood in Libby's house to suggest a foul end. The man deceased in Emery's kitchen, who, like his still-at-large killer, hadn't yet been identified. And four men shot to death in the shadow of gleaming farm machinery.

Does her family hate you?

Having learned of Voyzey's kill plan, Joanne's parents had offered their pity to Libby. There was no evidence that Joanne's rich father, Devin, had had any part or knowledge in the fiasco orchestrated by Voyzey. Joanne's mother had even invited Libby to the upcoming funeral. She wasn't yet sure if she'd go.

A curious twist was that Devin had offered to buy Libby's house for much more than it was worth. He hadn't said why, but she had a suspicion. His daughter's killer had lived there. He had washed her blood off his skin there. Libby believed Devin planned to erase the house from existence. She was happy to sell it and not just to appease him. It was a murder scene and she could never return. Emery's place was going on the market for the same reason. Currently the sisters shared a flat in a nearby city, where so far they had been left to their own devices.

Is it true then that there was a Brazilian hitman?

Alain? He wasn't from Brazil – people were obviously connecting him to the old rumour about a killer-for-hire licking his lips at an alleged £100,000 bounty on Joel's head. But apparently Alain *was* a bona fide hitman, or as close to the movie depiction of one as you could get: shadowy, travelling the world, operating under various aliases and disguises.

There was no trace of him as yet, but police had various CCTV images of the man as well as his fingerprints and DNA from certain crimes scenes. He was now highly wanted in the UK as well as other places in Europe, in Canada, Ukraine, and the USA. It was possible he'd left the country if he had false ID other than the Detective Inspector Alan Manvers pseudonym.

Some suspected Alain was his real name, but others were doubtful. Detectives investigating a drive-by-shooting in Detroit, America had the name Neil Waterson from a discarded bank card. In Prešov, Slovakia, scene of a strangled businessman, he'd rented a scooter as Robert Kuciak.

Do you still love your husband?

No, she didn't. Did she miss him? No. Did she pity him and wish he was still alive? That was a tough one. Despite being a killer himself, he didn't deserve to go out the way he had. Nobody merited such a death. He had grieving parents who'd done nothing wrong.

Emery hadn't mentioned Joel's demise when they first spoke after he was murdered. Libby had wondered why and had assumed all manner of dark intentions. Since then, of course, they had had time to discuss their feelings. Emery had admitted that, yes, she had wondered if Libby knew more about Joel's evil than she'd let on. But she'd quickly regretted this and, by way of silent apology, had sworn to not bring him into conversation until Libby did so. Both sisters had waited for the other to go first, basically, and in time had managed to see the funny side of this.

Recently, they had asked each other the same question: are you happy he's dead? Libby had to be honest and admit, if only to herself, that the world was a better place without him. She could easier move on with her life now he wasn't part of it. The whole sorry debacle would be forgotten by the public quicker now he was dead. Was it selfish of her to think that way? Was it wrong not to care if the answer to that last question was an affirmative?

And Emery's stance? The same. They couldn't erase Joel from their history, but that day the sisters swore to make sure he played no role in their futures. It was easy. He wasn't the person they'd been led to believe. That guy had never existed, only a monster playing a role. And if that outlook was nothing but a coping mechanism, so be it. Whatever worked to get them from one day to the next.

And, finally, the million pound question: *Where's Quinn?*

The police now knew a lot more about him. The man called Alain had been correct when he'd said Quinn would be hiding away under a rock.

Two years ago, Quinn had fled South Yorkshire because he had a target on his head. Apparently he had held a woman captive for over a week. He had resettled in Birmingham, living with a male homeless group in an abandoned, dilapidated house. He made good money from criminal activity, but he couldn't enjoy it. He had to remain in hiding, like a fugitive from justice, in case Franz ever found out he was alive.

Once Quinn's face was in the news, the woman he'd held captive had come forward to tell her tale directly to police, so he was now wanted for that crime. His housemates had also come forward to tell tales. According to one, Quinn had had no contact with Joel since he'd left Franz's employ. They had been close friends and Joel had talked about Libby often. In turn, Quinn had kept Joel's secret from Franz. But once Quinn was gone and Joel was aware of his crimes against women, he cut contact. The public found that bizarre given what Joel would later do.

However, the two years Quinn was in hiding did nothing to dampen his feelings about Libby, perhaps because there was no other woman on scene. Quinn had talked about her often to his new friends, and had even claimed he was in love, despite having never spoken to her or seen her in the flesh. Preposterous, but there you go. But she was out of reach, up there in the lion's den, where he'd be killed if he ever showed his face.

Until she wasn't out of reach. Until her life shattered and she became single, and he saw a chance for them to be together. Quinn believed fear for her life and future would compel her to hook up with him and abandon the life she knew. According to one housemate, Quinn's parting words as he left Birmingham for Sheffield, had been, 'I'm going to go get my girl.' Scary.

She had assumed he wanted nothing sexual from her because he hadn't given a single hint during their time together... but it was all part of the scam. Once they were locked up together in the cottage in Cullerton, he increased her perception of the danger enveloping her and pretended her one anchor to her old life – Emery – was gone, all to make her dependent on him and as pliable as warm putty in his hands. Then his real intentions came to the fore.

But when his dream of a relationship, a life, with her faltered, he got desperate. His phone had been found, undamaged, in the burned cottage, and it exposed him. Quinn had said the property was one of Franz's safe houses, but this claim, like so many others, had been a lie. He'd located it by searching the internet for holiday homes to rent and by sheer luck it sat empty. He had pretended the door key was lost so he could bash in a back window.

Monroe had shown Libby proof that the WhatsApp group apparently involving rogue members of the Covert Policing Command had been set up by him. He'd created all three profiles and the messages the trio posted. He had even rented web space and been in the process of constructing a fake news website, probably to exhibit stories that would convince Libby she was in mortal danger from all directions. There was also evidence of an attempt to find a fake passport for her. Maybe he planned for them to escape overseas and start a new life.

Until that moment when he finally realised he would fail to win her heart. Then he tried to sell Libby to Voyzey for his freedom.

Now, four days since rescue, Libby found her new resolve faltering at this latest mention of Quinn. Asking about his role was one thing. After all, the media and the public still retained an interest in the Joanne Yeowell story, especially after chapters involving new deaths and kidnaps were added. But hinting that Libby was still in danger from him was another kettle of fish. Nobody else mentioned him for the remainder of that shift, but that one time had been enough to deaden her mood. After the sisters had packed up for the day and they were driving home, Emery sensed the change in Libby.

'Still worried about him? I heard that twonk earlier. The one who said Quinn was in Edinburgh. You know not to take that shit seriously now.'

It had been just four days since he vanished, yet Quinn had apparently been sighted in at least a dozen cities across the country. On one day alone he reared his ugly head in London, Cardiff, and here in Sheffield. Hence her joke about Flash, the superhero.

She had believed the first sighting, in Nottingham. She had been in two minds about the next, in Bradford, suspicious about his subsequent appearance in Peterborough, and had rejected the following claim that he was on Nemesis at Alton Towers in Stoke-on-Trent. The police were also doubtful, yet had to check them all out. They had kept her up to date, usually with terms like 'false alarm'.

Alarm was a good word. Because she was on edge a lot. The first sighting, the one she believed, made her happy.

Nottingham wasn't Sheffield. So Roy wasn't here. Wasn't watching her. But that feeling didn't last long. She wanted definitive proof that Roy was elsewhere, for without it she couldn't be sure he wasn't lurking in a tree on her street. Nor could the police. They broadcasted this worry by posting a car outside her house for the first two nights.

How bizarre this turnaround, that she might be in danger from the man who'd once protected her?

Roy's fugitive status and the story of their time together was obviously massive news, and of course she hated it. But it did allow her to learn what the public felt about her. She was surprised by the result. They felt sympathy. This time there was no doubt she was a victim.

So, it had been four days since her rescue. The police didn't think anyone from the gangs of Voyzey or Franz would come for her and so far they'd been right. The media chaos had settled a little. Joe and Jane Public were focusing on their own problems. Libby felt it was about time she believed she could get on with her life without issue.

Could she? It depended on whether or not Quinn would seek revenge because she had obliterated his plans.

Some people felt this was impossible because Quinn was dead, maybe at the hands of former enemies. Libby got the feeling she was supposed to be happy about this. But would she be? As he'd reminded her so many times, he'd saved her life that fateful night. Without him, she'd already be dead. She wasn't sure how she'd feel if he turned up as a corpse.

When Emery entered the bedroom, she screamed in shock. Libby barely heard it, and she didn't turn to face her sister. Her eyes could not be dragged from what was right before her. Next came actual words – 'Libby, please, let's go, come, please, get out' – but again her voice had zero power against what had magnetised Libby.

Finally, her hands. They clamped down on Libby's arm, to pull and twist in her effort to remove her from the room, but the result was the same. Libby was locked in place. Emery was nothing but a ghost, a mirage, a dream. Maybe this whole scene was in her mind.

The police earlier warned Libby about pranksters who might knock on her door: 'I don't want to scare you, Ms Mytton, but I saw that Quinn on this street a minute ago.'

They expected fools to post letters: *Hello, baby, I'm Quinn, and tonight and I'm coming for you.* They said she might get dodgy phones calls from people pretending to be him: *I'm waiting for you back at your house, darling.*

The car that had defended her home for two days was long gone, though, so the police hadn't taken their own warnings too seriously.

Behind her, Emery fled the bedroom, no doubt to go call the police and let them know they should have been more vigilant.

Now it was just Roy and Libby in the room.

She reached out a hand and touched his arm, just to make sure he was real. It was no trick of the mind.

He'd punched a pair of big holes in the ceiling in order to loop the rope over a joist, so it would support his weight. There was no toppled chair below him and the bed was too far away, so she stared and wondered how he got the rope around his neck.

Later, the police would theorise that Roy had help and they'd start scouting for an accomplice. Libby would be worried about such an accomplice returning, but soon she would learn of a neighbour's CCTV that showed Quinn approaching her home alone and on foot.

When wood splinters are found in his fingertips, the next and accepted theory would be that Roy arranged the rope in place then leaped to grab the joist through the holes bashed in the ceiling. He pulled himself towards the ceiling and held that position with one hand while he fed his head through the noose.

Then, with his face pressed against the ceiling, he didn't just release his grip. He pushed, to accentuate the speed of his drop and guarantee what one officer would call *traumatic spondylolisthesis of the axis*. Detective Monroe would be kind enough to offer another term for it: hangman's fracture. Over 1,000 pounds of torque on the neck, cleanly broken, with death occurring quickly.

Libby pulled on his arm. His body hung at ninety-degrees to hers, so she saw only his left side. Her tug slowly turned his corpse on the rope, until he was facing her.

Unfortunately for Roy, a hangman's fracture required a lot of momentum and a body could only achieve it by plummeting roughly five to nine feet. The post-mortem would say he suffered a short-drop hanging. Not quick, and not painless.

The police would also theorise that Roy came here to kill her and then end his own life, for he knew the net was closing. He had a steel outdoor knife, although he might have brought it solely for the purpose of jimmying the back window he got in via.

Upon finding she was out, they would say, Roy panicked and opted instead to progress to part two of his plan. Emery would second this opinion. The public would eat it up.

Libby wouldn't agree. Because she would recall his words, which came to her as she stared at his bloated, colourful face:

Look into these dead man's eyes. They're going to haunt you forever.

Those eyes were wide open with the fear and pain of his final moments. She stared right into them. It was what he wanted. Once upon a time, they'd been the eyes of a knight in shining armour. And this prompted just one, all-important question.

Would those dead eyes get their wish and haunt her forever?

END

ACKNOWLEDGEMENTS

It's a long process from initial idea in my head to putting a book in a reader's hands. I couldn't have written this without some frontline aid. So thanks go to:

Microsoft – for the word processing software (Word).

Hovis and Tetley – for the sandwiches and tea that fuelled me.

Google and Waterstones – for the research material.

My part is over when I type THE END and email it off. Other hands then take hold and do their bit to make the final product something I am happy to put out there. The main culprits are: Hannah Baxter-Deuce, Tara Lyons, Clare Law – for tireless grind in editing and promotion and formatting and all the other stuff. Everyone else at Bloodhound Books and Open Road Media – for back office work beyond my realm. Betsy Reavley and Fred Freeman – for giving me a shot in the first place.

Since it's a lengthy deal to write a book, life sometimes gets in the way. So, finally, a list of the people/things/situations that delayed me. You would have had this book much earlier if not for the following:

The kids – for wanting things like food and clean clothes and help with far less important writings like homework.

My boss at the other job – for a contract that says I belong to him for 40 hours a week.

Dying Light: the Beast – for making the end boss well hard.

A NOTE FROM THE PUBLISHER

Thank you for reading this book. If you enjoyed it please do consider leaving a review on Amazon to help others find it too.

We hate typos. All of our books have been rigorously edited and proofread, but sometimes mistakes do slip through. If you have spotted a typo, please do let us know and we can get it amended within hours.

info@bloodhoundbooks.com